"You are such a good man, Eric," Amy said softly.

She was touched by how easily he figured out a way to include her grandparents in their idea for a spur-of-the-moment backyard barbecue. "In no time at all we have ourselves a plan."

Eric stared at her with a faint smile. "I guess we do."

Amy looked at the sky framing the trees and water downriver. Something about this moment, this day, held a meaning she couldn't quite define. She knew only she wouldn't forget it. "How about a short bike ride tomorrow?" Amy said. "Maybe around town before Cassie gets home."

"Sounds like another plan." He opened his arms and she stepped into them. "What a great day, huh?" He kissed her cheek and slowly released her.

Amy got on her bike. How was she going to convince Grandma this wasn't a romance in the making? She couldn't even convince herself. She couldn't let this go on.

Dear Reader,

Thanks for joining me on my third trip to Bluestone River, a community that cherishes its history and natural beauty and where love is known to blossom. With the town on the upswing, many who left Bluestone River years ago are now happily back home. Amy Morgan is one of them, and she has nine-year-old Cassie with her. Amy once abandoned her dreams for a marriage that fell apart, but now she's determined to believe in herself again as she builds a new life for herself and her daughter.

Eric Wells just started his new job as principal of the school Cassie attends. Eric liked Amy a lot during their high school years, but she gave her heart to someone else. Now he has to deliver bad news about Cassie's classroom troublemaking. Fortunately, Eric understands the fourth grader's anger and unhappiness. Like Cassie, Eric had a father, but never a real dad.

As Eric and Amy's friendship deepens and a romance seems possible, their biggest challenge is to put their fears and failures behind them and open their hearts to new dreams and the promise of love.

Please visit me on Facebook and Twitter, and sign up for news and updates at viriginiamccullough.com.

Once more, to happy endings!

Virginia McCullough

HEARTWARMING

A Bridge Home

———

Virginia McCullough

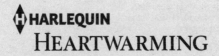

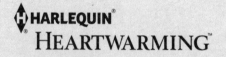

Recycling programs
for this product may
not exist in your area.

ISBN-13: 978-1-335-88984-3

A Bridge Home

This edition published by arrangement with Harlequin Books S.A.

For questions and comments about the quality of this book, please contact us at CustomerService@Harlequin.com.

Harlequin Enterprises ULC
22 Adelaide St. West, 40th Floor
Toronto, Ontario M5H 4E3, Canada
www.Harlequin.com

Printed in U.S.A.

Virginia McCullough grew up in Chicago, but she's enjoyed living in many places, including the coast of Maine, western North Carolina and now northeastern Wisconsin. She started her career writing magazine articles but soon turned to coauthoring and ghostwriting nonfiction books. When fictional characters started whispering in her ear, she tried her hand at writing their stories. Now, many books later, Back to Bluestone River is her second series for Harlequin Heartwarming readers. When she's not writing, Virginia eagerly reads other authors' books, hangs out with family and friends, and plans another road trip.

Books by Virginia McCullough

Harlequin Heartwarming

Girl in the Spotlight
Something to Treasure
Love, Unexpected

Back to Bluestone River

A Family for Jason
The Christmas Kiss

Visit the Author Profile page
at Harlequin.com for more titles.

To Keri Vellis, a dedicated and tireless mom of many and a fierce advocate for children.

CHAPTER ONE

WITH A BASKET of clean clothes balanced against her hip, Amy Morgan climbed the basement stairs humming the opening bars of "My Funny Valentine." A slightly off-key rendition, especially on the high notes, but what difference did it make? The song had looped through her head all day, no matter how hard she tried to purge it from her brain. There was zero chance of that happening, since Valentine's Day plans were the buzz at work that afternoon.

As the River Street Salon's receptionist she had a front row seat to the daily small talk. Every woman who came in that particular day was expecting her special someone to show up with a bouquet of her favorite flowers, a box of chocolates or both.

Amy carried the basket of still-warm clothes into the kitchen and plunked it down on a chair at the end of the long table. "Happy

Valentine's Day to me," she muttered under her breath.

Oops, her words came out louder than she intended. Grandma Barb glanced up from where she stood unloading the dishwasher. "Did you say something, Amy?"

"Nothing important, Grandma. I was just talking to myself—again." Amy injected an upbeat lilt into her voice.

"She does that a lot," Cassie said. Amy's nine-year-old sat at the table swinging her legs and tapping her pencil on her math worksheet.

"Oh, you, don't exaggerate." Amy made a face at Cassie before plucking a pair of her grandpa's jeans off the top of the pile. "How's that homework coming?"

"Boring. I *told* you I'm not good at math."

"You used to be." Amy immediately wanted to snatch those words out of the air. Couldn't she have come up with something a little more original? She only seemed to remind Cassie about how her life "used to be." But whatever she said was the wrong thing lately, and Cassie never thought twice about telling her so.

She waved the worksheet in the air. "My teacher said this is harder than what I did last semester in my old school. It's *three*-digit multiplication."

"You'll catch on, honey," Grandma Barb said. She pulled a chair out from the table and eased herself down. She reached out to pat Cassie's arm.

Amy smoothed the wrinkles out of the jeans and braced for another argumentative answer from Cassie, but none came. Good. If she'd done one thing right, it was drawing a line in the sand when it came to Cassie's great-grandparents. They were to be treated with respect—and only with respect. No back talk, no antics. Ever.

"As soon as I'm finished folding these clothes, I'll heat up the stew, Grandma."

Grandma tilted her head toward Cassie and smacked her lips. "And then we'll have red velvet cake for dessert."

Cassie smacked her lips back and grinned.

At least Grandma Barb could bring a smile to her little girl's face. So could Barb's gray-and-white cat, named Cloud because her coat resembled white clouds against a gray sky. At the moment, Cloud sat on her haunches next to Cassie's chair, apparently in the mood to accept whatever attention anyone in the house chose to heap on her.

Amy took a deep breath and squared her shoulders. She had to fight off her own cloud of gloom and doom. She kept a watch on Cassie, who fidgeted with her braid, but kept her head down and finished up the remaining math problems on the page. Then she lifted the pencil high in the air and let it drop onto the paper. "I'm done, done, done." She slid off the chair and hurried out of the kitchen and into the living room.

Phew. Amy exhaled in relief as if she'd finished *her* homework.

"I know you're worried, sweetheart, but your little girl will be fine." Grandma Barb spoke in a confident tone.

She meant well. Amy gave her that. Her grandmother seemed to have an unending supply of optimism. But Grandma hadn't read the message from Amy's teacher about the nine-year-old's *adjustment* issues. Or rather, maladjustment. Grandma hadn't been on the embarrassing phone call with the school's office manager to set up an appointment with Eric Wells, the new principal. As if Cassie's bad behavior wasn't bad enough, Amy had gone to high school with Eric. They'd even worked together as coeditors of the high school newspaper.

"Maybe so, Grandma, but you don't have to slink into the school tomorrow morning and hope no one notices you showing up at the principal's office to meet with *Mr.* Wells." She grabbed one of Cassie's pullovers from the pile and quickly folded it and set it aside in a growing pile of Cassie's things. Her daughter was old enough now to put away her own little pile of clothes, even if she griped about it. Amy herself had lived with her grandparents most of her childhood and doing a bunch of chores was part of a regular day. She'd rebel against them occasionally, but Grandma would shrug off her complaints. Now Amy found herself doing the same thing with Cassie.

Grandma pointed to the window. "Look at that snow. I doubt anyone's going to be having meetings at the school tomorrow. We'll be buried by morning."

Amy turned to look out the picture window behind her. Grandma could be right. The snow was forecasted as barely deep enough to cover the half foot of snow that blanketed Bluestone River a few days ago. But the wind had picked up and blew the snow horizontally. They were in the midst of a whiteout now. "You could be right. Maybe we're in the path of that giant storm after all."

Grandma's eyebrows lifted almost to her forehead in amusement. "I'm sure Les will tell us at dinner."

Amy chuckled. "In great detail." After a stroke forced her Grandpa Les to slow down, he'd become even more dedicated to news and weather watching. Unfortunately, it took a little effort for him to move around, but he balked at using a wheelchair, at least in the house. On the other hand, in his eighties now, like Barb, his mind hadn't lost a beat.

Amy returned the piles of folded clothes to the basket and set it aside to put away after dinner. She took out the pot of stew she'd made that morning before work, and while it heated, she warmed the rolls in the oven and brought bowls and plates to the table. Grandma could finish setting the table without having to get up from her chair.

"We have our system, don't we?" Barb smiled as she plucked silverware out of the wire basket on the table.

"Like the old days." As happened so often since she'd been back in Bluestone River, a wave of nostalgia gently rolled in. Some-times she couldn't help but long for the simpler days of her childhood with Grandma and Grandpa, whose unconditional love had nurtured her when her parents wouldn't—or maybe couldn't.

"Speaking of systems…" She smiled at Grandma and went to the arched entry into the living room. "Time to come to the table, you two. Do you need help, Grandpa?"

"Nah." He inched to the edge of the chair and braced his hands on the arms to lift himself to his feet. "Cassie will walk next to me. Maybe she'll let me hang on to her hand."

Cassie nodded eagerly. "You bet, Grandpa."

She sounded so sweet. How could this be the same girl who'd refused to make valentines in class that day? Even worse, she'd dumped art supplies in the trash? It hurt knowing that today's episode wasn't the first. The other day, Cassie had instigated a name-calling match with a boy in her class.

"Hold on to your hats, girls," Grandpa Les said as he sat in the chair Cassie pulled out for him. "Just saw the weather update. Winds are picking up." He tapped the tip of Cassie's nose. "I bet you'll be home tomorrow and helping me put together that puzzle we've got going. What do you want to bet they call off school?"

"Lots of Valentine's Day plans up in smoke, too, I suppose," Grandma said.

"Not ours," Amy said, trying to sound upbeat. She looked at her grandparents and her daughter. The three of them were her holiday plans. "Pass the bowls and I'll dish up the stew."

"And eat fast," Cassie said, "so we can have cake."

Grandma and Grandpa jumped in with their usual teasing about Cassie's sweet tooth, so like their mother's they'd say fondly. Amy couldn't deny it. For the next few minutes, she enjoyed the comfort of the warm rolls topped with melting butter and a generous dollop of honey. The scent of thyme and garlic in the hot stew on the cold night made all her problems seem a little less serious.

After they'd cleared away the cake plates, her grandparents opened the cards Amy bought to give them, one from her, one from Cassie. She'd had some warning about Cassie acting out in the previous days when she couldn't coax her daughter to even glance at the cards they were giving to her grandparents. Cassie cared about one thing only, and that was choosing the valentine to mail to her father, who apparently hadn't bothered to send his daughter a card. At least nothing had arrived in that day's mail. Cassie had checked yesterday and the day before, and she'd do it again tomorrow. It remained to be seen if Scott bothered to call before Cassie's bedtime. She stopped trying to predict her ex-husband's actions. Scott had been a major-league sweet talker before they were married, but those days were long gone.

Nothing could excuse Cassie's outburst at school, but Amy had a pretty good idea what had prompted the hostile behavior. If only she could convince Scott that Cassie's disappointments had piled up. Amy had resolved to at least try to stop keeping score of Scott's broken promises, both to her and to Cassie, but she couldn't expect her daughter to do the same.

Later, she leaned against the doorjamb of Cassie's room and looked on as her daughter put her clean clothes away. She even took time to even out the piles of clothes in her dresser. Cassie claimed not to like anything about her new home or school, and Bluestone River was just a dumb little town, but for all that, she kept her room as neat as could be. Like mother, like daughter.

Amy had the sudden urge to bypass her

meeting with the principal and pull Cassie out of the class and homeschool her. That would keep her out of trouble.

And let me save face.

ERIC WELLS STOOD at the window and cheered the blinding white snowdrifts that were frozen stiff under a sunny blue sky. More sharply angled drifts blocked his driveway and made the street impassable. He didn't care. In all his years of teaching, and now in his new gig as principal, he'd never be this happy about a snow day. It wouldn't solve any problems. He knew that. But at least he had a reprieve. He could avoid meeting with Amy Morgan that morning.

Eric texted his mom to let her know he'd be over in a couple of hours to clear her walk and driveway. Then, warm in a down vest and heavy work boots, he pulled his heavy wool hat over his ears and got to work. First, he shoveled his back steps and the short path to the garage behind the house. Then he dragged out his brand-new snowblower and cleared the way down his driveway and front sidewalk, where he joined one of his neighbors in making a dent in the snow blocking other houses on their side of the street.

Before he started the trek to his mom's house a few blocks away, he dug his phone out of his pocket and took a couple of pictures of the front of his two-story brick house. The deep snow reached the first floor windows and even the drifted snow on the roof looked like whitecaps frozen in time against the blue sky. Cool.

This house, the first he could call his own, needed repairs and upgrades inside and out, but at the moment the snow hid the shabby exterior. That was okay. It wouldn't look bad for long. Eric had spent many years teaching math in a town a couple of hours south of Bluestone River. He'd lived in a one-bedroom apartment in a large complex, but always had a goal to buy a big, rambling house of his own. He'd found it and closed on it a couple of days before Christmas. He'd made the leap from renter to homeowner only when he'd landed the principal's job at the Madison School, the largest of the grade schools in Bluestone River.

Taking another shot of the snow-covered spruce trees in his front yard, a sense of satisfaction surged through him. He'd finally checked off two boxes on his list of goals. His time in the classroom had been rewarding enough, but he'd always tucked away ambitions to move into administration. The home was on tree-lined Oak Street, and with four bedrooms, a roomy attic and a big backyard, all the house needed—besides a major renovation—was a family. *He* needed a family.

His picture taking done, Eric set off down the cleared sidewalks to his mom's house on another one of the "tree streets," Birch Street. He'd spent his teenage years in that house on Birch and had intentionally bought his own place in the central and older part of town behind River Street. He liked being able to stroll over to the diner for a quick dinner or in decent weather walk the mile or so to work.

As he made the turn onto Birch, he spotted his cousin Seth getting out of his truck in front of Eric's mom's house. He picked up his pace and caught up to Seth on the sidewalk.

"You here to help me?" Eric asked, gesturing to the blanket of snow burying the stairs up to his mom's front porch.

Seth held up the giant shovel as his answer. "And when we're done digging your mom out, I thought we could hang out at your place and start ripping out those ancient bathroom fixtures."

"Good thought," Eric said. "I won't turn

down the help." Seth was getting his own construction business off the ground and remodeling Eric's house was a good filler project. Seth was painstakingly documenting progress with dozens of before and after photos he'd cull later and turn into a display on his website. At the moment, he and Seth were in the before stage, but they'd started messing things up worse in order to come out on the other side.

The two got to work removing enough snow off the stairs to get to the front door, where Eric's mom stood watching until she could open the door and let them in.

"The school principal gets a day off, huh," she said, giving Eric and Seth a quick hug each, "but poor me, my plans were all canceled."

"Tomorrow is another day, Aunt Monica," Seth teased. "I'll bet it's crammed full."

"Maybe so, but this morning's French class was canceled," his mom said, "but, I'll be all right. I'm just glad my boys are here to help me out."

He and Seth exchanged an amused glance when his mom called them "her boys." Before Eric left for college the cousins had lived two blocks from each other, but with their reddish blond hair and blue eyes, they looked a lot like brothers. Not so surprising since their mothers were fair-haired, blue-eyed sisters.

"Trust me, Mom, you won't miss much. You'll be back to your schedule by tomorrow." After nearly forty years in nursing, including a twenty-year stint as the nurse manager of a medical practice, his mom had retired. That didn't translate to slowing down, though, not with two book clubs and volunteer work for regional blood drives. Her French class at the community college was supposed to help her get ready for her dream trip to France next fall.

"Your efforts won't go unrewarded," she said. "I'll have lunch ready by the time you're done."

An hour later, his mom could come and go from her house and the town's road crews had made their way to the back streets. Eric and Seth were digging into giant BLTs.

"By the way, did you see what the storm did to the bridge?" his mom asked. "It's awful."

"I haven't heard anything about it." Eric assumed she was talking about the covered bridge spanning the Bluestone River. One of the town's historic landmarks, the bridge was an important tourist draw. "What happened?"

"From the pictures, it looks all but destroyed." She pulled a photo posted on a local radio station's website and handed her phone to Eric.

"Wow. You weren't exaggerating." One side of the bridge had caved in, leaving the vertical wooden wall slats in a heap on what was left of the plank bottom. At least a foot of snow sat on top of the roof, now mostly collapsed. "That looks fatal," he said, passing the phone to Seth.

"Not so fast," his mom warned. "With all the improvements in town, you can bet Mayor Mike is putting a plan together to repair the bridge as we speak."

Eric shrugged. "I suppose." He'd gone to high school with Mike Abbot, better known now as Mayor Mike. Like so many of his classmates, Eric was among those who had scattered after they graduated. But many, like Mike and now Eric himself, had made their way back to their hometown. Unbeknownst to Eric until yesterday, Amy Morgan had added her name to that group.

"Let's go have a look at the bridge before we head to your house and get to work," Seth suggested.

The idea was a welcome distraction from mulling over Amy and her troubled daughter.

After a quick goodbye hug, Eric and his cousin climbed into the truck and Seth drove the few blocks down River Street toward the park and the river. "I see we aren't the only ones here to gawk at the damage," Eric said, nodding to the dozen or so trucks and cars in the parking lot.

Even through the snow-covered branches of the trees separating the parking lot from the playground, Eric saw a piece of the roof hanging off the one intact side. "The photo didn't do the wreckage justice, huh?" he remarked as they started down the slope. "Mom could be wrong about the solution."

"What do you mean?" Seth asked.

"Cooler heads might prevail and they'll tear the thing down before the wooden bottom completely sinks into the river from the weight. It's sort of a relic, anyway."

"An important relic. I guess we'll soon find out," Seth said.

As they got closer, Eric noted clusters of people standing by the riverbank looking at the bridge and pointing this way and that. With everyone bundled up in hats and scarves and puffy coats, Eric couldn't immediately recognize anyone. Some of the kids were running around, more interested in the snow than the bridge. A little boy put one foot into a deep pile of snow and struggled to lift his other foot. Another kid followed closely behind and tried to plant her feet in the deep footprints the boy made. Even with a scarf covering half the boy's face, Eric knew he was Mike Abbot's son, Jason. An easy ID, since Eric also spotted Ruby in the crowd. Even before he'd moved back to Bluestone River, his mom had told him his old friends Ruby and Mike had married. Now they were raising Mike's son and had a new baby girl of their own.

Ruby was in the midst of an animated conversation with another woman who nodded along. She looked familiar, that other woman. Something about her reminded him of Amy Morgan. Whoa. It was her. He was almost certain. When she suddenly pulled off her hat and a mane of straight dark hair fell down her back, he was certain.

He grabbed Seth's arm to hold him back. "Stop, stop. We have to get out of here."

"Huh? Why? What's wrong?"

"That's Amy Raskin. I mean, Amy Morgan. She married that guy in our class, Scott

Morgan." His heart beat faster as he spoke. "I don't want to see her."

"Why? What's the deal?" Seth asked, letting himself be pulled back. "I thought you liked her. Since like *high school*."

"C'mon." Eric hurried through the snow toward the truck. "I do like her, Seth. But I was supposed to have a *disciplinary* meeting with her today about her daughter." He shook his head. "Forget I said that. I shouldn't be talking about a student or a parent." He held up his hand for emphasis. "I mean it. Don't repeat that."

"All right, man, calm down," Seth said. "It's not like it's an emergency. And you know you can trust me to keep my mouth shut."

Eric exhaled a heavy sigh. Seth was right. He'd overreacted, but he couldn't help it. "I don't want to be shooting the breeze with her about the busted up bridge with her one day and talking about, you know, her kid's problems the next." He climbed into the passenger seat, feeling over-the-top relief, like he'd escaped from some kind of danger.

Seth still eyed him with curiosity, but Eric kept quiet until they were at his house and had hauled Seth's tools inside.

He led Seth into the old barn of a bathroom with its broken tile and ancient wallpaper. "My job can be tough sometimes." He braced his hand on the doorway, his mind still on Amy and her daughter. "Being a principal in a small town means I run into people while I'm in the supermarket tossing bags of chips into my grocery cart. It's inevitable." He couldn't help but chuckle at the memory of the very scenario last week. As he greeted the mom and dad, the first grader couldn't keep his big brown eyes off tortilla chips and dark beer in the school principal's cart.

"Goes with the territory, I guess. You better get used to bumping into people you knew from way back when," Seth warned. "Lots of the kids you graduated with are back in town now. And it's not only your crowd. I was two years behind you and now my classmates are turning up everywhere. People seem to drift back for all kinds of reasons."

"I can handle Ruby and Mike—and the others, too," Eric said. "They were friends of mine. I could even handle knowing Amy is around if it weren't for her daughter. No mom likes to hear her kid is a troublemaker and disrupts the classroom." He hesitated, but then said out loud what Seth was being tactful enough to leave alone. "I know, I know. I'm familiar with the problem. I spent more than my fair share of time sitting in the principal's office, too. And my mom had more sleepless nights because of me than I like having on my conscience."

"That can be an advantage, though, right?" Seth asked. "In a way. You were a handful for quite a few years. It can't hurt to understand firsthand what the parents are going through."

"True enough." Eric gave the loose tile on the wall a bump with his fist. "Let's make a dent in this mess. Later, burgers and shakes at the diner will be on me."

Seth picked up a scraper from the plastic bin of tools he'd carried inside. "Okay, then, start scraping that wallpaper, buddy. It's already half-disintegrated."

Eric grinned and took the tool from Seth's outstretched hand and got to work. It didn't take long before the first strip of the old yellowed wallpaper was at his feet. History. Like that old high school crush he'd had on Amy.

CHAPTER TWO

AMY SAT IN the chair across from the school's reception counter. She and Heidi Archer, the office manager, had filled the empty minutes with small talk about the piles of snow around town and the next blizzard in the forecast. Now she sat quietly in her red pantsuit, her job interview suit. As she fidgeted with her onyx beads, she tried to transform the fact she knew Eric Wells back in high school into something positive, rather than the negative coincidence dominating her thoughts.

In theory, being an old friend of Eric's was better than talking to a complete stranger about her daughter's bad behavior. Right? Not necessarily. Not when even hearing his name brought up regrets. Although more than twenty years had passed, Amy remembered how proper Eric had been when he asked her to one of their high school dances. She'd said a firm no, but he'd tried again. Both times she'd brushed him off without giving his feelings a second thought. It could have been awkward between them, but by sheer luck, they'd worked exceptionally well as the team of coeditors of the school newspaper. That's all Eric had ever been to her. A casual friend and someone she worked with. She'd had no time for him beyond divvying up the work to get the paper out every two weeks.

She smoothed the pad of her thumb over her freshly polished nails, a deep but shiny midnight blue. The new nail tech at the salon said that color was in big demand this year. Well okay, then, she'd give it a try. Amy had to admit her manicure gave her a tiny lift on a day that otherwise triggered a lot of self-doubt. She wished Eric would open his office door this minute. She was prepared to listen to what he had to say, respond as best she could and make the meeting a done deal.

As if on command, the door opened and without a word Eric waved her inside.

"Uh, congratulations," Amy said, momentarily thrown when she looked into Eric's bright blue eyes. She almost gasped. Out loud. She'd all but forgotten those eyes, his most striking feature. Way back when she'd joked that between his eyes and his hair, all he needed was a kilt and some bagpipes to look like an authentic Scot. But putting the kilt fantasy aside, it was hard to miss how good he looked in a gray suit coat and red tie.

She hadn't remembered him as especially athletic, but he had the broad shoulders and flat abs of a guy who cared about his fitness—and looking good. "On your new job," she said. "It's quite an accomplishment." She struggled to stop studying the man Eric had become. "I guess Cassie and I moved back to town about the same time you did."

"Well, thanks. Seems we made our way back to Bluestone River in time for winter. It's good to see you, Amy." He pointed to the chair. "Please, have a seat."

Amy nodded and sat on the edge of the chair across from the desk.

"I wish we didn't have to do this," Eric said. "I mean—"

"I know what you mean," Amy said, her tone more impatient than intended. She nervously tapped her lips. Eric's raised eyebrows were evidence he hadn't expected her to interrupt. In a softer voice she said, "To be honest, I've been dreading this for three days now, so let's get on with it."

Eric raised his arms in mock surrender. "Okay, then. So you know that Cassie's teacher, Skylar Morse, says she complains a lot and is *contrary*—one of those favorite teacher words for difficult kids who aren't especially pleasant to deal with. Teachers usually do their best to ignore that stuff, but apparently, Cassie's now openly defiant."

"She drags her feet when we ask her to do things at home," Amy added, so Eric didn't have to ask about that. "That seems kind of typical. She's certainly unhappy at times and pouts." She took a deep breath. "I don't expect you to take my word for it, but she wasn't always like this."

Eric glanced at the notepad in front of him. "So, you're telling me she can be difficult to deal with at home, too?"

Amy stiffened in the chair. "Well, no, not really. That's not the impression I want to leave. But we also live with my grandparents. You might remember, Eric, they raised me. My parents were, well, let's just say they were gone."

Eric nodded. "I remember. Uh, how are your grandparents?"

"Okay." She paused. "As far as it goes. Les had a stroke and it affected his walking and it took time to get back the full use of his left arm. But luckily, his mind is sharp as ever.

I'm helping them now that they've slowed down." She glanced down at her hands. "They're helping me out, as well."

"I see." Eric opened his mouth as if he had more to say, but apparently changed his mind.

Amy had a feeling she knew where he wanted to take this conversation, so she went ahead and filled him in. "Scott and I are divorced, which is why I left Chicago. The move works for me and my grandparents, but Cassie doesn't see Scott as often. She misses her school—and her friends. But she doesn't act out around her grandparents."

"She saves it up for school, huh?" Eric said dryly.

Amy nodded, conceding the point. "She's still upset over our divorce." She'd leave it at that for now, rather than blaming Scott, who wasn't helping any. She swallowed hard to keep from voicing a litany of complaints about her ex.

"What about Scott? Does he know what's going on? Has he talked to her?" Eric pushed the notepad aside and rested his forearms on the desk.

Her thoughts flitted from one way to answer the legitimate question to another. She'd rather avoid even talking about Scott. Ironically, though, when Eric mentioned him, her first instinct was to cover for Scott—and for herself. Talking to Eric like this brought back her high school days in Bluestone River when she had eyes only for Scott.

"As much as possible, this conversation is confidential, Amy," Eric said, frowning. "I'm not going to ask probing questions to be nosy."

She smiled and exhaled. She'd been holding her breath and didn't even know it. "I trust you, Eric. My reluctance to open up is about me." She let out a nervous snicker. "Who wants to talk about their failures?"

He didn't respond in words, but gave her an understanding look.

"Here's the thing. Scott never was much of a dad. He did the bare minimum. If that." She'd just said the words out loud. She admitted the biggest mistake of her life was choosing a man who was an indifferent dad. With her face growing hot, she skimmed away the beads of sweat forming on her hairline without being too obvious about it. What a mistake. Her stylish and flattering wool pantsuit was the wrong thing in the hot, dry air in Eric's office. A sundress would have been better.

"I'm sorry, Amy," Eric said. "That's tough."

She'd let her shoulders droop and curl forward again as if she were trying to hide. Not the picture she wanted to paint of herself. She quickly squared her shoulders and shifted in the chair. She'd told an ugly truth. So what? The floor hadn't opened up and swallowed her whole. The earth was still spinning. She was alive and breathing.

"The worst of it is watching Cassie wait for his calls and then when they don't come, she asks me if she can call him." She lifted her chin a notch and added, "And he lets her down. He breaks his promises and rarely calls, even to just say hello. It's heartless. Sometimes, he doesn't show up for visits at all."

"Which is why she acts out," Eric said through tight jaws, leaning back in the chair now. "No wonder she hasn't adjusted."

Blunt words, but she couldn't argue. "I think that's the reason behind the behavior that landed me here talking to you today."

Eric nodded, but didn't speak. He got up from his chair and stood by the window. "No matter what's gone on, Cassie has to learn boundaries. She's not a little kindergartener."

"I could take her out of school," Amy blurted defensively. She immediately regretted her suggestion. What if he agreed? She'd have a whole set of new problems. Still, she barreled on. "I have a part-time job at the River Street Salon. I could arrange my life to homeschool Cassie. I'd do a good job, too."

"I'm sure you would," he agreed, cocking his head quizzically, "but what would that solve?"

Amy shrugged and pushed loose strands of hair behind her ears. "It would keep you from suspending her or telling me to find a new school."

"*What?* Where did that come from? I'd *never* suggest such a thing. Especially not at this stage, Amy." Eric's voice rose on every word. "Besides, do you really think taking her out of school would solve her problems?"

"No, not really." She conceded the point, but her patience with the direction of the conversation was wearing thin. Besides, she was even more frantic now about solving Cassie's problems than when they'd first started talking. "So give me a better idea," she challenged.

Eric braced his hand on the window frame, and for the next few minutes he talked. Amy listened. Would his ideas work? She couldn't say. She heard a lot about consequences, but nothing about punishments. He never even said the word.

"So, if it's okay with you, let's get Cassie in here," Eric said, moving to the door.

When she nodded, he pressed a button on the phone and asked Heidi to arrange for Cassie to come into the office.

When Eric sat down behind the desk, Amy's heart pounded fast. No matter how she tried to spin it, she couldn't shake the humiliation, made worse because of a shared past with Eric, no matter how superficial. If only her ex hadn't been someone Eric knew back in high school. Scott had been an arrogant teenager, full of himself. She'd mistaken his bravado for confidence and found his swagger a sign of a guy destined for success. But the more she'd elevated Scott, the more she sold herself short. It was still painful to accept she'd thought Scott Morgan's attentions were special and a gift he bestowed on her. After all, who was she back then? The girl whose grandparents had to take her in because her parents were too selfish and inept to take care of her.

"It shouldn't be long," Eric said, breaking the silence.

His words and reassuring smile pulled her out of her dark self-talk. For no other reason than to change the subject, she said, "The damage to the bridge is really something, isn't it? I wonder if it can even be repaired."

Eric gave her a blank look. "Yeah, I hear it's a wreck."

"Oh, haven't you seen it?" Her forehead wrinkled in a frown. "I thought I saw you down by the river after the storm." She waved him off. "There were a lot of people down there. It was probably someone else I saw."

The knock on the door interrupted their conversation and Eric hurried to open the door.

A RELIEF, THAT RAP on the door. It saved Eric the need to either lie or banter about the bridge. Seth had been right about his overreaction. But he had to brush that aside. Feeling a little foolish was irrelevant now.

Eric stepped back and held the door open for Cassie to come inside. "We won't be long," he said to Heidi. He pointed to the empty chair and Cassie followed. "Okay, Cassie, I've got two questions for you," he said, keeping his tone measured. "Do you know that throwing art supplies in the trash is against the rules? And do you understand it was disrespectful to your teacher and your classmates?"

Cassie nodded. "But Ms. Morse told me I had to make valentines for someone at home."

"I see." Eric deliberately avoided catching Amy's eye. "I guess you're not a fan of Valentine's Day."

Cassie folded her arms across her chest. "It's okay, but I told my teacher we already had cards for my grandparents. My mom bought 'em."

"And then what happened?" Eric asked.

"She said then I could make one for my dad." Cassie's face scrunched up in her struggle not to cry. "But I already mailed him a card. To his house in Chicago. He doesn't live *here*."

He glanced at Amy, who was gnawing her lower lip as she watched Cassie. The mother-daughter resemblance was striking. The same long dark hair and eyes that highlighted their heart-shaped faces. Cassie's eyes were a striking greenish brown, where Amy's were darker. He remembered those eyes that belonged to a really cute teenager. What a knockout woman she'd become.

Eric pulled his attention back to the situation. "But you could have made another choice. Right?"

Cassie shrugged. That and her deep frown told him she hadn't caught on.

"Let me explain. You see, how you act, what you do, is all about choices. You could have kept it simple and made another valentine." Eric held up one finger. "Maybe for your dad. Or another card for your mom." Two fingers. "Or, for your two grandparents." He flashed a big grin when he held up four fingers. He glanced at Amy and caught the smile tugging at her mouth. "Wow, Cassie. I came up with four choices in about four seconds."

Cassie looked at him and then at her mom.

"Do you understand what Mr. Wells is telling you?" Amy spoke in a soft voice and lightly rested her hand on Cassie's arm.

"He doesn't know me," Cassie said, pulling her arm away. "He doesn't know I hate it here."

"Maybe so," Eric said quickly before Cassie's response changed the subject. He had other plans for that. "We'll get there. But we were talking about choices. We could come up with more and not even break a sweat."

That grabbed Cassie's attention, so he continued. "Did you know you and I came here about the same time," Eric said. "So, I'm getting used to my new school, too."

Cassie's expression reflected her surprise.

"The thing is, Cassie, this isn't the first time you had choices," Eric said. "I get it. You're having a hard time with a new school, new house, new town and making new friends."

"I don't have any friends."

"Yet," Amy interjected. "We talked about this. It takes time to meet new kids."

Cassie tightened her crossed arms and hunched her shoulders. "They all know each other, like, since kindergarten."

Eric looked at Amy and smiled. "I know all about that, don't I?"

"You sure do," Amy said. "Mr. Wells was the new kid in my high school class, Cassie. I remember when he started."

Eric exaggerated a groan. "And I had no friends. It was awful at the time. But eventually, I made friends. I got to know your mom." *Not so much your dad.* He cleared his throat. "So, all that aside, I want you to know—" he tapped his temple "—up here, that trashing art supplies, refusing to do projects and calling other kids names aren't going to help. And all those things break the rules. And we have the rules to help make this the great school we all want it to be."

Eric let that sink in a minute and noted the tiny bit of progress. Cassie hadn't loosened her arms and she still stared at the floor, but her scowl was gone."

"Sometimes we have to adjust to things even if we don't like them," Eric said. "The way I see it, this is one of those times in your life." He turned to his open laptop. "But, let me see what I've got here."

He shot a look at Cassie, who was watching him at the computer, more curious in the moment than defiant.

"I thought so," he said, flopping back in the chair. "It says here you're in the highest math group. *Wow, will you look at this?* You've already started three-digit multiplication."

"I got a perfect score on my last test," Cassie boasted, "and it's hard to multiply all those numbers."

"I'm proud of you," he said. "Keep that up."

"I will," Cassie said. For the first time she sounded almost happy.

"So, here's what we'll do," Eric said. "You'll come to see me first thing on Monday morning to start your week and again on Friday afternoon to see how your week went. These are our *appointments*. Understand?"

Cassie looked at her mom and nodded.

"You'll check in with me to make sure you're staying on track. That means no name-calling or arguing with Mrs. Morse. You'll follow *all* the rules."

"Sounds good," Amy said, nodding at Eric.

When Eric studied Cassie, he saw a little girl more relaxed now than when she'd come in. That was something to take away from the meeting. He pushed the chair back and stood. "Okay, Ms. Archer will get you back to class."

He turned to Amy. "I'll make the arrangements with Ms. Morse to have Cassie here first thing on Monday. I already have a couple of other kids meeting with me. We'll try it for two weeks."

Eric addressed Cassie as if no one else was in the room. "Do you know what's expected of you? Do you understand why you have to meet with me?"

Cassie nodded. "I have to follow the rules."

Eric nodded. "Then we have a deal?"

Cassie again answered with a nod.

"I want you to think about choices." Eric kept his voice low, but matter-of-fact. "You make small decisions every day. It's up to you to think about them and make good ones."

"Okay, sweetie." Amy steered Cassie to the door. "I have to get to work."

As she followed Cassie out, Amy looked over her shoulder and mouthed, *Thanks*.

He acknowledged her with a quick close-mouthed smile. Then Heidi left with Cassie and Amy hurried away. He dropped in his chair to give himself a minute before moving on to whatever was next on his to-do list.

If only Cassie knew how well he understood the way her anger covered deep sadness. The kind she was too young to understand and didn't have the words to express. But he was sure she felt betrayed by her dad. It wasn't about being angry with her mom or hating a particular school. Without being able to say as much, deep inside Cassie likely believed there was something wrong with her. Otherwise, her dad would call. He'd visit. He'd find ways to let her know how much he cared about her.

Eric sighed. As a teacher he'd dealt with too many Cassies. They were the kids who had dads who painfully resembled his own. He shook his head in disgust.

AMY SORTED THROUGH her jumble of mixed feelings when she opened the back door of the River Street Salon and shrugged out of her heavy coat and hat. She pushed her hair off her face and tried to balance her failures with a surge of renewed hope. The meeting itself was so much easier than she'd imagined. Thanks to Eric. Somehow, he made the rules clear without making Cassie feel like nothing more than a troublemaker. He'd hit a few high notes, too. Praising her math skills right before sending her back to class lifted the energy in the room. Amy hadn't seen that coming.

The only thing she found odd was his blank face when she'd mentioned seeing him at the bridge. She was certain Eric was the man she saw with Seth, his younger cousin. Since they looked so much alike they were hard to miss.

"Well, well, look at you all dressed up." Georgia Greer, owner of the River Street Salon, came into the break room and gestured to Amy head to toe. "Special occasion?"

"Only if you call a meeting at the principal's office special," she said in an intentionally light tone. She filled in a few details about the meeting, keeping her tone optimistic. "I admit it's been a big—and difficult—adjustment all around."

Georgia nodded. "But you have no worries here. You're doing a great job, and I know you're capable of doing a lot more."

She thanked Georgia, knowing her boss probably had no idea how much those words meant to her. Amy followed Georgia into the salon and up to the reception desk where a customer was coming inside. Teri, the new stylist and nail tech, joined them.

"Busy day," Georgia said to the customer. "The storm meant a lot of rescheduled appointments."

"And it's going to mean a big fight over the bridge, or so I hear," Teri said as she led her customer to her chair.

Fight? "What's to fight about?" Amy said. "I picture Mike Abbot—and Ruby—already figuring out how to fund repairs. That's the impression I took away from talking to Ruby down at the river the other day."

Georgia frowned. "I assumed that, too. But I went to the diner this morning and heard some rumblings about rethinking the bridge, maybe tearing it down and building a two-lane road to the land on the other side."

Fat chance of that happening, Amy thought. "There's nothing on the other side except acres of prairie and a couple of unpaved roads. I'm quite sure Ruby and everyone else who came to have a look were talking about saving it."

"I hope you're right," Georgia said, ending the discussion when she greeted one of her regular clients coming inside.

By the time Amy started home a few hours later, she'd scheduled a dozen or more appointments and confirmed more than a dozen or more with phone calls. When she wasn't on the phone or processing payments, she unpacked newly arrived stock and resupplied the shelves of the bath and body products Georgia carried.

The scent of the new coconut and lime shower scrub and body lotion added to her improving mood as the afternoon passed. Eavesdropping on the conversations going on around her, she noted almost everyone had something to say about the storm damage, but fallen trees and mangled signs didn't attract the same degree of attention as the landmark covered bridge.

Funny, in early January when Georgia hired her part-time, she'd been of two minds about the job. Relieved to have a job, she'd also accepted the position a little grudgingly and felt defeated. She'd been assistant manager at an upscale cookware shop in Chicago, so working as a part-time receptionist in a hair salon starkly reminded her of questionable decisions in her past.

Amy assumed she'd miss supervising a crew of sales associates and yearn for the fast pace of retail. As it turned out Georgia and the two part-time stylists and nail techs made her feel glad she was back home. Now she'd met lots of new people in town and had even bumped into a few old classmates. She'd felt like a girl slinking back home without much to show for her life, except her child, but that was slowly morphing into the pleasure of living in Bluestone River again.

When she let herself in the house, she heard voices in the living room. She unwound the scarf from around her neck and got out of her coat and her wet boots, but she stopped at the doorway into the kitchen when she heard Cassie's voice. She was telling her great-grandparents about her dad coming all the way from Chicago to pick her up next Saturday morning. They were going to have an adventure. All day. And, Amy thought, Cassie would go on about it all week.

Her stomach turned over, a familiar feeling now when Cassie talked about Scott. *Please, Scott, don't let her down. Again.*

CHAPTER THREE

ERIC THOUGHT ABOUT calling Amy while he cut up a pile of vegetables and boiled rice for his stir-fry dinner. He mulled it over later when he took a claw hammer and crowbar to the decrepit cabinets in the bathroom and later when he carried the debris out the back door to the construction bin Seth had left on the porch. He was still thinking about Amy—and Cassie—when he opened a bottle of dark beer and settled down on the couch in the living room and flipped on the TV. He clicked the sports channels until he found a basketball game to give his brain some background noise to distract him. He could only hope.

It had been a week since he and Amy had met in his office and she'd told him what kind of man Scott had turned into. As if Eric couldn't have predicted that. He'd always seemed like a guy who'd be all take and no give—a lot of talking and not much substance. That wasn't sour grapes, either. Scott hadn't won in a fair fight over Amy way back when. That was because Eric had never had a chance with Amy in the first place. She'd never given him a second look.

What bothered him now was that Amy blamed herself for what Scott had done—or not done. He'd watched that kind of burden weigh heavily on his mom. Like Amy, his mom had married a guy who was not only a mediocre partner, but a dud as a dad. From seeing the sadness in Amy's brown eyes when she sat across from him, he guessed she carried more than her share of the blame for her marriage hitting a wall.

Eric checked the time on his phone. If he was going to take this step, the time was now. "You've got to quit overthinking this," he muttered.

He made the call and seconds later he heard her voice. "Eric?"

He could barely hear her over the background noise on her end, but it gradually faded. "I hope I'm not calling too late."

"No, no, I was just with my grandpa watching cable news." With a soft snicker, she added, "Les calls himself the most well-informed old man in town."

Eric wanted to know more about this

grandpa and grandma who raised Amy, but if he started down that road he'd never get to the point. "Listen, I called for a specific reason. I mean, I didn't…" Tongue-tied. But why did he find this so difficult? The old attraction? His worries for Cassie? Hard to say. Once he was in his professional groove the other day, he'd handled the situation with Cassie pretty well. His aim was to adopt that tone in this call.

"Eric? You've got me curious now."

"I'm sorry. To be honest, if this were another student, I wouldn't be talking about what I'm about to bring up." He paused. "Because it's personal. It's different this time because I already know you." He hesitated, but added, "And I knew Scott. That's why I'm calling."

"I'm listening," Amy said. "I'm in my room now with the door shut, so I can talk freely."

"You likely aren't aware of a few things in my past," he started. "One of the reasons I think I understand children pretty well— maybe kids like Cassie in particular—is that I was always in trouble, especially when I was around her age. For a few years, I spent almost as much time in the principal's office as I did my classroom."

"I'm stunned," Amy blurted. "Really. It doesn't match anything I know about you, Eric." She paused. "Or thought I knew."

He'd expected that reaction. It wasn't the first time someone had a hard time seeing him as a troubled kid. "It's true. A whole lot of teachers and principals were more or less forced to give me a fair share of their attention."

Amy scoffed. "It's so hard to believe because you were like the *peacemaker* in our class."

"Much better than the troublemaker."

"I recall that homeroom teacher we had senior year, Ms. Shaw," Amy said, her voice still expressing surprise. "She pointed to you as an example of a boy with fine manners. Ha! You even got teased over that one."

He snorted. "Yep, that was me. The guys ribbed me relentlessly for weeks. Even the hotshots like Mike Abbot had a good time with it. What seventeen-year-old wants a teacher heaping praise on him for his manners?"

"I get it," Amy said, clearly amused, "but look at you now."

"When I moved to Bluestone River for my sophomore year, I'd already turned around.

With some major help." It was his mother who'd drilled the whole manners lesson into his head, claiming that no one liked rude people, no matter how good-looking or smart.

"Really? You went from being labeled a so-called problem to who you are now?"

"I was motivated to become a teacher because I wanted to help kids make the best of the situations they found themselves in, no matter how difficult or hurtful," Eric said, knowing his honesty could sting. "They can't control their parents, but they can learn to navigate through tough times. It's what I want for Cassie—and all the other kids, too."

"I believe you," Amy said softly. "But can you tell me more about what happened to you?" Amy asked. "I won't pass on anything you tell me. I promise. You know I have a complicated past myself."

Her earnest, curious voice made it almost hard to breathe. "It's not so complicated, really. My dad packed a bag and walked out one day. No explanation, at least not to me. Of course, my mom said all the right things about him leaving her, but not leaving me."

Amy groaned. "I know that drill. Your mom wanted that to be true. I can say that for sure."

"I suppose you can. But I wouldn't call if this was only about your divorce," Eric said. "That's none of my business. But I'm confiding in you because from what you said last week, I have a feeling Scott could be a lot like my dad."

Trying to stick to the facts, Eric explained that his father lost interest in keeping up any kind of relationship with him, let alone a nurturing, supportive one. He made promises about everything from camping trips to fixing up a room in his apartment. Almost nothing he talked about ever materialized. Once he left his mom, his dad never again went to parents' night at school. Eric lost count of the number of birthdays he ignored—claiming he had a bad memory for details like that.

"As for the twice-a-month weekends I was supposed to spend with him, he canceled way more often than he showed up," Eric said, getting to his feet and walking around the living room and then into the kitchen. "And, man, did I lash out. I was *openly*, no-holds-barred defiant. The things I did weren't exactly like Cassie destroying the art supplies, but I was nasty and aggressive," Eric said, wincing against the memory of himself as a boy in turmoil. "That's what put me inside the principal's office many times."

"That's awful. I can only imagine how hurt you must have been." Amy's voice revealed her empathy as much as the shock at hearing this unknown part of his story.

"Anyway, this went on for years." He paused, aware he had to be careful about what he said to wrap this up. He didn't want to alarm Amy about the path he'd taken. On the other hand, everything he'd said was sadly accurate. If these hard facts could help her cope with Cassie, or more to the point, Scott, then it was worth spilling them. "Eventually, when my dad finally showed up for something, I refused to see him."

"All the time we worked together on the newspaper," Amy said, "I thought your dad had died."

Eric moved to the living room window and pushed the ancient drapes aside and looked out to the quiet street where the snow glistened under the half-moon. "Of course you did. I let people assume that." None of this mattered so much anymore, but Cassie did. "What I really want to say is that when I was a miserable kid acting out, my mom had the same regrets you talked about the other day in my office." It had taken his mom too many years to stop feeling like she'd messed up his life. "My dad died for real when I was about to graduate from college, but by then I'd softened my attitude enough to see him once or twice a year."

"So, taking this from A to B, your experience with your dad eventually led to your check-ins with kids going through hard times. Children like Cassie." Amy stated it as a fact, not a question.

"More or less. When I was thirteen a baseball coach in a park league finally got me to see I was burning bridges one after the other." He shook his head, even all these years later regretting his bad attitude. "You see, I'd already earned myself a reputation as one of the bad guys. Avoid Eric, other parents told their kids. But the coach got it. I was lonely and angry. Coach White was patient. I finally figured out that being obnoxious hurt me, not my dad."

It hurt his mom, too, but he didn't need to go into all that with Amy.

"The coach drilled in the idea about making good or bad choices. It stuck. That's why I use it in my work with kids."

Neither spoke for a few seconds, but that

was okay. It was a comfortable silence, even on the phone.

Finally, he took a deep breath and broached what he knew could be a tricky subject. But it had been nagging at him. "Didn't you have to navigate through some bad times? When you were a kid, I mean?"

"Hmm…sort of." She let out a long sigh. "My parents left the first time when I was around three years old," Amy explained. "They were gone a year or so, came back, hung around for a while, but then left again, when I was about five. In and out a couple of times, but eventually they stopped pretending they were going to come for me."

"That's tough, Amy. Must have been awful."

"It was for the best, as it turned out." She paused. "That's the adult Amy talking, though."

"Exactly," Eric agreed.

"I'd already spent most of my time with my grandparents. That's because Mom and Dad were always busy chasing the next big thing."

"Big thing?" Eric asked. "What does that mean?"

This time Amy broke the tension with a laugh. "I meant that sarcastically. Let's just say that one winter they ran off to take jobs on a cruise ship. They were supposedly looking for some exotic far-off place for us to live a simpler life."

"You mean like on a tropical island?" Eric asked.

"Yep. I remember them saying we were going to live in a tent on the beach or some such thing." She paused. "Looking back at it now, they made it sound exciting to live like hunters and gatherers. Hunt fish, gather seaweed."

This was all news to him. And her offhand tone didn't fool him. She'd never said one word about her parents when they were teenagers working on the paper.

"I'll tell you more about it some other time," Amy said. "At least the parts I remember. I try not to think about them much now. Not long after I married Scott we got word they'd died in a boating accident, but we hadn't heard from them in years. We didn't know where they were, and my grandparents didn't have money to hand over to private investigators to find them."

His gut tightened. "Wow, Amy, that's terrible."

"And in the past," she said, her tone firm

now. "Unfortunately, Scott is the present. Or he's supposed to be, at least for Amy."

"That's the worst part of all this, I'm sure," Eric said, sensing she was making it sound like a cut-and-dried story because she didn't want to talk about her parents. "You've got a lot on your mind. But call me if you want to talk about...well, any of this. I mean it. Anytime."

"I'm grateful you phoned," Amy said. "You give me hope that Cassie and I can get through this."

Eric smiled. That was the idea. "'Night, Amy. I'll keep you updated."

Not long after the call, he'd turned off the TV and all the lights, yet, he was restless, his mind racing through the memories he'd stirred up. Slamming doors and locking himself in his room were the least of it. It was how he sneered at any adult who tried to talk with him that still made him ache when he thought about it. Until Coach White persisted in pushing past his hostility, Eric had felt isolated, hopeless.

He ran through the whole conversation with Amy, hoping he'd said the right things. She claimed it helped her, and he took her at her word.

"WHAT DO YOU want to do first?" Eric asked the question in a tone that managed to be warm but not overly familiar. His blue eyes fixed on Cassie, she had his full attention.

"I don't know, Mr. Wells," Cassie responded shyly.

Amy stood back and let the conversation between Eric and Cassie unfold on its own. Cassie's eyes still red from her earlier tears broke Amy's heart, but what could she expect after Scott called and canceled the adventure he'd promised Cassie. The one that was supposed to last all day. Right.

Something came up. That's all he'd told Amy when she'd lifted the phone out of Cassie's grip. Work stuff. Besides, more snow was on the way and that meant the roads between Chicago and Bluestone River would become treacherous. Oh, really? Amy hadn't heard that weather report.

Thinking of her recent conversation with Eric, it was clear that Scott still didn't get it. It was better not to make promises to Cassie in the first place. Somehow, he chose to blame Amy, claiming her decision to move back to Bluestone River made it even harder for him to see Cassie. A bogus excuse. He'd never been that interested in his daughter even when they were a family. She couldn't say that out loud, though, not with Cassie standing right next to her. But not seeing his daughter very often was Scott's choice.

Even talking to him brought up the harsh judgment she directed at herself for being such a big fool to fall for a man who couldn't be bothered with his own child. Talk about a bad choice.

After speaking to her dad, Cassie had run off to her room, brushing off efforts from Amy or her great-grandparents to comfort her. Distraught herself, Amy had paced the kitchen trying to figure out what to do. That's when Eric came to mind. She mulled over his offer to call him if she wanted to talk. At first, she convinced herself that was a ridiculous idea, way out of line. Finally, she decided to take him up on his offer mostly because she couldn't afford to wallow in regret or waste energy while Cassie was feeling so terrible.

When she'd caught Eric at home, she'd expected him to listen and offer advice. But Eric skipped over the advice part and suggested they go to the Snowball Fair over in Laurel, a town about thirty minutes away. *It will get her mind off her dad*, Eric had offered.

Amy had been so surprised she'd barely

managed to sputter an objection to let him off the hook, but seconds later he'd convinced her to drop her guard and say yes. Now she stared at the display of ice sculptures and snow forts on the field behind Laurel's crowded expo center. Kids and adults were coming and going from the building, where carnival music blared through loudspeakers. Adults dressed up as polar bears, walruses with exaggerated tusks and penguins roamed through the crowd, greeting visitors and passing out flyers about the event.

Amy pointed to the adults and kids making all sizes and shapes of snow people at the edge of the tents and covered entrance inside. "Let's see what's doing over there."

"Good idea," Eric said, "unless you'd rather build a snow fort." He nodded to a field where people were making elaborate forts, some complete with moats and snow ladders.

"What's it going to be, Cassie, snow forts or snow people?" Amy asked.

Cassie looked at the forts and then at the field of snowmen, some finished, some in progress. "Snow people." She took off down the path and ran through the clusters of snow people, many with traditional carrots for noses and walnuts for eyes. "Come on over here," she yelled, waving both arms over her head.

"Looks like she found a spot." Eric chuckled. "I liked how she gave some thought to the choices you offered her."

"It was a very big decision," Amy said, giving Eric a sidelong glance. "Let's hope she'll take that much time to consider some of her other choices."

Eric laughed. "I'm with you, but it was still amusing to watch her weigh her options."

Cassie's voice calling out to her grabbed her attention, and Eric's. She was pointing to a family of four who were adding a football helmet to a very tall snowman whose round head sat on shoulders they'd packed and shaped to look like pads. They'd tucked a football under one arm.

"Let's make a snow lady next to him," Cassie said when they caught up with her.

"You've got it all figured out," Eric said.

"I see some plastic bins of supplies by the tent, Cassie. Let's go see what we can find." With Eric following, she and Cassie went to the bins and rummaged through them. Amy found an old red felt hat and some plastic flowers to stick in the brim.

"Hey, Mom, look at these." Cassie giggled

as she held up a wide stretchy belt with red sequins in one hand and a purse to match in the other.

"Very chic," Amy said, nodding. "We've got plenty to get us started."

"Look at these cool shoes," Eric said, holding up a pair of black Mary Janes.

"Where will her feet be?" Cassie asked.

"I'll let you know once we get started," Eric said, grinning.

Amy laughed. "I'm curious myself."

He leaned toward her as if confiding a secret. "I have an excellent idea, but I can't take any credit for it. My mom came up with this when Seth and I were little. You'll see."

"It's a mystery, Cassie," Amy said.

"Okay, you two, let's get to work. Cassie, why don't you start the big snowball for her body? Your mom can start with the head." Eric lowered his voice to sound extra serious. "I'll get going on the mystery pieces."

Amy watched Cassie steadily work to turn the blob of snow into a larger and larger ball. Her face looked both determined and blissfully happy. Amy stopped what she was doing to take it all in. During cherished moments like these, all the worries about Cassie melted away and Amy could relax and just enjoy being a mom.

Between the three of them, it didn't take long to get a giant snowball for the body and one for the head. "I think that's big enough, Cassie," Eric called. "Time to give this lady her head."

Amy picked up the smaller ball and plunked it on top of the body.

"Okay, are you two ready to be impressed?" Eric teased, smiling at Cassie.

Cassie nodded. Amy held back a laugh when she saw what Eric was up to.

"Well, then, watch this." Eric rolled into place two long thin rolls of snow and tucked them up against the body. Then he packed the snow into a firmer shape and carefully crossed one piece over the other. Suddenly, the snow lady was sitting on the ground with crossed legs.

"Look at her, Mom." Cassie clapped her hands. "Hardly any snow people have legs, but ours does." Her eyes widened. "I can make feet so she can wear her shoes."

"Very clever," Amy said. "I'm impressed."

Cassie used both hands to pack snow and shape it into two blocks that would pass for feet. Amy took out her phone and captured

Cassie putting the Mary Janes on the snow lady, with Eric standing next to her with a huge smile on his face. Then she and Cassie arranged the hat on their creation and stuck the red and yellow flowers in the brim.

"Uh-oh, she doesn't have a waist." Cassie held up the sequined belt.

"We'll have to make one for her," Eric said. "Let's see." He took one end of the belt and Cassie had the other and they wrapped it around the middle part of the snowball body and cinched it.

"Wonderful," Amy said as she took pictures of the almost finished product while Eric and Cassie went back to the bins. They pulled out a couple of dowels for arms, sunglasses and red wax lips for a mouth. Eric declared the lady finished when Cassie hung the red purse over the dowel.

"So smart to wear sunglasses on this bright, sunny day," Amy said, taking a final picture of Eric and Cassie looking triumphant standing with the snow lady between them. She sent a couple of her best photos to Eric's phone. "Her crossed legs and shoes make her very special, Cassie."

"I love her," Cassie exclaimed, clapping her

hands and jumping up and down. "She's the best snow lady ever."

Eric nodded and looked around. "I agree. She's one of the best of the bunch out here."

"Let's go over to the tent and officially enter the contest," Amy said. "But first, don't we have to think of a name for our creation? I'd say she needs a fancy name."

"Hmm, what do you think, Cassie?" Eric asked.

Cassie shrugged. "We could name her Hat Lady." Then she bounced up and down and clapped her hands. "I know, I know. She's Miss Sparkle. Because of her sequins."

Amy laughed. "I like that. What do you think, Eric."

Eric echoed her laughter. "Nice going. She's definitely the most sparkly snow person out here."

"I think she likes it." Cassie waved at Miss Sparkle. "Bye-bye, see ya later when we win."

Cassie ran ahead.

"Win or lose," Eric said, "she had a lot of fun making her snow person."

"Absolutely," Amy said, wondering if any of this seemed odd to Eric. He obviously found Cassie amusing, but he was sacrificing his day off to spend time with a child who knew him only in his role as the principal. He was not only saving the day for Cassie, but for Amy, as well. It had all happened so fast. One minute she was telling him about Cassie's heartbreaking tears and the next he was pulling up to the door to take them out for the day.

"I enjoyed it, too," Eric said, his expression thoughtful. "As much as I work with kids, I don't get to spend this kind of carefree time with them very often."

"I suppose not, but you're sure good at it." Amy almost added a remark about what a great dad he'd be, but she caught herself in time. She didn't know him nearly well enough to get that personal, even after he'd opened up about his troubled relationship with his own dad.

Cassie reached the tent ahead of them and was talking to a woman at the table while she and Eric caught up.

"You all having a good time?" the woman volunteer asked. "Your little girl is thrilled with her snow lady."

"Now the big question is, what's next?" Amy said, sliding past the implication that the two of them were Cassie's parents.

"The petting zoo," Cassie said. "I know where it is. I saw the sign."

Amy patted Cassie's shoulders. "You don't miss a thing."

"We'll see you later when we put ribbons on the snowmen and announce the winners," the woman said. "Have fun with Mom and Dad at the zoo."

"He's *not* my dad," Cassie said, as if that were obvious. "He's Mr. Wells, the principal of my school. My dad couldn't make it today."

"Well, okay, I'm sorry. My mistake." The woman drew out the words and exaggerated her sheepish expression. She glanced at Eric apologetically.

Eric's normally pale cheeks turned pink as he waved off the apology.

The truth was hard to face. She'd had more fun with Eric over the last couple of hours than she'd had with Scott in a long time. It had taken her ex years to finally admit the awkward truth: he wasn't really into family time.

"The petting zoo is this way," Cassie said, pointing past the ice sculpture garden to the largest tent on the grounds. It extended from the open expo center doors.

"We can warm up inside the tent," Eric said.

"But first, we have to see the ice sculptures." Amy pointed to the largest one in the middle of the garden, a polar bear and two cubs. She called for Cassie to follow her. "I want to get some shots of you standing with the bears."

With the ice glistening under the sun, the sculpture garden stood out dramatically against the blue winter sky. The dozen or so sculptures were mostly renditions of marine creatures. Dolphins and whales seemed to be leaping up from ice blocks shaped to look like ocean waves. A couple of ice penguins with exaggerated smiles drew a huge crowd of picture takers. A whimsical troll couple looked on as if they were the guardians of the scene.

"Looks like I'm not the only person with a phone camera," Amy joked as she weaved through a crowd of many dozens of people enjoying the sculptures. She told Eric and Cassie where to stand while she took a couple of pictures of them and a few of Cassie alone. Then Eric took several shots of Amy with Cassie. A little performer at heart, Cassie liked nothing better than striking poses for photos.

Amy tried to ignore thoughts of Scott intruding on her good time. This was supposed to be Scott's time with Cassie. How sad that he'd forfeited his right to have such a fun experience.

She felt the same way when they went into the petting zoo, set up in a heated tent. As they walked inside, Cassie started happily skipping ahead. "I haven't seen her so excited, even buoyant, in a long time." Amy tried to ignore the lump in her throat at the sight of Cassie swinging her arms as she bounced along.

Eric nodded. "I'm glad she's having a good day."

Amy pointed to Cassie, who was standing on a horizontal slat in front of a wooden pen. "I might have known she'd only have eyes for the horses. Cassie used to love the Farm-in-the-Zoo in Chicago. We'd go there just to see the horses in the barn."

"Hmm…a horse enthusiast," he said, his forehead wrinkled in thought. "Now that can be a positive thing, especially for girls. I've heard from some of our parents that girls who ride and even own a horse mature in good ways. It's like sports. Keeps them occupied and out of trouble."

"Hmm." For all the good it would do her. Even looking ahead a couple of years the expense of owning and boarding a horse would be out of Amy's reach.

His low voice broke into her thoughts. "I didn't mean to suggest you should buy a horse, Amy."

He could read her mind? "I didn't think you did. It's just that when I see her around horses it's like looking at myself at the same age." She met Eric's gaze. "I didn't ride as a little girl, but in high school I worked as a summer nanny. I managed to put aside some money and took a few riding lessons. It was kind of a high point for me. I wish…" She shook her head and decided not to go into it. She wished a lot of things.

"I don't recall us ever talking about you and horses," Eric mused, "you know, back when we were in school."

"We were pretty focused on the newspaper," Amy said, keeping her eye on Cassie, who was leaning over the top of the fence and stretching out her arm to coax the two horses to come closer. Both were gorgeous dark brown mares with white markings.

When Amy reached her, Cassie pinched her nose. "It smells just like the horse barn in the zoo, huh?"

"I suppose it does," Amy said, smiling, "but you know I kinda like that horsey scent."

"It's not so bad." Cassie kept her eyes on the mares. "Aren't they pretty? They're the color of chocolate bars."

"I know. They're beautiful, sweetie." Amy put one arm around Cassie's shoulders and extended the other toward the horse closest to her. "Let's wait a few minutes and see if she'll come over. If she does, I'll pat her neck and she'll stick around and maybe come a little closer." Within minutes, one of the mares ambled over and pushed her nose into Amy's hand.

"Maybe she'll like this," Eric said, coming up from behind with an apple in his hand. "The owner of the horses said we could give the mare a treat. Only one apple, though, or she could get a stomachache. Lots of people are offering treats today."

"Go ahead, Cassie, give it a try," Amy said. "Put it in your palm and see what happens."

Sure enough, the mare made short work of the apple and then seemed to kiss Cassie's palm and make her giggle. "It tickles."

"Like a little feather," Amy said, stroking the horse's smooth neck. "A horse can nibble at your palm without hurting you."

When the mare wandered off, Amy turned to find Eric. He was next to a small pen where a man had parrots perched on his arm. "Hey, Cassie, let's go see the parrots."

They got to Eric just when the man moved one of his parrots from his arm to Eric's.

"All you need is a hat and an eye patch and you'd be transformed into quite the roguish pirate," Amy said, grinning.

Eric flashed a teasing grin at Cassie and said, "Aye, but I need me spyglass and me ship, don't I, lassie?"

Amy laughed at his tortured accent, and was about to say something about it, but the parrot beat her to it.

"Me ship, me ship," the parrot said.

"Oh, so you're finally talking today," the parrot owner said to the colorful bird on Eric's arm. "Seemed to take a little person coming around to make him lively."

"Do the parrots get cold?" Cassie asked.

Good question, Amy thought.

"They're toasty warm inside the tent," the man said, "but I don't carry 'em outside to have a chat with the snowmen."

"They've got really pretty feathers," Cassie said shyly.

"Would you like to have this one sit on your arm, lassie?"

The parrot owner lifted the brilliant-blue-and-golden-yellow bird off Eric's forearm and put it on Cassie's.

Giggling, Cassie said, "Me ship, me ship."

When the parrot repeated the words, Cassie laughed and turned to a couple of teenagers who'd joined them at the table.

"He really talks," she said.

"Looking eager for a turn, are you?" the parrot owner said to the other kids.

"I don't know about you two, but I'm getting hungry," Amy said, stepping back from the table. "How about we get some lunch indoors?"

When Cassie nodded, the parrot owner switched the bird from her arm to the arm of one of the teens. "Thank you," Cassie said, waving goodbye to the bird and the man.

"Wow," Eric said, "that was fun. I've never had a parrot perch on my arm before."

"Me, either," Cassie said, running ahead through the open doors to the expo center.

Games and craft tables were set along the far wall, but most of the people in the crowd were wandering toward the musicians on the stage.

"Live music," Eric pointed out. "I'm impressed."

So was Amy. The jazzy sound came from the dozen or so teenagers playing saxophone and trumpets, with two bass players and one on piano.

"Look at that," Amy said, pointing to the banner that read The Jazz Band of Laurel West High. "They have enough talent to have their own jazz group."

"Let's get closer and have a look," Eric said.

The musicians were arranged at the back of a stage, which itself was decorated with a set right out of a fairy-tale movie. The painted snowy forest background was lit with white lights and circled the limbs and branches of a realistic-looking tree attached to the edge of the stage.

"We got here just in time for the dancers," Amy said, pointing to the troupe of teenagers filing onto the stage. They were dressed in white bodysuits trimmed with ice-blue fleece.

The rows of folding chairs were full, but there was room on the side and at the back to stand. Amy positioned Cassie in front of her and lightly cupped her shoulders. When the performance started, Amy found herself mesmerized by the sound of the tap shoes on the wooden stage, the synchronized movements, all dozen kids, eight girls and four boys moving as one. It was like watching an old-fashioned Broadway musical.

When it was over, the dancers got a standing ovation and loud cheers.

"It's like the talent shows back in high school, huh?" Eric said. "Only better."

"I have such good memories of doing a dance routine with a bunch of girls junior year," Amy added. "We weren't nearly as good as these kids are."

Watching them perform another number, she was touched *for* the kids, as much as *by* them. They bowed and waved in response to the clapping for their second number. She hoped the kids' sense of triumph would last, her own similar memory acting like a safety net in the bad times. *Talk about projecting*, she thought. The further away she traveled from those high school years, the more clearly she saw the missed opportunities to feel good about what she'd accomplished.

Cassie turned to Eric. "I want to dance like that someday. I like ballet, too. My dad took me to see *The Nutcracker* once. Mom couldn't come. She had to work."

"That was a couple of years ago," Amy said. "I was sorry to miss it. I love that ballet."

"Hmm…tap dance, ballet, horseback riding. Lots of things to choose from, Cassie."

Irrationally annoyed, Amy gave Eric a pointed look. She could manage a dance class, but riding lessons were beyond her budget. No sense getting Cassie's hopes up. But she couldn't expect Eric to get that, even knowing she had a part-time job.

Amy sniffed the air. "What is that I smell? Could it be burgers or pizza, maybe fries?"

"I want a burger," Cassie said. "What about you, Mr. Wells?"

Eric pretended to consider Cassie's polite question before inhaling deeply and expounding on the aromas in the air. They got in line at the food booths and all three ordered a burger basket and sodas, a rare treat for Cassie.

While they waited for their food, Eric recognized a couple and their kids. When he waved to them, the kids called out, "Hello, Mr. Wells." They quickly approached Eric, but the adults only reluctantly followed.

When the woman stared at Amy quizzically, as if trying to place her, Amy introduced herself and Cassie.

"Great event, isn't it?" Eric glanced over at Amy. "I'm glad we were able to get here for it."

Sounds pretty cozy, Amy thought. This was going to get awkward fast. Fortunately, they were saved from having to make small talk. A woman at the counter called number thirty-two. "That's our lunch," Amy said.

The family wandered off and she and Eric picked up their order and settled at a table with their burgers.

"Was that weird for you?" Amy asked when Cassie was preoccupied with people watching and dipping fries in ketchup.

"Not so bad," Eric said. "When I was a teacher I'd run into people in all kinds of places. It went with the territory. It shouldn't be different for a principal, but somehow these chance meetups are a little more awkward now."

Amy snorted a laugh. "The kids didn't care. They were just happy to see Mr. Wells."

"Do *you* care?" Eric asked with curiosity in his voice.

"Nope." She gestured around her. "Certainly not here. Besides, my job doesn't come with an image to maintain." She paused, but then added, "Your position is entirely different."

Eric shook his head. "I'm not really concerned. Let's just say I'm getting used to having a new crop of parents and kids to bump into. I've been surprised that I'm a little more on display than I anticipated." He dropped his voice lower. "Bluestone River is a pretty small town."

Eric was sending her a message, Amy thought. But she didn't know exactly what it was and didn't care to ask directly. What did it matter? He didn't need to concern himself with others seeing them together. Besides, this threesome trip to the Snowball Fair was a one-time thing. That's all.

Amy stood and began gathering their paper plates and cups. "We should go over to the snowman field and see what's doing?"

Eric checked the time on his phone. "Yep, they should have given out the ribbons by now."

Amy gave Cassie's hat an extra tug over her ears when they got ready to go back out into the cold air. "Lead the way," she said to Cassie.

"I hope she's not disappointed with the result," Amy said when Cassie was a few steps ahead.

Eric shrugged. "We entered the competition and disappointment goes with the territory—at least, sometimes."

"I know that, but c'mon, Eric, I'm just thinking like a mom."

"I guess I did sound a little cavalier," Eric admitted with a sheepish grin. "But I deal with tests and contests and winning and losing all the time."

True enough, Amy thought, but that didn't always make it easy for kids to handle in the moment. "Grandpa Les was big on saying, 'win some, lose some.' For years, I thought he'd made up that cliché."

Cassie's happy voice carried across the field. "We got a yellow ribbon!"

"I don't know exactly what that means," Amy said with a laugh, "but I'll take it."

They hurried to Cassie and sure enough, a yellow ribbon was tacked to Miss Sparkle's hat.

"It says 'special mention,'" Cassie bragged. "A few of the snow people got yellow. That big one got a blue ribbon."

"I see," Amy said. "It's pretty terrific." It was a skier complete with snow hands holding poles and was built on skis.

After Amy got a picture of Miss Sparkle sporting her ribbon, they walked over to the tent, where a volunteer gave Cassie a ribbon to take home. "Our snow people will be on display until the snow melts. Since you won a Special Mention ribbon you can choose a stuffed animal from the shelf." She pointed to the collection of stuffed animals sitting next to the table. They were mostly whales and polar bears.

"You mean we won something more?" Cassie said, holding up the ribbon.

"Yes, you did. We had a first place, second place and then we decided we'd have six Special Mentions."

"What's it going to be, Cassie?" Eric asked as they examined the shelf of animals.

Amy wasn't surprised when Cassie picked up the one lone seal that looked like it was smiling. It was tan with big black eyes and whiskers. All-around adorable.

"I like this one," Cassie said.

Amy took one last photo of Cassie standing with Miss Sparkle and holding her amusing seal before they left the snowmen. "We should let you get on with your day, Eric."

"This was a much-needed break from all the hard labor I'm doing on my new house," Eric said as they strolled toward the parking lot with the dwindling crowd. "Well…actually it's an old house." He grinned. "I had a great time. I should be thanking you. We should do this…"

Bad idea, Amy thought, as Eric caught himself and stopped talking.

When they reached the SUV, Amy gave him a one-arm hug and whispered, "You saved our day." She pulled away quickly, though, and turned her attention to settling Cassie in the car. She didn't need a mirror to know that simple hug had made her blush.

CHAPTER FOUR

ERIC MOTIONED FOR Seth to follow him to the
row of empty chairs in the back of the community room, where the town council meeting was about to start.

"I've only come to a few of these meetings," Seth said, "and I've only seen a crowd
like this once or twice. Even the meeting to
give the okay to expand the river trails didn't
draw this many people."

Since he'd moved back to town he'd been
struck by how many people ran scared about
changing anything in town. Like the outdoorsy side of Bluestone River with the river
and the nature center was all there was to the
place. The town had taken advantage of every
feature it had to draw visitors, which added
up to much more than that old covered bridge.
He wouldn't have supported the idea of tearing it down if it was still in one piece and in
decent shape. But what good was it now that
it was all but destroyed. Why not let it go?

The room filled up fast and Mike Abbot soon banged the gavel on the podium to quiet the crowd.

"Seems funny to think of Mike as the mayor now," Eric said, "but Mom says he's doing a good job bringing the place back to life."

"The Great Bluestone River Revival some call it," Seth said. "Ruby has a lot to do with it, too. And her partner in crime, Emma O'Connell. Now Mike's zeroed in on River Street."

"The old diner may have given itself a face-lift," Eric said, "but the burgers-with-the-works and the milkshakes haven't changed a bit. Thank goodness." He got a kick out of seeing the everyday diner food advertised as part of the town's charm.

Eric kept his eyes on Mike as the mayor dispensed with the small stuff in less than two minutes. A new stop sign was up in Eric's neighborhood and the town had added a snowplow. Good news, but not the reason so many people had turned up. He waved the printed agenda, which was projected onto a screen behind him. "As you can see, we're here for an important reason, folks. I called this special meeting after the bridge was damaged in the storm two weeks ago. So, tonight we're here to *explore* ideas around the issue of the covered bridge, plus the possibility of developing some land on the other side of the river near the bridge."

Loud groans rippled through the room, but were mixed with some scattered applause. Next to him, Seth scoffed. "It's going to get ugly before this is over."

"Hey, everyone, emphasis on *exploring*. We won't be making decisions tonight. Not after one meeting."

"Why not, Mike?" a man in the front asked. "We need to get our plan together to fix the bridge before it deteriorates any more than it already has."

"If we fix it at all," a woman yelled from the back.

"Whoa," Eric said, surprised by the shouts and boos erupting. "This already isn't going well. I feel a little bad for Mike."

Even in high school Eric had taken to Mike. And Ruby Driscoll. They'd returned to town separately, but around the same time. Hmm... like him and Amy. But that's where the resemblance ended. Mike and Ruby were one of those irresistible high school love stories. Torn apart as kids, they reunited twenty years later after discovering the fire still burned between them. They were a family now. Eric pushed away those thoughts before envy got its hooks in deeper.

"It's fair to say everyone here brought their strong opinions and ideas with them. I want all of us to have a chance to speak," Mike said, "so form a line by the mic and that way we'll all hear what you have to say."

It didn't take long for the line to form and the debate to begin. At first, most of the speakers in line argued for saving the bridge.

"Seems like a done deal," Eric whispered to Seth, "but I have to wonder if it's worth it."

Seth shrugged. "I'm eager to hear other ideas. Stuff that's good for local business. I get a little tired of driving to Clayton for a decent hardware store."

Eric paused. "Hey, that would be good for me now that I've bought myself a fixer-upper." A couple of gas station markets offered a few things, but at high prices. Meanwhile, the old supermarket near the highway, small by today's standards and not close to up-to-date was steadily losing business.

The pro-bridge crowd gradually gave way to people with different ideas. A lot of them revolved around building a two-lane bridge for cars, arguing it would be needed eventually anyway if the town was going to continue its growth spurt.

Eric's thoughts turned to Amy. He wondered what she'd think about that idea. If he had to guess, she'd likely want to nix it. As the line thinned, he glanced around the room. A few people had left, but most stayed. He spotted Georgia Greer first, and then noticed Amy sitting next to her, her gaze fixed on the next speaker who stepped up to the mic, notebook in hand.

"Bernie Kirkland here." His voice boomed through the room. "I know many of you. But for those I don't, I farm six hundred acres on the other side of the river. I own fifty more acres near the bridge. Thought I might put that into corn but changed my mind. I hung on to that land, though. At least, until now." He glanced at Mike and held up a bunch of papers.

"Wait a second, Bernie," a voice shouted from the council members' tables on either side of Mike.

"Let Bernie finish," Mike said, banging the gavel once.

"But I thought Emma O'Connell owned that land." The man pointed at Emma. "Right?"

Emma stood and held up her hand to Mike. "Let me clear this up. At one time, my family owned that land. But I sold it to Bernie about ten years ago."

"And now I've got an offer from a couple of developers." Bernie waved the papers. "It's all here and it's what I want to talk about tonight."

"We'll see." The councilman punctuated his obvious skepticism when he leaned back in the chair and folded his arms.

"Who is that?" Eric asked.

"Jim Kellerman. He's been on the town council for many years, I think." Seth frowned. "Something's changed. In the past, every time I've seen him he's argued for more development—even at Hidden Lake. He's a builder. Or used to be."

"Go ahead, Bernie," Mike said. "Make it short. We're just listening to ideas tonight."

"Okay, then, here goes." Bernie glanced around the room. "Don't go shouting at me all at once."

Eric snickered. "Man, not a great start."

Over the next few minutes, he was proved right. Mike had to bang the gavel a couple of times while Bernie laid out the plan to knock down the bridge and put in a road across the river to a strip mall the developers wanted permission to build on the land Bernie was prepared to sell.

"He lost the crowd at 'knock down the bridge'," Eric mused, thinking that Bernie was a kind of charismatic guy, starting with his deep voice. Tall and muscular, he exuded all kinds of power, but not the power of persuasion.

"Looks like Georgia Greer has something on her mind." Seth nodded to Georgia who rose and walked to stand behind Bernie at the microphone.

Bernie moved aside and Georgia acknowledged the smattering of applause, a lot of loud cheers, with a low hum of boos breaking through. "Most everyone here knows I come down on the side of keeping one of our best tourist attractions," Georgia said. "But there's more. Whatever development we do beyond the bridge repair, let's not jeopardize the progress we've made on River Street. We fought to bring new life into our downtown businesses and so far it's working."

"Here we go with the downtown talk," Bernie said in a long-suffering tone. "I have an idea. Why don't we do things to make the town work for the people who live here?

Sometimes I think the only thing you people care about are the tourists passing through."

That was enough to punctuate the split in the crowd. Eric watched the way Amy cheered for Georgia, leaving no doubt where she stood. She greeted her boss with a big smile and a double thumbs-up when Georgia came back to her seat.

"I can relate to Bernie," Seth admitted.

Eric mulled that over, wondering why Bluestone River couldn't be more than a tourist town, but still be a beautiful, peaceful place.

"I see we've reached the end of the line," Mike said, speaking over the noise of a hundred or so people all talking to somebody sitting next to them. He gestured to the council members sitting on either side of him. "We'll adjourn the meeting now. We'll put out a summary of the ideas we've heard and call another public meeting." Mike banged the gavel one more time. "Patience, everyone. We're doing our best, no plan will be rushed through."

The council followed Mike's lead and moved to adjourn. When Eric stood and grabbed his jacket he saw Amy walking toward him.

"Hi—I thought I saw you with Georgia," he said. "Quite a night."

Amy greeted Seth, who excused himself to go talk to someone he knew. "I'll say. I hope there'll be enough people to crush the stupid idea of abandoning the covered bridge."

"You feel that strongly about it, do you?" Eric teased.

"Of course." Amy jerked her head back. "Don't you?"

"Hey, hey, I'm not trying to start a war." He smiled. "Let's just say I have an open mind."

Amy smiled sheepishly. "Fair enough. Let's just say I'm passionate about the bridge." She turned and pointed to Georgia, who was huddled with a couple of other people. "And River Street."

"How's Cassie today?" Ironic that Cassie was a safer subject than a landmark bridge. He'd had his first Monday morning meeting with her and it had gone well.

"So far, so good. She mentioned meeting with you on Monday and has been pretty quiet about school since." She leaned in closer, as if telling him a secret. "Well, except for a little bragging about her advanced multiplication skills."

"She has a right to brag," he stage-whispered back.

"Speaking of Cassie, the stuffed seal she won is officially named Nancy." She lifted her hands in the air. "Don't ask me why. She's added it to the collection of dolls and stuffies she likes to sleep with."

Eric smiled and nodded, thinking once again what a good time he'd had with Amy and her little girl.

"Speaking of Cassie, she's with my grandparents tonight." Amy sighed. "She's probably wearing them out. They're typical grandparents, you know. Indulgent and easily manipulated. She usually thinks of all kinds of excuses to stay up. Five more minutes putting in puzzle pieces with Les and ten more minutes reading to Barb."

"Oh, she likes reading to people, huh?"

"Oh, yeah. She should be an audiobook narrator. Very expressive."

Like her mom, Eric thought, animated and easily amused. Amy's brown eyes sparkled as she spoke. "I have no trouble hearing her strong voice in my head."

"I better go say goodbye to Georgia. Let me know if anything comes up with Cassie at school."

"Of course."

He watched her move through the room in her puffy coat, jeans and knee-high boots. Her hair hung loose down her back. After saying a quick goodbye to Georgia, she ran into more people she knew and stopped with each one long enough to say a quick hello and move on. At the door, she put her hat on and tugged the edge down over her ears. Then she was gone.

"You can come back into the room now," Seth said, stepping up to his side.

Eric groaned. "You caught me. I suppose I'm turning red."

"Yep, like apples," Seth kidded. In a more serious voice he said, "You have it bad for her, don't you?"

"C'mon, I don't even know her anymore," he blurted. "I shouldn't be thinking of her as anything other than the mother of a student. A woman I went to school with ages ago."

"Maybe so," Seth said. "But that's not the vibe I'm getting."

"Vibe, huh?" It was hard to deny, but Eric decided he had no choice but to brush off remarks like that. "You sound like my mom. She says stuff like that."

"Smart woman, your mom."

"That she is," Eric said, giving Seth a slap on the back. "Let's go down to the diner. I'll buy you a coffee."

"Okay, we'll change the subject."

The air was cold and crisp as they walked down River Street with a sliver of a new moon bright in the clear sky. Even with the streetlight interfering he could clearly see the stars forming Orion's Belt and part of the Big Dipper. The sky diverted his attention from Seth's good-natured ribbing, which was nothing more than his cousin—and close friend—simply being himself. But Eric couldn't say he was wrong.

THE HOUSE WAS quiet when Amy opened the front door. A little too quiet. Amy went into the living room where Grandma Barb sat in a comfy chair reading her latest romance novel. Cloud was stretched across her lap. "Uh-oh," Amy said, "you'll be up half the night until you finish your book."

"Probably," Grandma Barb said, "but I hope you're not. Cassie was sneezing a lot earlier. Came on out of the blue. I took her temp, but it's only a little above normal."

Not the news Amy wanted to hear. "It must have been sudden. She was fine earlier. Maybe it'll go away by morning. A good night's sleep will do the trick, I hope."

Grandma Barb put the open book aside. "Tell me about the meeting."

"Lots of people showed up," Amy said, frowning. "But I called this one all wrong. I assumed Mike would fill us in on raising funds to repair the bridge, but there were lots of rumblings about other plans."

"Well, like you said before, Georgia's been concerned ever since the storm brought it down," Grandma Barb said.

"I doubt she guessed how many people in town aren't particularly invested in it. Quite a few people floated other ideas and plans." Amy was still surprised by Eric's casual attitude about the bridge. "Even Eric seems to see the bridge as part of Bluestone River's past, but not necessarily its future."

"Really?"

"He seemed indifferent to restoring it." She shook her head. "I don't get it."

"What's the objection?" Barb asked.

As best she could, Amy explained the way the town seemed divided over what kind of development the town should go after. She found it troubling, as if she—and probably

many others—were taking the issues personally. Too personally.

"I guess Mayor Mike is going to face his
first big challenge."

"Looks like it." Amy paused. "Some of
the land in question was originally owned
by Emma O'Connell's family." She explained
the current owner had some offers to develop
the acres on the other side of the river. "A
number of people blamed Emma because she
sold the land in the first place."

"Emma, another one of your old pals from
high school," Barb said.

Amy nodded. "And right in the thick of
everything. And engaged to Parker, the guy
who runs the bird sanctuary."

"That so?" Barb said. "Well, I'm sure it
will sort itself out, honey. Not much you can
do about it."

An annoying answer. Amy wasn't sure
how to counter it. But for once in her life,
it struck her that she wasn't powerless. She
didn't know exactly what she'd do, but she
wasn't going to sit back and watch other people take over and solve the problem. She was
about to say as much to Grandma Barb when
her attention was pulled away to loud cough-

ing from Cassie's room. The kind of coughing Amy associated with a bad cold.

"I'll go see if she's awake." Amy bolted down the hall to Cassie's room.

"Sounds a lot worse than earlier this evening," Barb called out.

"She hasn't been sick in such a long time it's taken me by surprise." Somehow they'd managed to get through the previous winter without Cassie missing even a day of school. Cassie liked tacking that perfect attendance ribbon on the corkboard in her room.

When she opened the door, Cassie was sitting up. Amy settled on the edge of the bed and put her palm on her little girl's forehead. "You're warm, sweetheart. I think your coughing woke you up."

Cassie nodded, but then a bunch of sneezes came one right after the other. Amy handed her a tissue from the box on the nightstand.

"My throat hurts."

"I bet it does," Amy said. "I'm going to take your temperature." She retrieved the thermometer and a couple of throat lozenges from the cabinet in the bathroom she and Cassie shared. Seconds later, she had her confirmation. Her temperature was up over one hundred degrees now. It was pretty clear there would be no school for Cassie tomorrow. "So, drink some water and then we'll get you back under the covers. I bet you'll go right to sleep."

Apparently too tired and sick to argue, Cassie slid under the blankets and tucked her two favorite dolls against her chest and made room for Nancy's head to rest on the pillow. Amy pulled the blanket tighter around Cassie's shoulders and kissed her warm forehead before she slipped out of the room.

Grandma was still up and turning pages when Amy went into the living room to say good-night. "She's not doing so well. It's probably just a cold, with the usual sore throat and cough. I'll keep her home tomorrow. Can you—"

"Of course, nothing changes. I'll watch her while you're at work in the afternoon. No worries, honey."

She'd assumed Grandma Barb would be okay with watching Cassie for the whole afternoon, but hearing her say as much sent ripples of relief through Amy's body. What to do when Cassie was sick had always been a tough issue. Back in Chicago, she or Scott would take a day off to stay home with her, although Scott made excuses why he couldn't do that. It was usually Amy who had to hope one of the sitters she had on her list would come to the house. When all else failed, she called in sick herself.

Grandma cocked her head and offered a reassuring smile. "You know we're not going anywhere. We'll be here for Cassie." She rubbed the cat's back. "Won't we, Cloud?"

"I know, Grandma, but I don't want to be a burden." Amy scoffed at the cliché, but it fit.

"*Same here.*" Grandma Barb gave her a pointed look. "But I'm afraid that's what we're becoming for you."

Amy waved her off. "No, no. Never."

"That's a conversation for another day," Grandma said. "But for now, I'm perfectly capable of taking care of Cassie for a few hours. And you're only a few blocks away."

Amy nodded. Sometimes she worried more out of habit than from anything real.

"Have fun with your love story—and Cloud. I'm off to bed." She squeezed Grandma's shoulder and went on her way.

Odd that Barb could stay up late and still be on her game the next day. But she claimed that with every birthday she added she needed less and less sleep. Maybe so.

Amy opened the door to Cassie's room and

heard her slightly raspy breathing. The shaft of light coming from the hallway illuminated Cassie's face. Amy leaned against the door-jamb and studied her daughter, so peaceful in deep sleep. It was hard to picture her calling anyone names, or being contrary and giving her teacher a hard time.

When her mom and dad left her with her grandparents and took off, Amy was only four years younger than Cassie was when Scott moved out. Instead of acting out, Amy tried hard not to be noticed. Like a little soldier, she'd obeyed all the rules. She didn't dare cause trouble—or so she thought. If she mis-behaved or talked back would her grandpar-ents keep taking care of her? What would happen if they said they were too old and she was too much? Raw, terrifying insecu-rity kept her in line. At first.

When her parents came back and left again weeks later, Amy's only consolation was her grandparents. As a little girl, she didn't know the term *forever family*, but she'd counted on Barb and Les to always take care of her.

For all the problems that had come up, Amy was grateful. Even if Cassie claimed to dislike her new school or town, her daugh-ter never questioned who she belonged to.

CHAPTER FIVE

THE TEXT FROM Cassie's teacher, Skylar Morse, came on Friday morning. Cassie had been home sick for two days and wouldn't be coming to the usual Friday meeting. What was up? he wondered, reaching for the phone to call Amy. He pulled his hand back before he tapped her number. He didn't make a habit of calling parents whose kids were sick for a couple of days. But, then again, he didn't know most other parents. They weren't his old high school friends. Wouldn't he feel the same way if Jason Abbot had missed a couple of days of school? Not really. Eric had to laugh at himself.

Amy was a different kind of friend, but still, it wasn't a good precedent. Whew, his better judgment had kicked in. Leaving his phone on his desk, Eric left his office for his morning rounds of classrooms. He started with kindergarten, where the kids were looking at the magnetic weather map and Brittiany Clark pointed to places where it was sunny and warm and other spots where the snow was deep. She covered the US, Canada and Mexico, and the kids were helping to pick out magnetic pieces to place on each area that matched the temperatures she called out. Florida and Mexico had beach umbrellas and a big sun. The Midwest had icicles placed all over it. She put multiple magnets showing falling snow up in Iowa and Minnesota. "The weather forecasters are warning us we have more snow on the way. Lots of it. What does that mean?"

"Snowmen," the kids called out, and she stuck snowmen across five or six states.

When Eric waved to Brittiany she smiled but kept on going, just like he wanted. He wasn't keeping tabs on the teachers, but he liked to know what the kids were up to in the classrooms. Listening to the five-year-olds making brrrr sounds when Brittiany pointed to Maine up in the corner made him smile. This was his favorite part of working with kids and now working with teachers, too. This was only Brittiany Clark's third year of teaching, but she had the attention of all twenty-six little kids sitting on the floor in a big circle.

Moving on, he listened to the first and second graders reading stories aloud from their textbooks. By third grade, most of the reading and writing was done on basic computers. Cassie's class was finishing up their math groups, four levels, by Eric's count. He imagined Skylar sending Amy the links to the lessons and homework Cassie was missing.

Between reports, meetings with individual teachers, and the Friday check-in with the small group of kids, the hours flew by. Then his car seemed to steer itself to the salon, where Amy was in front of the computer and on the phone. When she saw him, her welcoming smile lit up her face. She held up her finger to indicate she'd be with him in a minute.

"Hey—nice to see you. What brings you here?" she asked, looking at him as if evaluating his need for a haircut.

Self-conscious, he swiped his hand down the back of his head. "It's not for a trim. That was last Saturday. I'm actually here to see you. I heard you had to keep Cassie home for a few days."

"She's been in bed or wrapped up in a big quilt on the couch in the living room keeping my grandparents and Cloud company."

"Is she getting better?"

Amy shrugged. "Not as of late this morning when I left for my shift here." She sighed. "I know it's only a cold, but I worry anyway."

"I'm sure you do," he said, realizing he'd been a little overly concerned himself.

"We'll see if she turns a corner over the weekend," Amy said. "Sometimes she gets well as quickly as she gets sick. If not, I'll take her to the doctor."

"Speaking of the weekend, I have it on good authority that we're getting more snow. Brittiany Clark was playing a cool weather game with the kindergarteners."

Amy groaned. "Snow? And it's the first week of March."

"Right. Like that matters in our part of the world," he said with a laugh.

Amy nodded. "I suppose. Looks like I'll be dragging out my grandparents' ancient snowblower. Sometimes it's easier to go back to old-fashioned shoveling."

When the salon's phone rang, Eric said a quick goodbye and mouthed, *I'll call you*, as he left. As he drove home, he thought about Amy being here in town trying to rebuild her life. Her grandparents and their home had always been her shelter, the place where she could always return. Now who was sheltering whom was more complicated. He guessed they all needed each other. They were tending Cassie, but when the snow came, she'd be the one to take care of the sidewalk and driveway. Her family moved him in a way he didn't have words to describe.

From his point of view, running off with Scott Morgan was Amy's huge mistake. He'd bet Amy would agree. Sort of. She'd argue that then she wouldn't have Cassie, the obvious light of her life. So much heartache, though. If only she'd seen Scott for the self-centered jerk he'd always been. *Stop, stop.* Totally irrelevant history. Today, Eric saw a woman doing whatever it took to give everything she had to her child and to the people who'd raised her. She was so much more than her brown eyes and pretty face. But then, he'd always known that.

"MAYBE THIS WILL be the last storm of the winter," Grandpa Les said at breakfast on Sunday morning.

"Let's hope so, Les," Grandma said. "I'd like to see a daffodil or tulip in the ground soon."

Amy smiled at the sweet conversation. She

glanced at Cassie, who had improved quite a bit by Saturday afternoon and woke up complaining about being cooped up. "I'll start clearing the drive and the stairs as soon as Cassie has had her fill of oatmeal." She patted Cassie's arm. "You're on your second bowl, so it looks like your appetite is back."

"Maybe you'll feel well enough to do your language assignment, Cassie," Barb said.

Amy wished Grandma hadn't brought up the assignment. The teacher wasn't worried about the math homework, since Cassie had more or less mastered the last unit. But the language class was different. She was supposed to write a story about a pet who has an adventure in a house. She could make it a cave or a mansion, and the pet could be anything from a dog to a snake. Cassie usually got a kick out of assignments like that, but not this time. Her response was listless at best. It could wait. Amy would rather have her playing with her dolls without any pressure, maybe watching cartoons and college basketball with Grandpa Les until she fell asleep on the couch.

Amy pushed back from the table. She was feeling the pressure of clearing the walks of snow. "I might as well get started." Had a grudging tone slipped into her voice? Probably. This wasn't how she wanted to spend her time, but what she wanted wasn't the point. It was the first in a list of chores that would fill her day. She stuck her feet in her work boots and pulled on her wool hat and insulated gloves.

The snowblower was heavy and unwieldy, but Amy fired it up. The engine groaned but it started.

"Hey, looks like I showed up just in time," a male voice called out.

A familiar male voice. Amy smiled, turned around and greeted Eric coming toward her, shovel in hand. She lightly slapped the snowblower. "It sings, but it's like me, slightly off-key, isn't it?"

"It sounds a little like it's in pain," he agreed, "but I've got mine in the back. I got out early to clear my mom's place. Again. Thought I'd swing by to see if you need help digging out." He waved in the direction of River Street. "I'm only a few blocks west of you."

Amy wasn't exactly sure how to react. A part of her was taken aback, unsure if she should accept his help. She'd reached out to him once already. That ended in a good time at the Snowball Fair. Now he was doing her another favor. Amy also wasn't big on surprises, or so she claimed. But she couldn't deny the pleasure of seeing him approach.

"Shouldn't take me too long—you can work on the stairs if you want to." He looked her up and down and grinned. "You're dressed for it. So, are you game?"

"Am I game?" she repeated, her finger on her chin, pretending to have to think hard about her answer. "I'm game as long as you'll come inside later and meet my grandparents. Let us give you a cup of coffee. I think we can manage a cookie or two." She stopped. "Wait, seems I recall you've already met them, haven't you?"

"Yeah, at the senior lunch," he said. "We sat at the same table and got our certificates for doing a good job with the newspaper. You met my mom, too."

She hadn't remembered the specifics, but he was right. "They were so much younger then." She took her gaze off him and stared at the house as if she could see them inside.

"I know," he said softly. "All those years ago, I didn't understand how important they are to you."

Wanting to avoid the trap of slipping into

the past, Amy told him how great they'd been during the days when Cassie was sick. "She's much better. She'll probably be at school tomorrow. I doubt she's fallen behind."

"No, I wouldn't worry about that." He took a couple of steps back. "I'll get the contraption started."

Amy started shoveling the back stairs and quickly brushed snow off the front porch and stairs. Between the two of them, the place was cleared in about a quarter of the time it usually took Amy by herself. Cassie and Grandma appeared in the front window to watch the snow pile up along the edge of the sidewalk. When he'd stowed his snowblower and the shovel, she led him inside through the back and into the kitchen. Cassie was waiting by the door.

"We hang out in the kitchen a lot, don't we, Cassie?" Amy remarked. "What can we give Mr. Wells for a treat? We need to say thanks for helping me out." She went into the living room where Grandma Barb was helping Grandpa out of his chair.

She heard Cassie say, "We've got cookies. Want one?"

Eric chuckled. "I've never said no to a

cookie, if that's the plan. Will you be joining me at the table?"

"Okay," Cassie said. "I've been sick. That's why I couldn't, you know, see you on Friday."

"Your teacher told me about your bad cold." Suddenly, his voice took on a note of disbelief. "What's this?" Amy came back into the kitchen to see him grinning and pointing to a photo of Cassie anchored on the refrigerator with one of Barb's magnets.

"That's me and Miss Sparkle at the Snowball Fair," Cassie said. "Remember, we got the Special Mention ribbon and we had burgers and fries."

"Oh, I do recall that day. As a matter of fact, I have the same picture on my fridge."

"Really?"

"Yes, really. And I also remember you and your mom feeding an apple to one of the horses."

"And we saw the parrots."

"Is that so, lassie," he said in his pirate accent.

Eric had such an easy way of bantering with Cassie—probably all kids. Cassie didn't seem nervous or like it was at all unusual for the principal to be in her kitchen.

With her arm around Les's shoulders, Amy helped him into a chair at the table.

"Well, I sure wanted to say hello to the man who showed up to help us out," Les said to Eric. "I'm thinking I met you a long time ago."

"You did, Grandpa. Eric and I were just talking about it. It was during senior year at an honors lunch."

"Grandma said Mr. Wells should come over for dinner one night," Cassie said.

"She did, huh? That sounds fun." Amy glanced at Eric. As much fun as it could be, this situation with Eric was getting a little dicey, way too entangled. She doubted he'd find the invitation enticing, anyway. He probably had much better things to do with his time.

She glanced up at him, expecting him to look ill at ease once everyone crowded in the kitchen. Grandma was getting cookies out and Cassie was trying to hold Eric's attention while Amy produced mugs and plates.

"Maybe you know my mother, Monica Wells," Eric said to Les and Barb. "She used to be the nurse manager in Dr. Kendall's office—Don Kendall."

"Of course," Barb said, as if a lightbulb had

just come on in her brain. "I didn't connect you with her. Les and I still miss Dr. Kendall—and Monica."

"She retired when he did. She does some volunteering for the blood bank now and again, but she's mostly enjoying herself. She's learning French for a fall trip she's planned with a couple of friends."

Amy glanced at her grandmother. That sounded like the kinds of things Grandma had done after Amy married Scott and left Bluestone River. She'd eventually quit her part-time job and volunteered at the community Halloween party and tutored young children after school. It was only in recent years that she'd gradually pared down her life and was more confined to home.

"Tell her to enjoy it all while she's still young," Grandma Barb said, smiling encouragement. "We do slow down eventually, you know."

Eric didn't respond in words, but his nod and his expression communicated empathy. He seemed to *understand* things. Maybe that was one of the valuable things that came from having troubles of his own. Over their coffee and cookies Eric talked to Barb and Les as if he'd known them all his life.

When it came time to leave, Amy said she'd clean up the cookie plates and mugs and her grandparents went back to the living room with Cassie in tow. Amy stood with Eric as he put on his jacket and the rest of his cold weather gear.

"Well, needless to say, once again I can't thank you enough. My grandparents enjoyed seeing you and hearing about what your mom is up to these days."

"Working for Dr. Kendall for so long, she knows a lot of people." He opened the door and stepped outside and pointed to the cleared walk. "As for this, it was nothing. Saved me from patching cracks in a couple of walls in my house."

"A little avoidance, huh?"

"Oh, a little," Eric said. "Honestly, though, I've been surprised by how much I'm enjoying all this scraping and patching. I'm becoming more familiar with flooring and tile than I'd have ever predicted. Seth keeps me focused like a laser beam."

With that, Eric waved and said he'd see Cassie in the morning. Watching him walk to his SUV, Amy was left feeling at loose ends. Wanting something she didn't have, an admission she didn't often allow herself.

Eric the man was as sweet as the boy in high school who treated her better than her more exciting boyfriend ever had. It made her wince to think of how she'd rush away when they'd finished the mock-up of the paper. Off to find Scott, the handsome guy who claimed he was so in love with her. Soon, soon, they'd break away from their "dinky little town" and head to the city where their "real life" would start.

She'd always known Eric did his best to skirt around Scott, never crossing his path if he could avoid it. On graduation day her coeditor gave her a hug and wished her well. She'd rarely thought about him again. Until now, when she couldn't seem to get his friendly, handsome face and bright blue eyes off her mind.

ERIC SPOTTED AMY entering the town hall's conference room. That's where he was headed. Thrown together again? For reasons he knew nothing about, he'd been asked to attend the organizing meeting for an upcoming event in town, The Fourth on River Street. Now he wondered if a similar request was what brought Amy to the meeting.

He caught up with her inside the room,

along with Mike Abbot and Emma O'Connell, Rick Russo, the owner of the diner, and Vivian Hopkins, who'd opened a new card and gift shop on River Street.

"We're missing Ruby, for obvious reasons." Mike couldn't get the sentence out without flashing a big smile so full of joy everyone laughed. The Abbots were still glowing over their new baby girl.

Amy raised her eyebrows when she glanced at Eric, as if both curious and surprised to see him. "Georgia asked me to represent the salon on the committee," she explained. "I didn't know it would be like homecoming week."

"We're the grown-ups now," Emma said, pleasantly. "It's our turn to keep this place going."

"I suppose so," Eric said, smiling at the truth of Emma's words. "I spotted you at the town hall meeting, but didn't get a chance to say hello."

"I heard you were back," Emma said, "and I figured we'd run into each other eventually."

Eric nodded, noting the cane propped next to her chair. His mom told him about Emma's fall, and that she needed a cane to walk. Like Amy, Emma had married one of their classmates, whose early death shocked everyone.

But she was engaged to Parker Davis, the new director of the bird sanctuary, an authentic center created by converting the old resort buildings.

"I'm not exactly sure why I'm here," Eric said. All day he'd been nervous about this meeting, which puzzled him. It wasn't as if he'd known Amy would be there. "But when the mayor asked me to show up, how could I say no?" he joked.

Mike laughed. "The seat of power over here. But, kidding aside, I've got plans for you, buddy. Ruby came up with an idea I like a lot. All will be clear, Eric, soon enough." Mike went on to say that he was only organizing the committee to get it off the ground. He wouldn't be convening it or having any role other than to see what they came up with. "And if you don't like my idea, we'll scratch it and come up with something else."

Eric met Amy's eye, seeing she also was curious about Mike's teaser.

Mike tapped the end of his pen on the table. "By the way, just to be clear, whatever gets organized for the Fourth of July is entirely separate from whatever happens to the bridge and the development plans, whatever they turn out to be."

"What? No controversy?" Amy quipped. "On the serious side, I hope this gets settled soon. We've already had another storm. And it's still only March. The bridge could get damaged even more."

"Good point, Amy, but we've got that covered." Mike said he'd sent a maintenance crew to the bridge to shore up the structure they'd already built around the bridge to prevent it from crumbling. "We're making sure nothing happens to it while we make sure everyone has a say. Not just about the bridge, but our future. Nothing you'll work on for the Fourth of July depends on development plans down the road."

Eric glanced at Amy, who frowned and leaned forward, as if she had something to say. Apparently, she thought better of it and relaxed in her chair again.

"Just as well we avoid the big fights." Rick thumped his finger on the table. "Let's keep the focus on our downtown."

Vivian had been quiet, but she chimed in to agree with Rick.

Rick and his wife owned the diner, Vivian owned the gift shop, but Eric wasn't a stakeholder like them. Puzzling.

As if reading his mind, Mike spoke directly

to Eric. "Ruby thought we should do something new and fresh with our parade, or I should say, the return of a real parade."

Bluestone River's Fourth of July celebration had dwindled over the years and had amounted to the high school marching band and some political candidates greeting the small number of people who turned out. His mom dutifully only walked down to River Street to add another spectator to the crowd that grew skimpier every year.

"We're thinking that since Memorial Day has its special focus to remember sacrifice," Mike explained, "we could choose a popular theme for the Fourth, something like 'education as the road to freedom.'"

"Now, that would be a change," Eric said, shocked by the idea. But he liked it. "The idea behind the theme happens to be true." *Don't get me started.* He could fill in the details in less than thirty seconds.

"Exactly. That's why Ruby thought of you for the committee. Let's just say, we were thinking we'll ask the town's teachers to march as a group in the parade. We'll include the support staff."

Teachers would swell a crowd, Eric thought, since they'd bring their families along. This could be good. Remind people that teachers were indispensable. "So, you want me to…"

"Organize that part of the parade. You would sign up the teachers. Now that we're bringing back a real parade, the historical society is interested in creating a float again—it's been years since they've participated. Same with some of the clubs at the high school. Apparently, for the last several years, they couldn't coax students into participating. But we're about to change that. Giving the parade a theme will help us make the parade an important community event. Like it used to be."

"That's it?" Eric grinned and lifted his hands. "That's all we have to do? Piece of cake."

"Well, that's the bare bones," Mike said, with a laugh. "You can run with it. Embellish a little. Ruby said you can count on her to volunteer to help. The baby will be older and she'll be out more by then."

"Sure, we'll want to get the kids involved in some way," Eric said. "Give them a stake in it. That'll drive up the numbers of people coming down to the parade."

"Then you'll join the committee?"

Eric didn't need to weigh the decision. He wasn't only a principal. He hoped to have his own kids in the Bluestone River schools one day. If he wanted to volunteer this would be the time. "Sign me up, Mike." He looked around at the others at the table. "Celebrating teachers is easy—and a little *overdue*."

"Eric's right about getting the kids involved in honoring *their* teachers," Amy said. "Give them some ownership."

"If everyone's on board, then why don't you build the festival around it?" Mike said. "Build it up with some other features and events. And don't forget the financial side. The council gives the okay for the budget."

"Pretty clever," Rick said. "Get the teachers and all these kids and before you know it, we have a crowd. And a big ol' parade."

"Don't think Ruby didn't calculate that," Emma said dryly. "She'll be happy to pass on her initial estimates."

Mike chuckled, as if embarrassed by Emma's remark.

Seeing the easy exchanges between Emma and Mike, and the others, Eric was struck by the foolishness of his pre-meeting jitters. This wasn't high school. He and his mom had moved to Bluestone River at the start of the school year and learned the first day that more than half the kids had gone to grade school together. He was the outsider. But Mike and Ruby, or Emma and Amy, or anyone in that crowd hadn't treated him like he didn't belong. He'd done that all by himself. To Amy, blind to his feelings for her, he was a kid she worked with on the paper, not an outsider. Serving on this committee handed him a chance to start acting like this town was his home...for good.

His attention was drawn to Amy, who was reading from some handwritten notes, mostly ideas Georgia wanted brought to the table about ways the businesses could promote River Street. "Georgia's all about coupons and specials and cross-promotion, too."

"I'll help with that," Vivian said.

"Then the two of you can write it up. Present ideas to the group." Mike swiped his palms a couple of times. "See? My work is done here. It's all up to you now. When it comes closer to the time, we'll put out a public call for volunteers to help you pull it off."

"It's a late start," Amy said in a warning tone. "We don't have much time to plan this summer shindig."

"Shindig, huh?" Eric chuckled at her

choice of words. "That's what we're calling it? Maybe we should make it official."

"Well, *gala* doesn't fit," she said, as if teasing back.

"Kidding aside, how about if we simply call this a celebration of education?" he offered.

"That's good branding, but it doesn't have enough snap," Amy mused, snapping her fingers. "We could use it in some of our press releases. But the headline should probably say something like, 'The Fourth on River Street—Join your friends and neighbors to help us celebrate our teachers at Bluestone River's Festival of Freedom.'"

"Nice. We're almost there," Eric said, nodding.

Emma smiled and pointed in their direction. "Listen to the newspaper editors batting around the right wording."

Eric glanced at Amy, realizing that's exactly what they were doing. For a few seconds, twenty years had dropped away.

"You two should be in charge of the publicity—flyers, press releases, ads," Vivian said.

"How about we meet next week," Rick said, standing and putting on his coat, "same day, same time, Wednesday, five o'clock or so?"

Only Amy frowned a little before answering. She was the only one on the committee who had a small child, Eric thought. Rick had kids in high school, Vivian's kids were grown and gone. Emma didn't have kids. "Will that interfere with your job?" Eric asked in a low voice.

"No. Georgia wanted me to be here on behalf of the salon, so she won't mind. I was thinking of Cassie and my grandparents. I'm sure they'll be fine looking after Cassie." She got to her feet and spoke to everyone. "I just had to think it through to make sure I wasn't missing something in my schedule." She checked her watch and grabbed her jacket. "Oops, I better go."

"I'll walk you to your car," he said.

"You don't need to do that. Besides, it's not here. It's over in the lot behind the salon," Amy said, pulling on her coat and gloves.

"That's okay," he said. "I walked over from the house."

"You did? A little cold for a stroll, isn't it?"

He held the door open, letting in a rush of the cool evening air. "If I waited for a warm day to walk around town, I'd be waiting a long time. Besides, I'm meeting Seth at the diner."

"You two are pretty close, aren't you?" she asked as they began to walk.

"Like brothers, really," he responded without hesitation. "When Mom and I moved to town, Seth and I morphed from cousins to best buddies. My uncle was the closest thing I'd had to a dad. I'm older, so I could help Seth navigate high school. He didn't like school so much. Not like me."

"And me." Her voice carried a wistful note.

"That was funny back there, the two of us playing with words. Reminded me of the old days, huh?" Or, maybe she'd forgotten about the fun they'd had putting the paper together. It was the first time he'd been in charge of something important to him. They'd shared the responsibility. And it had been sink or swim.

As if reading his mind, she said, "Working with you on the paper helped me later when I had to manage a retail team. Covering all the hours, training, running a smooth customer service operation was like managing the production schedule."

"And you liked it?"

Amy gave him a tentative nod. "It was great at first, I mean, I really took to it and liked those jobs. But I want different things now."

"That's intriguing."

"And all I'll say on the subject—for now. I'm always mulling over ideas," Amy said, "but none will work right now. Cassie is my focus. Nothing else really matters."

They were steps away from her car and she clicked to unlock it. He got the message. She didn't care to linger.

"Say hi to Seth for me," Amy said, climbing into the driver's seat.

"Will do." He waved as she started the engine and backed out. *She wanted different things, huh. What things?* he wondered, as he meandered from the lot to the diner.

CHAPTER SIX

AFTER THEY'D HAD their manicures, Ruby and Emma lingered at the counter to chat.

"I haven't had much chance to catch up with either of you," Amy said, "even though we're working with the Fourth of July committee."

"It didn't take you long to volunteer," Ruby said.

"That was Georgia's doing. She has a big stake in what happens to this town." Amy smiled. "Enough with the committee and all that. I want to hear about the two of you. I get the feeling that life is humming along nicely for the both of you."

Emma nodded knowingly. "Turns out nothing could keep Ruby and Mike apart."

Ruby nodded. "And Emma's right in the thick of things—and planning her wedding, too."

Amy stared at Emma's diamond and garnet ring. "It's gorgeous. Congratulations, Emma."

Was it possible to be happy for her two old pals and still be a little green with envy?

"I never thought finding love would ever happen for me." Emma's gaze was warm and reassuring. "We're planning a fall wedding and you and your little girl are invited."

"And we accept. I can't wait." In the Ruby-Emma duo, Ruby had always seemed like the livelier one, a force of nature. But in her quieter, more subdued way, Emma conveyed understanding, empathy.

"We know you're going through a lot," Emma said. "If you ever want to talk, I'm here."

"Me, too," Ruby added.

Touched by the message her two old friends were sending, Amy was about to respond when a woman's voice boomed from the back. "Who do we have here? Emma O'Connell!"

Amy saw that the voice belonged to Maisie Green, one of Georgia's customers. She wore a salon cape and her curly hair was wrapped in a towel. "You ought to be ashamed of yourself." Maisie didn't speak the words, she hissed them.

"Do I know you?" Emma asked.

Georgia gave Amy a look that warned of

trouble ahead. "This isn't the time or the place to argue, Maisie. If you have a bone to pick with Emma, please do it somewhere else." Georgia put her hand on Maisie's arm, but the woman stepped away. "Listen, ladies, I don't want the controversy over the development to poison the atmosphere in my feel-good salon."

"I understand, Georgia," Emma said. "Ruby and I are done here anyway, so we'll be on our way."

"Not until you tell me why you sold those acres of prairie to Bernie Kirkland." Maisie had lowered her voice, but not by much.

"What business is it of yours?" Ruby demanded. "It was her land. She had the right to do whatever she wanted to with it."

Amy groaned inside when another woman came to the front ready to pay, but she was taking her time getting her credit card out.

"My family has been in this town a long time, too, Emma. And I would bet a ton of money your family wouldn't have wanted to see a giant mall go up on fifty acres of valuable farmland."

"No one's talking about giant malls, Maisie," Emma said. "Really. I don't have to justify myself to you. Bernie wanted to farm the acres, so I sold them. But things change. Farms change."

"But you used to be for preservation," Maisie went on. "Do you think we don't know your money keeps the sanctuary open? A couple of years ago, you funded the new trails."

Amy finished processing the customer's bill, but the woman made no move toward the door. Another customer came up to the counter and listened in.

"So, that's no secret, Maisie," Emma said, keeping her voice low. "Everyone knows I have a foundation. I fund things. Big deal."

Maisie was about to say something, her mouth open to speak, but Emma interrupted. "I'm at the sanctuary almost every day. Contact me if you really want to talk." Emma slung her handbag over her shoulder. "But I'm done here. You have no right disrupting Georgia's business like this."

"If some giant ugly development happens on those acres, you'll be sorry."

That sounded like a threat, Amy thought.

"Maisie," Georgia said, "this conversation is over. C'mon back now."

"We'll see you soon," Ruby said to Amy as she followed Emma out the door.

Georgia disappeared with Maisie, and the two customers left the counter area.

Amy took a deep breath, feeling the tightness in her chest give way. She'd had to break up the occasional fight in the shops she'd managed over the years, but this incident was different. She was shocked. Impressed, too, by how well Emma had kept her cool.

When most of the customers had left, Georgia came up to the front and greeted her with, "I saw that argument coming a mile away. Maisie is stuck in the past, I'm afraid."

"Emma and Ruby are the exact opposite, aren't they?"

"Oh, yeah," Georgia said. "But Emma doesn't get personal about it. She doesn't pick fights, that's for sure. But ever since her sale of those acres became known she's had to answer for it."

"I liked what you said about this being a feel-good place," Amy said, smiling at Georgia. "That's exactly what you've created. I noticed it right away."

"Well, I meant what I said." Georgia slung an arm around Amy's shoulder. "I'm not shy about saying what I believe is good for Bluestone River. But I don't want that kind of ugliness to ever happen again in here."

"I get it," Amy said, glancing at the door, where one of Georgia's newish customers was coming inside. It was back to business when Georgia walked the customer to her chair.

Over the next two hours or so, Amy did all her regular work and straightened out displays. Maisie paid for her haircut and left without a word.

Georgia greeted Kyra Murphy, a customer Amy hadn't met before today. The first thing Amy noticed were her striking gray-blue eyes, accented by wavy blond chin-length hair framing her face. She'd been friendly, even exuberant, when she first came in for her regular trim, but now she stood at the counter holding a credit card in her slightly shaky hand. Amy finished up with the customer ahead in line and then started running Kyra's card, commenting that the computers had been uncharacteristically slow so far that day.

"Are you running late?" Amy said as Kyra checked the time on her phone and then again on the salon's wall clock.

"I am. I made a big mistake." Kyra nervously scratched her cheek. "I didn't allow enough time for my appointment, and now school's out. I have to pick up my little girl. Fortunately, Madison School isn't far away."

"That's where my daughter goes to school. She doesn't take the bus, huh?"

Kyra waved her off. "No, no. She can't. I mean, not yet. One day she will. But Lottie's my foster child." She impatiently patted the counter, her eyes filled with fear. "She's only been with me a few weeks. She always sees my car the second she comes through the school doors. If I'm not there, she might be scared or upset." Kyra rubbed her forehead. "I don't know how I let this happen."

Amy noted the time on the computer. The kids were likely streaming out of the building at that very moment. "Let me call the principal. You know Eric Wells. He's a friend of mine. I'll let him know you're on the way."

Kyra groaned. "Why didn't I think of that?"

"Because you're worried, that's why," Amy said softly. *Panicky is more like it*, Amy thought, as she made the call. *Pick up, Eric, pick up*, she said to herself.

"Amy? Uh, what is it?"

She heard his impatient tone. This was a busy part of his day. "I need your help." She quickly explained the situation. "Kyra is about ready to leave. She'll be in front of the school in a couple of minutes."

"I understand. I know who Lottie is," Eric said. "Tell Kyra not to worry. I've got it covered."

"Thanks, Eric." She ended the call and exhaled as she watched the muscles in Kyra's face visibly relax. "It's taken care of. Eric is seeing to Lottie. She'll be fine."

"I got myself so worked up over this." Kyra scribbled her signature on the credit card receipt and slid it across the counter. "I feel really stupid about cutting it so close. Next time I'll allow more time."

"You can breathe easy. I'm sure Eric is reassuring your little girl right now."

Kyra flashed a big smile as she rushed to the door. "Her name's Charlotte Leigh. She goes by Lottie."

Then she was gone. Amy went to the window and watched Kyra get into her car and zoom down River Street.

"Everything okay?" Georgia joined her at the window. "I had to take a call from one of my kids or I'd have come up front to see what was going on."

Amy explained the situation, but she couldn't shake off the emotions the situation triggered in her. Kyra's fear, the relief, the proud smile when she said her full name.

"I don't know exactly how old I was, but my grandparents became my foster parents, officially, I mean." Amy was conscious of her heart beating hard in her chest, as if she'd been Kyra, or maybe Lottie. She wasn't sure which. "At some point, my grandparents needed the authority to act like parents and make decisions for me. That meant admitting my mom and dad had abandoned me."

"Is that so?" Georgia said, surprise in her voice. "I had no idea."

Amy propped her elbow on the counter. "It's not something I talk about much. But needless to say, I owe my grandparents everything. Without them, I could have ended up in the foster care system myself."

"And now you live with them again," Georgia said. "Will you move into your own place eventually?"

Amy shook her head. "Probably not for a long time. I came to Bluestone River for Cassie and me, but my grandparents needing some help now sealed the deal. They're giving me a hand with Cassie. My grandparents are her after-school day care. I'm their driver and shopper and, I guess, part-time housekeeper."

"I see, an arrangement that works for everyone."

"I *know*," Amy said, stretching the word out to lighten the mood. "My grandparents really, really want to stay in their house. They never had visions of sunny Arizona or Florida beaches." She smiled at Georgia. "I'm their assisted living." She turned her attention back to the desk, sensing Georgia studying her. Again.

"Since it's quiet right now, come to the back with me." Georgia waved in a big "follow me" gesture. "I want your opinion about some handmade soap. Locally made—that's always a plus."

"As long as it smells good, I'm in," Amy said.

When they got to the back, Georgia spread sample blocks of scented soaps on a tray she put on the card table she'd set up to fashion a break room in the storage area. Over the next few minutes, Amy inhaled the fragrances of pine, rose and lavender, and oohed and aahed her approval to all of them, only hesitating over the dusty bluish-green soap because it was unscented. But it had a perfect name, Rushing River.

"Clever to name her soaps for things that

feel close to home." Amy picked up one of the blocks and held it in her palm. "We have a small lavender farm nearby, so Lavender Fields is a perfect name. So is Climbing Roses."

"You're right," Georgia said with a laugh. "We've got our own Rushing River, a perfect fit, but none of the usual references to sea breezes and ocean spray."

The soap was more than a scented product, Amy thought, freeing her imagination to picture the soaps arranged in pyramid fashion in a corner of the reception area. "The display could sit between the lotions and the shelves of shampoos and styling products. We could make a sign emphasizing the local connection."

Georgia lowered her head in a decisive nod. "I'll put in an order today."

Amy had another idea, but not wanting to overstep she held back. On the other hand, Georgia had asked for her opinion. "What if you bought a large number of mini samples and packaged each one with the coupon and business card ready to hand out at summer festivals and farmer's markets. That way, everyone walks away from your table with a little gift from the salon."

Amy heard her phone buzz, but let it go to voice mail. She wasn't about to end the conversation, especially since Georgia's expression was focused and thoughtful as she picked up one of the soaps and turned it over in her hands.

The jingle of the bell on the front door broke the silence and Amy moved toward the front of the shop.

"I can see why your former boss gave you such good recommendations. You have quite the flair for this sort of thing," Georgia called out.

"Thanks," Amy called back. Then, seeing Eric standing at the counter, her surprise registered as a jolt. "Hello. I didn't expect to see you here."

"I'm meeting Seth at the web designer's office down the street. You probably know her, Maggie Hall." Seth explained, "Now that he has a growing supply of before and after pictures of my house, he's finally going to produce a real website for his contracting business."

"And he wants your advice, I bet."

"I get a say in picking the worst of the before photos and the best of the after."

"Must be some project," Amy said with a laugh. "I'd like to see those photos myself."

"You can do better than that. You'll have to come by one day soon and get a formal tour," Eric offered, his fair skin coloring a bit.

"It's a deal." How soon was soon? She'd love to see what he was up to. For that matter, she'd love to see him.

"Uh, I stopped by now to let you know it was really good that you called me about Lottie. I found her, but she was already upset that she hadn't seen Kyra's car in the line." He set his thumb and index finger about an inch apart. "Lottie was this close to a meltdown, I'm afraid."

Amy's chest tightened in a sadly familiar way. It was as if an old memory she didn't know she had suddenly surfaced. "No kidding."

"Kids were passing her by on their way to their parents' cars or getting in line where the buses were loading. It all looked typical. An ordinary day. But seeing it through Lottie's eyes, it was a much different scene. She looked frantic."

Amy covered her mouth with her fingertips and swallowed hard. "She must have been relieved when you told her Kyra was on the way. Here at the counter I saw how quickly Kyra panicked because she didn't want Lottie to worry."

"I'll say. She rushed over and hugged Lottie. She was so sorry." Eric turned to stare out the window. "She said it over and over."

"I only met Kyra today and don't know anything about the situation, except she said Lottie hadn't been with her long."

Eric shook his head. "Maybe not, but she's completely devoted to her." He narrowed his eyes and gave her a long look. "She reminds me of you."

Had he read her mind? Lottie's reaction had triggered Amy's memory. In an unwelcome way. But how could Eric know that? "Me? How so?"

"Kyra was being so hard on herself. It was just a mistake. She misjudged the time. Even when it turned out okay, she still blamed herself."

He meant Kyra, she realized with a start. Not Lottie. Relieved in a way, she rolled her eyes to make light of it. "Funny how that works."

"I call it like I see it," Eric said, shrugging. "Well, I better go. I only wanted to tell you all went well. Mission accomplished."

Then he was gone. Amy braced her hands on the counter and lowered her head to take a couple of deep breaths. She'd seen herself in Lottie, he'd seen her in Kyra.

WHEN AMY STEPPED into Rick Russo's house, a rush of warm air took the sting out of the damp, cold wind that held no hint of spring. She unwound her scarf and hung up her jacket on one of the many hooks arranged on the wall for visitors' coats.

"I set us up in our family room," Rick said, leading the way to a room next to an open stairway to the second floor. "Eric's already here, so you're the second person to arrive."

"Wow, that's a fantastic feature," Amy blurted at the sight of the free-standing stone fireplace dominating the center of the room. Her eye was drawn to the serving dishes and plates on the table. Rick and his wife, Kristen, had said they'd supply food to make this a working dinner. She and Eric had suggested meeting at the diner, but spreading out in this comfy home was so much better.

Rick smiled in obvious pride in this new home. "Kristen and I are like kids with a new toy. We like having people come over and enjoy our new place with us."

"Come join me," Eric said from his place on the stone bench circling the fireplace.

Eric asked about her day and she asked about his, and it struck her that she'd missed this kind, casual banter about ordinary things. He made it so easy to spend time with him.

He was talking about measuring the growth in Bluestone River by the number of new students they'd enrolled, more than a dozen since January. He looked like he had more to say, but Rick came back with Emma and Vivian and they soon lined up to fill their plates. Mac 'n' cheese and baked chicken. Fresh corn bread with honey. Comfort foods. But, surprise, surprise, Amy thought, she had no need to look for comfort. Not that day. She'd had a lively shift at the salon. Cassie was safe at home having fun with her great-grandparents. Now Amy was part of a River Street event. She was sure the five of them on the committee would create Bluestone River's best July Fourth ever.

By the time they finished an hour of brainstorming, Amy was revved up. She and Vivian were in charge of lining up the vendors and handling the business association's promotion plan for the event. Emma volunteered to help Eric organize the teachers. The city would handle the setup for the kid-size Ferris wheel and rides set up beside a stage at the end of the commercial section of River Street. Mike had finalized arrangements with the high school band to march in the parade. Eric approached the other music teacher who was thrilled to include the high school chorus in the event. It was her idea to sign kids up from all the grades to join the chorus and make it even stronger. The drama club wanted to read the Declaration of Independence—in costume. Some other high school clubs had expressed an interest in floats, so that looked promising.

Vivian and Rick were in charge of coordinating the contingents of veterans and political candidates, and others who'd want to participate. They'd work with Mike on the program and a couple of speakers. Eric thought they could lure more families to be involved if the school kids marched in the parade, but also gather in a tent before the parade and make posters for the teachers to carry.

Eric nodded to his laptop screen. "I'll organize what we've done and send a copy to Mike and the council. With Emma handling the logistics, like arranging for food booths and staging and putting out calls for floats and displays, we're underway."

"If anyone is going to object, we might as well find out now," Emma said.

"What's there to object to?" Amy asked. "The costs aren't that high."

"People don't need a reason to complain," Rick said with a laugh.

"Maybe so," Amy conceded, "but no one is going to rain on my parade. This is going to be great."

Amy had no trouble picturing the day, right down to Georgia handing out soap samples and coupons at the salon's table. Georgia planned a drawing to win baskets filled with hair and skin care products.

"I hope you're right," Vivian said. "But Bluestone River isn't in such a good mood right now, what with the rumblings just below the surface."

Amy raised her hands in mock surrender. "Okay, okay. I hear you. I'm forewarned." Development controversies had yet to be settled. It had created an odd tension in town, as she and Georgia had witnessed in the salon the other day.

Once outside, Emma and Vivian backed down the driveway first. "I'm good with your optimism." Eric gave her a quick close-mouthed smile as they walked down the driveway to their cars. "From what I've seen over these last years, and heard from Seth and Mom, too many people had been complaining about poor Bluestone River's slump. They were waiting for something to happen. Now we have people jumping into a debate about the town's future."

Amy paused to look at Rick's house, which sat on the edge of many acres still blanketed with snow. Beyond that land the woods of the Hidden Lake Bird Sanctuary rose from the prairie and changed the look of the gently rolling landscape.

"Rick has a nice life, doesn't he?" Eric remarked. "A couple of lively kids. He and Kristen seem to have a good thing going, separate from them working together at the diner." He stared at the house with longing in his face.

At least that's what Amy saw. But maybe she was only projecting and seeing in Eric what she herself felt inside. She left his question—more like a statement—hanging in the air and said a quick goodbye and hurried to get into her car.

CHAPTER SEVEN

ERIC OPENED HIS office door, and one by one, wished the three students a good day. Heidi was ready to take them back to class, but he asked her to tell Skylar he was spending another couple of minutes with Cassie.

Cassie scowled when he went back to his desk. "Why do *I* have to stay longer? I'm not in trouble."

"Didn't say you were," he shot back. "But I'm still a little puzzled about something. So, I wanted to ask you about it."

She squinted, giving him a wary look. "Okay? What is it?"

"What is it about *art* class that gets you riled up? From what I hear, you do good work in every other subject. Even *exceptional* work sometimes."

He paused, giving her time to react to his words. A smile? A little pride? Her features softened a bit, but not much.

"Not art, though. You have to be pushed.

Ms. Morse has to remind you about the consequences of refusing to do the assignment." When Cassie's expression darkened, he quickly said, "That's the *choice* you're making."

"So?"

"So, your art teacher ends up spending her time with you, rather than the class."

Cassie lowered her head to avoid meeting his eye.

"You see, hearing this made me curious. What is it, I ask myself, about that particular class? Why not math? Or reading or writing in your journal?" He shrugged and gestured to her. "Go on, talk to me about art."

"It's a big waste of time."

"I see." He didn't see at all. He encouraged her to continue. "Because…"

She wiggled in the chair. "It just is."

"Not good enough, Cassie. I expect a real answer, not a fuzzy one. I want to understand your *choice*."

Silence.

"Did someone tell you art is a waste of time?"

"My dad." She reinforced the hint of defiance in her voice by sticking her nose in the air.

"Ah, I see," he said slowly. "Not your mom?"

She shook her head. "Nope."

"Hmm. That's a curious opinion. Of course, your dad has a right to believe as he chooses. But did you ask him why?"

"Sort of."

A tentative response. "There's no right or wrong answer, Cassie."

"He says it costs too much money."

Eric got his completely unsurprising answer. Eric could almost hear Scott talking about who was paying for worthless art programs in the schools. Hardly an original thought. Scott's attitude was more common than Eric liked to think.

"Music, too," Cassie added, as if bragging.

"Oh, no," Eric said. "And here I assumed you'd be singing with the other kids on the Fourth of July. You know, down on River Street."

Cassie responded with a blank look.

"Did your mom tell you about the Fourth of July festival?"

"She said kids were going to draw posters for the teachers to carry in the parade."

"That's right. And you'll get a chance to be part of the parade and perform with the high school chorus." Cassie lifted one shoulder in a quick shrug. Very quick. Eric could almost see her brain cells firing while she figured out how not to refuse to sing, but not exactly give in, either. The time had come to offer her an escape.

"Don't worry, Cassie, I'm not going to try to convince you to *like* your art projects. And if you don't think singing is fun that's okay, too. That's your choice." He watched the tension in her face ease.

"What I'm asking you is to let a couple of ideas roll around in that fine brain of yours." He tapped his temple. "Agreed?"

She hesitated, but couldn't manage to hide her curiosity. "Okay."

"You see, art can be much *more* than drawing pictures or molding clay into animals or faces. It can also mean a chance to have fun with other kids. Even making posters for a big parade. And singing with other students is like throwing a party where everyone gets to have a good time." He had her attention. She even followed his hand gestures with her gaze. "And do you know what happens then?"

Cassie frowned and shook her head.

"Everybody wins," Eric said, exaggerating a happy face.

That got a laugh out of Cassie, so he quit while he was ahead and got to his feet. "I've kept you long enough. Your teacher will wonder where you are." Before Cassie left, he added, "Can I count on you to think about what I've said?"

Cassie gave him a quick nod and a wave. "Bye, Mr. Wells."

Eric returned to his desk and sank into his chair. Maybe he'd loosened a brick in the wall Cassie had constructed around herself. He'd known something was up with her. He'd never met a fourth grader who balked in art class. Insecure about how good they were at sketching or drawing, yes. But in his experience little kids almost never said no to a chance to paint or dig their hands into a lump of clay.

Eric guessed Scott didn't limit his negative attitudes to art and music. Cassie probably picked up on his resentments and identified with them all too well.

Did Amy know? He'd have to be careful about how he brought it up. It was one thing for her to make disparaging comments about her ex. It might not sit well if those same opinions came from him.

"It just makes me mad," Eric said, "to think of this jerk who ignores his kid most of the time, but then puts all kinds of garbage in her head when he's with her."

"No one likes paying taxes, Eric," Seth teased.

"Maybe not, but most parents like to display their kids' art on the fridge." He let out a mock groan. "And music. My mom put up with the terrible racket I made blowing on the trombone. "If I have kids…correction…*when* I have kids, I'll want them to have the same chance to make my head pound in pain."

Seth chuckled. "You made your point, buddy."

He couldn't even kid himself. This whole conversation was really about Amy and Cassie. He couldn't get the mom and her daughter off his mind.

Eric was trying to distract himself with scraping the ancient wallpaper from what would be his dining room one day, as Seth gave him a hand. He had big plans for this space.

"Okay, no more kidding around," Seth said. "I know you're worried about Cassie."

He shook his head. "Not just worried. It's worse than that. I *like* her spunky ways. But I also know what hurts that little heart of hers."

"C'mon, man, admit it. You're also talking about her mom."

Eric scoffed. "For all the good it does me."

"Stop with the 'poor me' stuff," Seth said, kicking away a pile of disintegrating wallpaper. "Why not just ask Amy out? See if she'll meet you for dinner at the diner one night."

"Wow, the diner," Eric said, not hiding his sarcasm. "Impressive. I'll show her I can go all out."

"Funny, Eric. But you know what I mean. Keep it casual. If you make it a big deal you might scare her off." Seth dumped debris into the trash bin that he'd wheeled into the room. "From what you said, she's busy with Cassie and her grandparents and her job, and...well, you know how it is sometimes."

Eric peered into Seth's face. His mind was a blank. "I know how what is?"

"Forget it. I probably shouldn't have said anything."

Now he was even more curious. "Don't leave me hanging. You have something on your mind."

"Okay, okay. Look, Amy got burned once and maybe she's taking her time. Maybe she needs a lot more time before she's ready to get involved again, and, you know, fall in love."

Eric mulled that over. Seth was right. From what Amy had told him, she'd been living on her own for about six months before leaving Chicago. Her divorce was final only days before she moved in with her grandparents on New Year's Eve. She was running scared. Like he could talk. He'd been terrified of relationships his whole life. "Yeah, well, the thing is, Seth, I don't want to just be that special guy friend who's good with her child, but nothing else."

Eric grabbed the push broom and cleared the wooden floor of the nearly empty room. "Our committee is getting together again next week. This time we're meeting with Mike in his office. You're right. I'll ask her if she wants to get a burger after the meeting." He gave Seth a pointed look. "Since the diner is a couple of doors down from Mike's office that shouldn't be too much of a big deal."

Seth nodded and kept watching Eric.

"What?" Eric braced his weight on the broom handle. Why had he barreled into this conversation, anyway? He always ended up frustrated. "You're itching to say something."

"I suppose I know you pretty well, Eric. And I can tell you're still stuck in that same rut that you've been in for years. You want a family, but you stop yourself from making that happen."

Eric fought back the urge to argue. He despised this topic of conversation.

"I wonder when you're going to stop being so afraid, buddy." Turning away, Seth added, "You're not your dad, Eric. You'll *never* become your dad."

Easy for Seth to say, he thought, on the defensive even with himself. He couldn't claim his cousin was wrong to call him on the fear he'd carried around. And hung on to much too long.

MIKE PULLED THE laptop toward himself and scrolled through the committee's notes. It seemed to be taking a long time for the mayor to review their plan. Amy wasn't the only one to notice. Rick caught her eye and frowned. Eric shifted in his seat, and Vivian and Emma, apparently tired of waiting, pulled out their phones.

Eric finally broke the silence. "Does it look feasible, Mike?"

"Yeah, yeah. It's fine. It's really good. It's just that I'm, uh, kind of restless. Frustrated, really. Haven't had much time to focus on the Fourth."

"We want to take this event off your plate, Mike. If you approve," Amy said. "We'll submit our proposal to the council. If they buy in, we'll take it from there."

"I know, I know." Mike closed the laptop and leaned back in his chair. "I can count on all of you. Fourth of July is covered as far I'm concerned. On the other hand, I never expected our old bridge would lead to such huge arguments. I got Bernie Kirkland pressuring me on one side, and the historical society board is on edge. Everyone's acting like the future of the town is at stake."

"Isn't it?" Amy asked, feeling a surge of energy in her body. She flashed a disgusted look toward Eric. "People are arguing that the bridge isn't worth the money we'd spend to save it. Can you believe it?"

Eric flashed a pointed look back. "She's including me in that camp. To be honest, yes, I think it's a fair question."

She was drawn to him in surprising ways. It seemed Eric went in and out of her thoughts all day. But he puzzled her, too. At least some of the time. Like now. Maybe it wasn't fair, but his indifference to the bridge troubled her.

"So now you see why I'm distracted," Mike

said. "I've been fielding calls and questions about this every day."

"Maybe we should concentrate on the things the people who live here can enjoy." Rick waved the pages of notes in his hand. "Like the Fourth of July festival. Nothing controversial about it."

Nice detour, Amy thought. Even Mike had to grin.

"We've got history teachers and the theater department stepping up," Vivian said. "They want juniors and seniors to do a reading of the Declaration of Independence on stage. What do you think?"

"I like it." Amy and Eric spoke simultaneously, and then chuckled. When they weren't at odds, they were side-by-side on the same page.

Mike and Rick agreed. "Great. Another part of the program taken care of," Rick said, moving to the next item on his list and the ones after that. When they were done, Amy had a long to-do list of her own and lots to share with Georgia.

"I hope this bridge and development issue will be solved before the Fourth," Rick interjected as he stood.

"Has to be," Mike blurted. "That's why I'm

pushing so hard. Everyone's entitled to their view no matter what it may be, but I hope you'll all come to our next public meeting. I'll beg if I have to."

"No begging necessary, Mike," Eric said. Then he looked at Amy. "Ready?"

"Uh, sure."

Suddenly self-conscious, she caught the curious stares from Emma and Mike.

"We're headed for the diner," Eric said, breaking the weird silence.

"We'll leave with you. Emma and I are headed there, too. We're meeting Ruby and Parker," Mike explained. "We've got the sitter for another couple of hours."

"My diner sure will be busy," Rick said with a grin as he headed out the door. "I'll see you there. You, too, Vivian."

AMY WALKED THE short distance with the others, as Eric stayed close by. He might have adjusted to the idea of them all eating as a group, but she was sure that wasn't what he had in mind when he'd asked her to join him at the diner before heading home. But they couldn't very well separate from the group now.

Once inside, Parker waved them over to

where Rick and a waiter were pushing tables together for them all. In a matter of minutes, the quick stop for a burger had turned into a party. *A noisy party, too*, Amy thought. The old-fashioned jukebox blasted hits from the 1950s and '60s and competed with the noise from the loud mixers turning out malts and milkshakes one after the other.

"I like to come in here just for the good smells." Amy lifted her nose and inhaled the scent of grilled onions and bacon for BLTs. She detected a hint of cinnamon and apples in the mix.

Eric nodded his agreement. "Those diner aromas keep me coming back." Eric pulled out a chair for her and claimed the one next to it. "With all the work Seth and I are doing on the house, we end up here for dinner more nights than not."

Amy nodded and reached for her water glass. Being part of this group dinner was safer. She'd been suspicious that this supposedly casual invitation was really a ruse for the *D*-word. He must have known referring to this as a date would put her off. In the weeks since she'd reconnected with Eric, she'd read his face, the way his gaze fixed on her sometimes, his blue eyes soft. And so appealing. No wonder she found herself blushing around him. But as much as she looked forward to seeing him, she didn't want him to get any ideas about them becoming more than friends.

Why? That nagging little voice intruded. It could be so insistent. It wasn't the first time it insinuated itself at the most bothersome times.

Because I'm not ready. She already knew what would inevitably follow this particular train of thought. One side of her would say that *ready* meant she was secure in herself, able to take care of Cassie and make a living. Translated, she had to make something of herself. And be there for her grandparents. But the argument refused to be put to bed. The little voice always put up another argument that said she was making too many demands on herself.

"Amy?" Eric said in a slightly raised voice. He leaned toward her. "What looks good to you? You drifted off to faraway land."

"Oops. Sorry." Almost dizzy from the dueling voices, she picked the first thing she saw on the specials board. "The meatloaf platter, please."

"Good choice," Eric said. "Make that two."

"Every time I turn around," Mike said, "I see another classmate, give or take a year or two ahead or behind us."

Parker, who had been quiet at the opposite end of the table, spoke up. "Some of us newcomers are happy to be included."

"Right, as long as we don't talk about the elephant in the room," Vivian said. "For one night, let's leave the controversy to the town meetings."

Mike laughed, but glanced at Eric. "We can try. No guarantees."

"I get it, man," Eric said, flashing a friendly smile, "but it can't be a smooth ride all the time. From what I hear, this is the first serious bone of contention you've run into as mayor."

"My grandparents said the same thing," Amy added.

"True, Mike's had a good run of luck," Ruby said, "but right now, all I care about is the dinner coming our way."

"A plate of meatloaf and garlic mashed potatoes beats an argument every time," Amy agreed.

"How right you are," Eric said, matching her lowered tone. "But while I have a chance, I wanted to mention a little good news. I have a hunch that Cassie's attitude is shifting some." He smiled, adding, "I might have put a chink in the 'I hate art and music' armor."

"No kidding?" As he told her about his meeting with Cassie, the emotions he stirred up in his gentle way didn't surprise her. "My daughter is turning into your biggest fan."

"I don't know about that," he said thoughtfully, "but even this little bit of extra attention is helping her. I can see it in her face. I watch her walking a little faster into the building. I was older when that coach I mentioned leveled with me about my behavior only hurting me. Cassie's a smart girl. She's learning that lesson much earlier than I did."

Amy enjoyed the scene forming in her mind. "Cassie actually gave you that song and dance about art and music wasting taxpayer money?"

Eric hooted. "So she has told you, too."

Amy wanted to come right out and ask what Cassie had said about Scott, but Parker called out a question about scheduling field trips to the nature center and the conversation took a different turn.

So much for Cassie and her dad. When the conversation rapidly shifted to other summer events on River Street, it was clear she and Eric weren't likely to have a private moment again. Especially when it came to Emma and Ruby's blatant curiosity about her and Eric. Amy almost laughed out loud at the knowing smiles that passed between the two of them, the glances from Eric to her and back to him. She hadn't seen Emma and Ruby together since the afternoon Maisie Green confronted Emma at the salon.

Had Eric even noticed how Emma and Ruby were watching them? She doubted it. Until he and Parker were immersed in work talk, Eric had been focused…hmm. He'd directed pretty much all his attention toward her, which is what Ruby and Emma probably picked up on in the first place.

When the dinner plates were cleared, Rick himself brought out a couple of platters filled with slices of the diner's famous cream pies and chocolate cake. No one was eager to break up their impromptu party and they lingered over their coffee. When it came time to pay, Eric picked up her check from the table. She started to protest, but he whispered a reminder that he'd asked her to have dinner with him. "We didn't know we'd end up in a group." Once outside the diner, there were hugs all around and then they split off to walk to their cars.

Amy thanked Eric for dinner, feeling a little deflated now that the evening had ended.

"Let's do something another time," Eric said when they reached her car. "Just the *two* of us."

Real subtle, Amy thought, amused. But she felt the same way. She was surprised how much she hoped to see him again soon. On the other hand, he shouldn't be wasting his time with her. She had a long way to go before she'd open her heart again.

Still, she heard herself say, "I'd like that." When he leaned down to kiss her cheek, she welcomed his warm lips on her skin.

When she got home, Amy knocked before opening Cassie's door, not wanting to wake her up if she'd fallen asleep. But the light was on and Cassie was reading, her two favorite dolls next to her, one a dancer, the other a Barbie, ever the equestrian in her jodhpurs and riding boots.

"I was waiting for you to come home," Cassie said, a hint of a whine in her voice.

Amy ran her fingers across Cassie's cheek. "I told you I'd be home after dinner. Is something wrong?"

"No, but there's a note for you. A girl in my class says her mom wants me to come over to their house after school tomorrow. It's a playdate."

Amy managed to squelch a shout of joy. Finally. Cassie had been at the school since early January and until now she hadn't mentioned any of the kids as a special friend.

"What's her name?"

"Lottie. You have to text her. She'll pick us up after school."

"Lottie?" Kyra's foster child. Another newcomer, like Cassie. This could be exactly what both girls needed. "So, I'll tell Lottie's mom you want to go. Right?"

Cassie responded in her low grandpa voice, "You bet your life I do."

Clapping, she said, "Good job, Cassie. You sounded exactly like Grandpa Les."

"Don't forget to send her mom a text," Cassie said.

"I'm going to do that right after I kiss you good-night." She planted a quick kiss on Cassie's forehead. "Lights out?" she asked, her hand poised on the switch on the bedside lamp.

"Yep." Putting the book aside, she adjusted her dolls and Nancy in the bed next to her, and closed her eyes.

Amy found Kyra's note on the kitchen

table. It mentioned the day in the salon and explained that later she'd made the connection that Lottie and Cassie were classmates. For Amy, a simple playdate was like plunking a cherry on top of what had been a good day.

Amy texted Kyra to finish the arrangements between them and received a quick confirmation back. She let out a happy sigh. She was done with her day. When she joined her grandparents in the living room, she wasn't worried about a thing.

CHAPTER EIGHT

AMY DID THE rundown on the spelling and math sheets in Cassie's backpack. "And finally, you have two dolls and a change of clothes."

"I don't need clothes. They're for Frieda and Kate."

Amy ran her finger down Cassie's nose. "I knew that, you silly." That brought a smile. It always did. "Okay, out the door with you. The bus will be here any second now."

After delivering one more hug, Amy opened the door and Cassie ran to the sidewalk and stepped around puddles of melted patches of snow to get to her pickup spot on the curb two doors down. Cloud jumped up on the windowsill. "Going to wait with me again, huh?" Amy said, scratching the cat's neck and listening to the loud purr. The three kids Cassie took the bus with were already there, but Amy stayed at the kitchen window until she saw the yellow bus come to a stop.

The sun glanced off the top of the bus thanks to such a bright morning.

The signs of spring were subtle, but the first robin had started a nest in a still-leafless tree in the front yard. These little promises were the grand prize for endurance. Not just for the cold and snow and ice. She'd made it through an uncertain winter, sometimes wobbling a bit, but so far her plans were working. Little triumphs. Like a job she really enjoyed with hours that allowed her to drive her grandparents to their appointments, maintain the comfy house, and fill the cabinets and fridge with food.

And keep everybody in clean clothes, she thought, giving Cloud a final pat before heading to the basement to start a load of laundry. As she filled the machine, she heard the floor squeak as Grandma moved around in the kitchen. She could follow her movements just from the sound of the footsteps above, from the coffeepot to the table and then back to the counter, where Grandma was making Grandpa's toast.

Once again, Amy was transported back to being Cassie's age when Grandma stood at the window and watched her get on the bus. Since seeing Kyra grow frantic about

Lottie, a mix of memories came and went, some fast and sharp, others more like a flower bud opening and revealing a tender moment. Those could go either way. The flower could open on a sweet memory of being a little girl and helping Grandma Barb fold clothes or it could be the dull ache of her reckless parents showing up and talking about an exciting life they had planned for her. But then they had to leave again to find this fantasy life. Three times they'd left with a promise to return. And without ever making her grandparents her legal guardians.

Amy hadn't talked with anyone about this slice of her past. At some point, when her parents hadn't been in touch for a year or more, Barb and Les took steps to become her legal guardians.

Once they'd put that process in motion, everything about her grandparents' lives had been scrutinized. First, they had to say the ugly word out loud. *Abandoned.* Barb and Les never used that word with her, of course. They left that to the lawyer and the court. But Amy remembered the undercurrent of anxiety in the house while her grandparents waited for an answer.

Amy's court-appointed advocate argued

it was obvious what her parents would have wanted. Hadn't they left Amy with her grandparents in the first place? Assuming her parents were missing, intentionally or not, it was clear where they wanted Amy to be.

Amy shivered at the thought that she could have suffered a different fate. But at some point her grandparents *officially* became her true forever family. She owed her life to these two people, both in their mideighties now. If she had one regret, it was spending too many years away from Bluestone River. She'd wasted those years on a man who wasn't capable of love. Not even close.

Now that she was back, she didn't intend to leave. Grandma Barb, especially, wanted to stay in this house where she'd lived most of her life. Amy promised to help them accomplish that. But Grandpa reminded Grandma— and her—that some promises could be hard to keep.

Amy chose not to argue, but something deep inside her said, *Watch me, Grandpa.* She meant to do whatever it took to keep them in the home they loved.

ERIC GRABBED HIS coat and went outside to the front of the school where two buses and a day care center van had parked and the kids were lining up to board. Walking down the line, he waved and nodded to make his presence known. He greeted the kids by name, knowing that just saying hello was sometimes enough to halt what he called skirmishes. A little push here and shove there could escalate, but not if they saw him waving and coming their way. Teachers milled about, too, watching for any sign of bullying.

He stopped randomly to ask a question or admire a picture destined to be refrigerator art. He usually saw Cassie in the bus line, but today she was with Lottie, another new girl in the fourth grade class. They were standing in the line where parents or babysitters pulled in to wait.

"Who's picking you up today, Cassie?" he asked.

Cassie jabbed her thumb at Lottie. "Lottie's mom. I'm going to her house."

"Good. That sounds like fun." Eric had been a little worried about Lottie, who was maybe too quiet and well-behaved, at least according to Skylar. Hmm… Cassie was one impulsive act away from changing that.

"Kyra wants me to make new friends." Lottie spoke matter-of-factly. "She says I could be with her for a long time."

"She explained about her mom. She's sort of a mom, only not exactly." Cassie spoke as if she was privy to some significant information.

"I get that." Eric smiled at Lottie, who for the moment looked content. He glanced down the line and saw Kyra Murphy's car. "Only two more cars ahead of you."

He waved to Kyra, who he could see was watching the girls from her car. For no particular reason, he waited with the girls until she pulled up. She buzzed the passenger side window down while the two girls scrambled into the back seat.

He bent over to say hello through the open window. "I hear you have some company this afternoon."

"I do. I couldn't be happier. It's a big day. Their dolls are being introduced to each other," Kyra said, with a grin.

"You have fun."

Kyra nodded. Without spelling it out, their short conversation was really all about good news. Amy also must have been happy to know Cassie had plans with another little girl.

He'd been concerned that she hadn't made many friends in her class.

Eric remained in front of the school until the last child was accounted for. Every day he saw rushed, stressed-out parents among the drivers in the line. Crammed schedules brought on lousy moods when a glitch threw a wrench into the carefully planned day. Whether he liked it or not, getting a glimpse into parents' problems went with the territory of his job. He'd grown up knowing having a family wasn't all fun and games.

But that didn't keep him from wanting one.

KYRA LED AMY to the sunporch, with its multiple houseplants hanging on hooks and lining the space under the windows. "I thought we could chat in here, especially after my meltdown in the salon," Kyra said. "I remember you from high school, but you may not remember me. I was a mere sophomore when you were a senior."

Amy responded with an embarrassed shrug because Kyra was right. But high school was too long ago to start apologizing for little slights. Instead, Amy admired Kyra's tiny brick bungalow, but with a sunporch that made the house stand out on the street.

"Do you work here at home?"

Kyra nodded. "Graphic design. It's a good thing I can do it at home, or as a single person, it would be harder to be a foster mom."

"Seems both girls were the new kids at the start of the term in January. I'm glad they found each other."

Kyra nodded and tilted her head toward Amy. "It's just her and me, so I'm afraid life is a little tame here alone with me. I think Cassie will be good for her. Are you alone with Cassie? I mean, no dad in the picture."

Before she could stop herself, she let out a cynical scoff. "Oh, she has a dad back in Chicago. But let's just say, he's not reliable. He was never a doting dad, but lately he's been breaking more promises than he keeps." She softened her tone when she added, "If I'm going to be a single parent, I'd just as soon be back in my hometown."

"I left St. Louis to come back home," Kyra said. "I can run my business anywhere. And I had a relationship there. But it didn't work out."

Amy stared at her shoes. "Well, I understand how things can go bad. I married a guy from high school. I'd known him all my life." She hesitated, unsure if she should go on. "Sorry. This is all ancient history now." Aware she was on the verge of rambling and saying way too much about her personal life, she changed the subject. "Cassie might have mentioned that we live with my grandparents. They're like parents to me."

Kyra looked at her with curiosity, but Amy left it at that. A longer conversation could wait for another day. "We'd love to have Lottie visit us after school one day. My grandparents watch Cassie until I get home from work. They're warm and lots of fun."

Kyra's eyes lit up. "Oh, that would be wonderful."

Flashes of Grandpa Les sitting at the card table with a puzzle spread out zipped through Amy's mind. He'd welcome another little girl joining him and Cassie. The two took those jigsaw puzzles very seriously. "We'll have her over. And you, too."

"Thanks for that." Kyra frowned. "I'm trying to bring Lottie out of herself, let her know she's safe with me and my friends."

Amy's stomach tightened. She understood those emotions so well, even after all these years. Tempting as it was to ask Kyra outright what she meant, Amy held back from crossing an invisible line. "We'll arrange something soon."

Kyra smiled broadly, as if pleasantly surprised. "I'll go get the girls."

Amy followed her from the sunporch to the living room that opened to a small kitchen and dining area. Kyra went down a short hall to Lottie's room. Such a compact house, but Amy's heart went soft just looking around. Lottie's art was on the fridge, and a calendar listing chores was on the wall next to the counter.

"Did you get here early?" It came out like Cassie was accusing her of doing something wrong.

Amy took the tone as a good sign. "Nope. I'm right on time. Speaking of time, we need to get home. It's my turn to fix dinner."

"Oh, you take turns, huh?" Kyra said.

"Mom makes pot roasts in the slow cooker," Cassie reported, as if it was a very important fact.

Amy and Kyra exchanged amused glances as Amy steered Cassie out the door. Her daughter was "Lottie this" and "Lottie that" on the drive home. But when Amy pulled into the driveway, Cassie's frantic voice pierced the air. "Oh, no, oh, no, I forgot Frieda and

Kate! I left them on the dresser in Lottie's room!"

"Do you want to go back to get them now?" Amy asked, fully expecting Cassie to say yes.

Cassie sighed. "Maybe it's okay if Lottie takes care of them until tomorrow." Cassie paused. "Lottie likes Frieda a lot. She doesn't have a doll like her."

Amy picked up her phone. "I'll text her mom right now. Then Lottie can bring them to school."

"Kyra isn't her real mom," Cassie insisted. "That's why she calls her Kyra."

"I know, sweetie, but a foster mom is like a real mom. I think of Kyra as Lottie's mom, you should, too."

"Lottie lived with a bunch of other families last summer and until right before Christmas," Cassie said. "She had to move a lot. Her real mom went away for a long time."

Amy's chest tightened. She knew zero about Lottie's story but hurt for the little girl anyway.

"Lottie likes Kyra. She told me she wants to stay with her forever." Cassie giggled. "Lottie likes that they have the same blond hair."

"So they do," Amy said, thinking it uncanny that the little girl's wavy hair was so like Kyra's.

As she walked up the driveway to the house alongside Cassie, she said, "I could see that Kyra loves having Lottie living in her house with her. It's nice, huh?"

Cassie didn't respond. She was already running ahead and then quickly pushed open the back door of the house. "Hey, everybody, we're home."

Yes, home, Amy thought, happy to hear the word easily roll off Cassie's tongue. At the same time, it was hard to brush off the heaviness of Lottie being buffeted about. *It wasn't the same as what happened to you.* Amy shushed that voice. Of course it wasn't.

But it was close enough.

ERIC HEARD THE knock on the door and said a loud, "Come on in." Skylar bolted in. Since he hadn't expected her, he jumped to the logical conclusion some sort of problem had come up.

"Is it Cassie?" he blurted, but quickly walked it back. "Not that she's the only fourth grader to have an issue now and then."

"Well, it's kind of about her," Skylar said.

"She's really upset with Lottie, but she won't say why. Lottie also clammed up."

Why was Skylar bringing this to him? It wasn't the kind of problem he'd normally step in to solve.

"I know what you're thinking, Eric. I handle this stuff every day. But in this case, I'm alerting you because if Lottie has *trouble* in school," she said, putting air quotes around *trouble*, "then I have to include it in reports I'm required to submit to Lottie's caseworker. You know how it is. We have to document everything."

Skylar had a point. If he asked Cassie to tell him what was going on, she'd likely trust him enough to do so. "Why don't I see Cassie right away? I'd rather get her side of the story before our regular talk later this afternoon. We'll have more time now."

"Good." Skylar crossed her arms over her chest. "I know it must seem like I'm being overly concerned, but there's something odd going on."

Eric grimaced. He hoped it wasn't anything serious. Cassie had been making such good progress. After Skylar left with Heidi, Eric sat down at the desk to wait. He flipped through a school board budget report, but absorbed almost nothing. He was too curious about what was going on with Cassie.

"I didn't do anything wrong, Mr. Wells," Cassie said before she was all the way in the door.

"Ms. Morse didn't say you did. She was worried about you, that's all." He pointed to the chair. "Sit a minute and tell me what's going on."

The words came fast and urgently, but it all sounded ordinary, even good. At first. Cassie had been visiting Lottie at her house. Playing with their dolls and making up a story on Cassie's tablet. Her understanding of foster care was a little sketchy, but that was to be expected. Amy picked her up and then came the bad news. The forgotten dolls.

"So, my mom texted Kyra about the dolls. Two of 'em. But then this morning, Lottie only brought one back. Kate." She raised her hands in the air in a helpless gesture. "The other one, Frieda, is still in her room. But she won't 'splain why."

"You don't think she forgot?"

Cassie shook her head with conviction. "I know she likes Frieda and wants to keep her."

"Let's wait and see, Cassie." Her story only reinforced his conviction that none of it needed to make its way into a report for a caseworker. But now that he was in the middle of the situation, he was obligated to follow through and get to the bottom of it.

Cassie narrowed her eyes and tried to look fierce. "I'm going to make my mom take me to her house and get the doll back."

Eric lowered his hands palms down to send a "let's take it down a notch" message. "I get it. You're upset. But I have a better idea."

Cassie grunted. "That's what you always say."

Eric chuckled. "Oh, yeah, and what of it?" He pointed to her with a little power behind his gesture. "Admit it," he teased. "I'm usually right."

His tough-guy tone almost made her smile. Good enough.

"You'll get your doll back, but I want to talk to your mom, and maybe to Ms. Murphy," he explained. "Most kids don't believe they can keep things that don't belong to them, Cassie. There's usually something else going on."

"I *told* you she likes that doll. That's because Frieda's a dancer."

"Okay, knowing that is a good start. So,

you can go back to class now," Eric said. "Not to worry, we'll sort this out."

As soon as the buses had left and the parents drove away with their kids, Eric headed to the salon, where he found Amy at the reception desk working on the computer.

"Did you have an appointment today?" she asked. "I didn't see it on the schedule."

"No, nothing like that." It would have made more sense to have called her, but now, seeing her at the counter he was glad he hadn't. "Do you have a minute?"

Her expression immediately darkened. "Is this about Cassie?"

Like a flash in his mind, he saw himself cupping her face in his palms and smoothing the worry from her face. "Yes, but it's not what you're thinking." It took only a minute or two to explain why Cassie was upset. "I'm telling you this because I had a feeling you'd want to talk with Kyra yourself. Skylar would like to see this settled quietly so she doesn't have to report it to Lottie's caseworker." Eric shook his head sadly. "Seems like a lot of fuss over a missing doll."

"You read my mind," Amy said with a sigh. "I should have expected something like this.

It's the kind of stuff that happens between kids."

"It would seem so. I suppose Lottie could have forgotten to pack the second doll."

Eric braced his hands on the counter. "Maybe Lottie acted impulsively, and now she's stuck, not sure what to do. But she must know she can't keep the doll."

Amy looked away, no longer meeting his eye. "I'll talk to Kyra. The two of us will handle it. I'll let Skylar know when we get it straightened out."

Was Amy aware she was wringing her hands? "I can see this upsets you, but in the end, Amy, it's probably just a one-time dustup."

"I know, but I had great hopes that these two new girls could become friends." She stopped talking and swatted the air. "None of that's important. I'll handle it."

The door opened behind him and Amy's face changed as she greeted an older couple, who joked about seeing Georgia for their usual his-and-hers haircuts.

With her attention elsewhere he had no reason to stay. When another person came up to the counter to pay, he quickly said, "Let me know what happens when you've talked with Kyra?"

"Of course." All outward signs of stress were gone now. She'd flipped a switch and was back into work mode. "I'll call you later."

Eric left, but didn't feel good about any of it.

CHAPTER NINE

LOTTIE'S EYES WERE already puffy from crying when Amy let her and Kyra into the house. The little girl seemed frail and hung on to Kyra's hand on the way to Cassie's room.

The girls sat on the floor and Kyra and Amy perched on the bed.

"Okay," Kyra started, "Lottie's got something she wants to say."

As long as she lived, Amy would never forget the moment Lottie pulled out the doll from her backpack and handed it to Cassie. Once she'd released the doll, she burst into loud, uncontrollable tears. She repeated one "I'm sorry" after another through sobs that almost choked her.

Kyra, tears shimmering in her eyes, gathered the little girl in her arms and held her tight. Looking at Cassie, Amy saw the sympathy, maybe empathy, in her daughter's eyes. It was clear to everyone, even Cassie, that what happened was about way more than a doll.

"It's okay. It's okay." Cassie's voice was high and thin.

Kyra tried to comfort Lottie with whispered soothing words. "It was a mistake, honey, but now it's over."

Really? Amy would have said it was far from over. She was still confused over what had happened, not just with the doll, but the bout of wrenching heartbroken tears. She watched Cassie put the doll with her others on the shelf next to the window.

"We're having pizza," Cassie said to Lottie, her voice still strained.

Amy made a show of looking at the time on her phone. "Ah, yes, it should be here any minute."

"You wait in here," Amy said. "I'm going to go set the table. We need to eat that pizza while it's hot."

"I'm going to go help her, Lottie," Kyra said. "Okay? Then we'll all eat."

Lottie had finally caught her breath and had scooted closer to Cassie.

Amy reluctantly left the kids alone, but maybe it was better. Lottie might get over this embarrassment and shame faster without adults in the room.

As soon as they were in the kitchen, Amy

said, "There's something unfinished. Something off. I can't put my finger on it."

Kyra leaned against the counter and rubbed her forehead. "I know what it is. Right before we left the house, Lottie finally dropped a clue about why she deliberately kept the doll. Apparently, there was a doll like Frieda at the second home she was in last year. It belonged to one of the kids in the family, so she couldn't take it with her when she was moved to the next place." She took a deep breath and said, "She loved that doll."

Amy put the plates on the table with a clatter that made her wince. "Wow. If you don't mind I'll tell Cassie a little about that later." She put her hand over her heart. "Even a child can understand why Lottie fixated on that doll."

Kyra blinked a couple of times, but her eyes still glistened. "Here's the thing, Amy. I don't care what anyone might say, but I'm getting Lottie a Frieda doll of her own." Kyra quickly wiped away tears spilling down her cheeks. "This situation really got to me. It was wrong for her to keep Cassie's doll. No question. But I didn't know the whole story, either. The doll had become some kind of anchor for her. Leaving without it was bound to be upsetting. Still, I didn't expect this melt-down."

"She's a lovely girl," Amy said firmly. "You're right to trust yourself. Let's just assume this came out of an insecurity she has. An impulse she obviously regretted."

"I hope they can stay friends."

"We'll declare the problem solved, over. Before you go home, let's look online for the doll." Amy chuckled and tried to shake off the hurt in her own heart. "Hey, today, it's a doll, soon it will be graduation dresses."

When the doorbell rang, Amy asked Kyra to get the girls while she paid the teenager delivering the two pizzas, a bag of salad, and another with the restaurant's special double chocolate chip cookies. Quite a splurge, considering her budget, but Amy would have paid anything to put things right between the girls. Neither she nor Kyra were naive enough to believe a pizza dinner would solve Lottie's issue, but it was a start.

Inhaling the aromas of garlic and tomatoes and cheese floating through the house, Amy went into the living room where her grandparents were watching the news. "Dinner's on the table."

"Everything smoothed over?" Grandpa Les asked.

She handed Grandpa his cane. "It is. I'll tell you more about it later. It's business as usual from here on in. I'm looking forward to this dinner."

The girls were side-by-side at the table. Lottie's red eyes were the only signs of the previous crying. She wasn't all smiles and laughter, but she was calm. Kyra dished out a piece of each kind of pizza, one topped only with vegetables and the other loaded with pepperoni.

As if determined to turn this dinner into a party, Grandpa Les saw the pizza on his plate and rubbed his palms together. "Thick layers of cheese and pepperoni, my favorite treat." He made a show of sniffing the air. "I think I smell chocolate cookies."

"Not your doctor's recommendation," Grandma Barb said, "but I guess it's okay once in a while."

Amy laughed when Grandpa Les rolled his eyes and looked at the girls for sympathy.

"With two more women at the table, I'm really outnumbered now," he said, winking at Lottie and Cassie.

Amy gave Lottie a pointed look. "Don't believe a word of it. He loves it when we dote on him."

"You bet your life I do." Giving Cassie an exaggerated wink, Grandpa said, "I never could fool your mom, Cassie. She's a smart one, she is."

"Oh, please," Amy said, laughing.

"Your eyes are doing that thing again, Grandpa," Cassie said.

Pretending to be surprised, he said, "Thing? What thing?"

"When you get silly your eyes twinkle."

Lottie and Kyra both giggled.

Cassie turned to Lottie. "He gets silly a lot."

That brought on more giggles.

With the heavy weight lifted from her shoulders, Amy dug into the food and added a comment here and there to the small talk around the table. She glanced across to Kyra, who was explaining her graphic arts business to Grandma Barb. Her work was mostly industrial—she specialized in updating logos and graphic themes for major firms across the country. She'd just finished up work with a Midwest airline, which impressed Amy's grandparents.

After passing a plate of cookies around

post-pizza, Amy insisted she would clean up the kitchen and shooed her grandparents back into the living room with the girls. Kyra stayed behind to help with tidying up. When they were done, Amy said, "Ready to go on-line? Do you want to get this done now?"

"Absolutely," Kyra said. "Let's have a look."

"Hey, girls," Amy called out. She gestured for the girls to come to her. "Let's go to my room."

Two adults and two kids in her small bed-room was a little crowded, but she grabbed her laptop and they all piled on her bed.

"What are we doing?" Cassie asked.

Kyra smiled. "You'll see."

Amy typed the brand name of the dancer doll in the search bar and a second or two later, a list of sites came up. "Whoa," she said when she clicked on a site for the company known best for these particular dolls. The dancer doll was an exact match for Frieda. "I think I've spotted what you're looking for." She handed the laptop to Kyra, who smiled and took it from there.

"Lottie, have a look at this. You, too, Cassie." Kyra turned the screen so the two girls could see it.

Lottie's eyes opened wide when she saw the doll on the screen.

"I didn't know before now that you once had a dancer doll to play with," Kyra said."

Turning to Cassie, Lottie nodded. "It was at another house."

When Cassie nodded as if she understood, a ripple of relief zipped through Amy.

"But, you're with me now," Kyra went on. "So I want you to have one of your own, Lottie."

"Really? You mean it?"

Kyra smoothed Lottie's hair. "Of course, sweetheart. I wouldn't say it if I didn't mean it." She waved her phone. "We're ordering it tonight."

Amy reached for Cassie's hand. Something important was going on and she wanted Cassie to remember it.

"But," Kyra said, cupping Lottie's chin, "you can't take other people's things. No matter what. I want you to promise me you'll talk to me about things you like. Now, I can't get you *everything* you could ever want, but I still need you to tell me how you feel."

"That's what my mom says, too." In a voice that sounded embarrassingly like Amy's, Cassie said, "'I'm not made of money, you know.'"

Lottie nodded.

"She's right about that," Kyra said and pulled up the website on her phone. "It's getting late. We need to place this order and head home."

Amy almost laughed out loud at the way Lottie and Cassie decided how they would tell their dolls apart. They batted ideas back and forth until Lottie settled on adding a blue—her favorite color—ribbon around her doll's wrist like a bracelet.

"You're sure?" Kyra asked.

Lottie nodded. "Yep."

"Then here goes." With Lottie looking over her shoulder, Kyra hit the "buy" command and made the payment. "Done." She lifted her arm in triumph. "It will ship tomorrow." She gave Lottie's shoulder an affectionate squeeze.

"Thank you," Lottie said, her voice muffled by leaning on Kyra's chest.

"Yay! I'm so glad." Cassie clapped her hands and Lottie followed her lead.

"But it's time to get to bed," Amy said.

Within minutes Kyra and Lottie had said their good-nights to everyone and left. Amy sent Cassie off to brush her teeth and then filled in her grandparents about what had gone on.

"It all turned out, though," Grandpa Les said, a thoughtful look passing over his face.

"Yes, it worked out." For now. Always left hanging in the air was the uncertainty about what would happen to Lottie—and Kyra. Grandma Barb was quiet, but held Amy's hand a little longer than usual when Amy kissed her cheek and said good-night.

Cassie was almost asleep when Amy went into her room. She opened her eyes long enough to say it was fun to have people over.

"I like having company, too," Amy said, taking Cassie's words to heart. She'd come back to Bluestone River convinced she had little in her life other than Cassie and grandparents. All her energies were directed to finding a way to make a good living and doing a good job of raising Cassie. But it turned out she could have a fuller life. Even friends.

Speaking of…she glanced at the time on her phone. She'd promised to call Eric with an update. She had a feeling he'd be pleased.

ERIC HURRIED DOWN off the ladder to catch the call before it went to voice mail. Amy. Good.

He'd hoped she'd call. He said hello and tilted his head from side to side to get the kinks out of his neck. Who knew even small sanders could get so heavy?

"You have news?" he asked.

Her joy came through loud and clear. "The best. I think we've put this incident behind us."

He listened to her tell her story without interrupting her, his mood rising. Mostly. Something didn't seem right, though, and was still nagging at him when she was done.

"I'm not saying Lottie's problems are over," Amy said, "but I believe the girls will be okay in school. That's good news for you and Ms. Morse. You won't need to worry about trouble brewing." She paused. "What do you think? Not bad, that pizza dinner idea, huh?"

She sounded almost giddy. But he couldn't let this bothersome thing go. "Uh, well, I think it's great that it worked out…"

"So why do I hear a 'but' coming?"

"My first reaction is that somehow, the same girl who caused the problem now has a doll just like the one she took…or, as Cassie put it, stole. I realize she's been in foster care—"

"Kyra is Lottie's fourth foster parent in less than one year," Amy interjected.

How had that slipped by him? "That's not good, I know. But it shouldn't seem like she's getting a reward...did I hear you right? You all picked out the doll together?"

"Yep, took care of it on the spot."

He had to admit the scene of Amy and Kyra with the girls tugged at his heart. But... "Cassie gets this? She's okay with it working out like this for Lottie?"

"Well, yes," Amy said. "Why wouldn't she be okay?"

"Because it seems like Lottie is being rewarded somehow, when she did take the doll."

"I get what you're saying and asking, Eric. But you didn't witness the heartbreak, the emotion. This child has been moved around..."

"Aren't you taking this a little personally?" Eric interjected. "I mean... I'm not sure what I mean." Why did he have an opinion?

The silence was only a second or two, but it seemed much longer.

"I'm not surprised you'd question Kyra's decision, but I am surprised you'd question my feelings about it."

"That's not... I'm sorry. I didn't mean

to imply your situation and Lottie's are the same. Really."

"But you did, Eric. More or less. It was Kyra's choice. It felt right to her. And that counts for something. None of this is about me."

Hard to argue with that.

"We'll have to agree to disagree about Kyra's solution," Eric said, "but I'm relieved Cassie and Lottie got through this bump in their friendship."

"How's the house coming?" Amy asked.

Her casual tone sounded forced, but an awkward shift in topic was better than no shift at all.

"I'm making good progress." He gave her the latest on his updated kitchen and added, "Are you up for the tour?"

"Sure. Whenever it works for you."

"How about tomorrow afternoon?" he said, responding to her eager tone. "You can bring Cassie. I hear it's supposed to be a good day. You know, like real spring." He strung those sentences together like he'd never have another chance.

"Stop, stop. You don't have to sell me. I like to go to open houses just to look around, so I'm eager to see what you've done to rescue your place. I won't be shy about critiquing your paint choices, and I'll even bring treats." Finally, their conversation was back to normal.

"Fair warning, though. I may need to bring Cassie if Scott doesn't show. Again."

"He hasn't been around at all, has he?"

"No. I'm treating it lightly with Cassie. I make everything that involves him tentative."

"For her sake, I hope he shows," Eric said, "but if he doesn't, she's always welcome to come along for the grand tour."

"Thank you for that," Amy said softly. She ended the conversation by saying she needed to check in with her grandparents before heading to bed.

The call over, Eric pushed away his disagreement with Amy over the doll incident. He wasn't in a position to second-guess and as long as the issue didn't spill into the school it wasn't his business anyway.

In one gulp he finished the bottle of water he'd been working on and took a last glance around his house before killing the lights and heading to bed. It was a good time to show off what he and Seth had done. From newly plastered walls and sanded woodwork, the house looked fresh and ready for a new era, but with some leftover charm. The original oak hutch was built in the side wall of the dining room and he'd chosen to keep the old-fashioned walk-in pantry in the kitchen. It was a bright, cheerful house on a sunny day, and warm and intimate when it was dark and rainy.

The place was so much more than its fire-place and woodwork and roomy kitchen and four bedrooms and an attic. He was turning it back into a home.

He was already looking forward to Saturday.

CHAPTER TEN

AMY PUSHED OPEN the front door, hearing the mixed sounds of pounding and buzzing. "Eric?" she called. "It's Amy." No answer. She stood in the entryway, bakery box in hand, and scanned both the mess and the obvious progress. Eric hadn't been kidding when he'd described the work he and Seth were putting into the place. But what a gem of a house. The wood railings on the curved stairway were stripped bare and exposed the gorgeous oak. Nice. She took a few more steps into the open area of the living and dining rooms. Only a couch, a coffee table, a treadmill and TV occupied the space. "Eric?"

Suddenly, he appeared around a corner in dusty jeans and T-shirt. "I thought I heard my name." He looked behind her. "You're alone? Scott showed up?"

"Part of it. He's taking her to the movies in Clayton and they'll have a quick dinner before he drops her off." She pointed to the porch. "I left my bike out there. Is that okay?"

"I'm sure it's safe. Your bike is a sign of spring." He grinned and used his forearm to push his hair back off his face. "We'll be calling it quits for the day soon. Seth and Brad, a guy from his crew, are almost finished installing fixtures in two of the bathrooms. I'm on the last leg of sanding the first-floor woodwork."

"Here. These are for you. Jelly doughnuts from Sweet Comforts. Every work crew deserves a treat."

"Thanks. How did you know they're the best jelly doughnuts in the Midwest?" He took the box from her outstretched hands and gave her an impish grin. "I may share with Seth and Brad."

Standing in the middle of the living room, Amy suddenly found it hard to breathe. Not from the plaster or the sanding dust. The house caught her off guard. There was something special about the open and airy space. "This house is incredible."

"Thanks. I still can't believe my luck."

Her eye caught the leaded glass windows in the dining room with their blue and yellow diamond patterns.

Eric followed her gaze. "I noticed those beauties right away, too. They're originals. Come with me. I'll show you around."

Amy followed him into the kitchen. She could see the markings where the wall had once closed off the room. That was gone now and vertical beams and a counter took its place. "I like how you've opened it up," she said, making circles with her arms. "My grandparents' house could do with fewer walls that shrink the layout."

"Speaking of that, I'm adding a deck." He pointed to the back door. "As soon as it's reliably spring we're opening up that wall and putting in long patio doors that will lead onto the deck."

She could picture every change he described, from his practical approach to expanding the closets to his ideas for updating the kitchen. He led her upstairs to the four spacious bedrooms and old-fashioned linen cabinets and drawers in the hall.

"As you can see, I wanted lots of room," he said.

"No kidding?" she teased. Everywhere she looked, every corner, every window, she saw potential…possibilities. Only the two skylights propped against a wall surprised her. "Where are you putting those?" she asked.

He pointed up to the ceiling. "The attic is almost finished. It could be a family room one day or a private space for a teenager. I just figure the more light the better." He grinned. "Who knows? My mom signed up for a watercolor class and is taking to it like a duck to water. Maybe she'll come around now and again and use the attic as a studio."

"Your mom is always up to something, isn't she?"

"Apparently, she defines the word *retiree* as 'never slow down.'"

"I used to say that about Les and Barb," Amy said, feeling nostalgic. "Years ago, they were more like your mom. But they're in their eighties now and ever since Les's stroke, they feel better staying closer to home. I'm glad I can be there to help keep them where they want to be." She abruptly stopped talking. This house was about the future, not the past.

Eric cocked his head to one side, but she didn't say any more. She wandered through the upstairs, room by room, looking out each window, open now on the mild day. She was conscious of Eric following a few feet behind and sensed his gaze on her.

"Did you and Scott have a house in Chicago?" Eric asked, breaking the silence.

She shook her head. "We rented a two-bedroom apartment. Wonderful neighborhood, but a house was out of reach." She rolled her eyes. "Well, not really." She walked to a window where the maple tree in the backyard was starting to leaf. "A year-round view. It's coming to life right in front of your eyes."

"I wanted a big yard. You know, like your grandparents' place."

"Living in an apartment, I missed that," Amy said. "But when Cassie was a baby, I practically lived in the city parks." Why did she sound so sad? Even to her own ears, let alone how whiny she must seem to Eric. All that was behind her now, that cramped apartment with its view of the brick building next door. The ongoing conflict with Scott, who insisted he wouldn't consider buying a house that ate time and money, at least not yet. It took years for her to accept that "not yet" meant "not ever."

Even with Cassie and a job she liked—and was good at—she'd always felt like she was camping out in Chicago, waiting, waiting. For what? For Scott to change.

"Speaking of parks, do you have time for a

bike ride on the river trail?" Eric asked. "It's the first springlike day we've had."

That pulled her out of her plummeting mood. "You bet. Matter of fact, biking is my thing. I spent a lot of time on those lakefront trails in Chicago."

"Meet you on the front porch," he said, looking down at his stained T-shirt. "I'll change and let Seth know I'm taking a break."

She carried her bike down the stairs, and while she waited for him she watched the kids playing on the street. A family of four went by riding single file on their bikes in the direction of the trail. She and Eric would have company down by the river. Hour by hour the day had warmed until it reached the high fifties in the afternoon sun.

"Ready?" Eric held up a paper bag and waved it in the air. "Donuts for later."

"Perfect," she said taking the bag from his outstretched hand. She stowed it in the rack behind the seat. "A reward at the end of the ride. The filling is my favorite, raspberry."

Eric wheeled his bike out the front door and braced one hand under the bar and carried it down the steps in one quick move. "No racing until we get to the trail," he teased, as he put on his helmet.

"Aw, you ruined my master plan," she quipped.

"Let's take the shortcut," Eric said as they went to the street.

"I didn't know there was a shortcut," Amy replied. "Lead the way."

It was only a couple of blocks to a cross street that took them over the river where a paved extension led down to a new stretch of trail. "This was just added last year," Eric called out. "Another Bluestone River improvement."

"I see that. Nice." This whole afternoon was nice, a break from real life, Amy thought. Like Cassie's bad mood while she waited for Scott to show up. Would he or wouldn't he appear? Beyond concern for Cassie, it seemed her grandparents' needs were always on her mind, and even that minor disagreement with Eric over the best way to deal with Lottie lingered.

Eric led the way down the slope. He seemed to know where he was going, so she followed along. They pedaled side by side at a leisurely pace until they reached the dusty road and parking area that was one end of the original trail. Now they took a turn down the farm road and another turn toward the woods.

He came to a stop at the edge of the forest where some fencing and a gate spanned a half mile or so of woods. "You weren't in town for the relaunch of the sanctuary and nature center, but the trails were extended through here. They opened the gates on Christmas Eve afternoon and lit up the boardwalk, another improvement. Some people parked in the fields and walked through the woods to the event."

"I missed the big launch by a week, but Georgia described it in great detail. It sounded wonderful. Cassie and I arrived on New Year's Eve, so we didn't get over here before the snow really piled up."

Amy hadn't been surprised to learn that Emma O'Connell had financed the extension of the trail system and had donated most of the money it took to transform the once neglected Hidden Lake Bird Sanctuary into a nature center for the community as well as the tourists. "I'll bring Cassie down here soon. Parker said they have lots of activities for the kids."

"It's a beautiful place, our Hidden Lake. I never worked out here at Mike's parents' resort," Eric said, "but Ruby and Emma did—

and lots of guys in school, too. I seem to recall you went away in the summer?"

He'd remembered that? She barely thought of it anymore herself. "I was a summer helper—a nanny, really—over near Moline. The family was related to Grandpa Les, so I wasn't working for strangers far away from home. I spent three summers in the family's vacation home on the Mississippi," Amy said, with a laugh. "I was mostly watching three little kids turn into prunes in the pool. That's what they wanted to do all day."

She'd wasted too much time daydreaming about living like that family. Their life would be her life one day, or so she'd thought. The husband and wife weren't too much older than her and Scott. But in her fantasies, she'd over-looked the fact the couple she worked for had lucrative jobs in a family business. She and Scott started out living in a cheap and dingy studio apartment while he went to college for accounting and she worked to support them.

"You lead the way back," Eric said.

Amy crossed the river again, but instead of heading to Eric's house, she went toward the covered bridge. *The poor dilapidated bridge*, Amy thought. Concrete barriers blocked anyone foolish enough to try to climb around the wreckage.

"I just wanted to have a look," Amy said, coming to a stop and getting off her bike. "Besides, it's donut time." She grabbed the bag from the rack and peeked inside before offering him first pick as he came alongside her. "Luscious, huh?"

Eric took a big bite out of the side of the donut. "Hmm...and messy." He licked sticky sugar from his upper lip.

"That's half the fun." Amy nibbled her donut around the edges. "You obviously don't know how to eat jelly donuts."

"Oh, really? You're the expert?"

"I am. The trick is taking small bites from the outside in," she said with a laugh in her voice. "Otherwise you risk losing the filling. And everyone agrees it's the best part."

Eric flashed an amused grin. "I'll take that under advisement."

As they polished off the donuts Amy's attention was drawn back to the bridge. She couldn't deny it was in bad shape, partially standing only because strategically placed beams shored it up and kept it from collapsing completely. Eric nodded to the bridge.

"So far, we've not heard about a solution to the problem," Eric pointed out.

"Of course there's a solution," she said. "Not jumping on it is the odd part. And the lack of urgency to fix it in time for tourist season is a mystery to me."

Eric gave her a skeptical look and pointed to the empty fields across the river. "I'm venturing into touchy territory, but can't you imagine a new road here extending off of River Street. It would veer off to a convenient—and attractive—shopping center?"

"Not if it means sacrificing the covered bridge," she said. "If you *insist* on developing that land, expand the park—put in a sports complex or an arboretum. Keep it a nature town."

"Okay, okay, you've said your piece." Eric surrendered with his hands up. He wasn't smiling, Amy noticed. "Like I said, it's touchy. Bluestone River can be a lot of things. It can have festivals and caroling in the park, but I wouldn't mind having a grocery store close by."

"Then let's lure a market to River Street," Amy said impatiently. "That's our neighborhood, yours and mine. Don't you want to see it grow?"

"A market would be great. The farmers' markets add a lot all summer," Eric said, matching her impatience, "but making the town more user-friendly for people who live here isn't a bad thing."

Amy opened her arms wide. "But the bridge is the symbol of the town itself."

Eric nodded toward what was left of the structure. "There are enough photos of that bridge to create a museum, Amy." He pointed from one end of the barrier to another. "You could create a glass display as long as those barriers to provide the history of the bridge. You could include photos when it was lit up for the holidays." He laughed lightly. "Some of the inside walls could be preserved, too. You know, the wooden sections where the teenagers painted hearts and carved their initials." Looking at the rubble, Amy couldn't deny he had a point. Besides, she didn't like the tension. "I concede the point." She exaggerated a formal tone. "I may not like it, but I get the logic of your solution. If the bridge can't be preserved, then making it into a historical landmark is the next best thing."

"Thank you," Eric said, matching her formality, though he smiled broadly. "You're not nearly as stubborn as I thought."

Huh? *Stubborn?* "Well, with that one word, you just dismissed my ideas."

"Wait, wait," Eric said, alarm in his voice. "I didn't mean to offend you. I was joking. More or less."

She waved him off. "No, I'm sorry. I know you didn't mean that in an insulting way. Forget what I said." The knot in her chest was familiar and scary. She was accustomed to having her ideas, her opinions, brushed away, sometimes with a quick flick of the wrist. If she complained, Scott accused her of having no sense of humor.

Eric looked puzzled, as if he didn't understand what she meant.

"We were exchanging our opinions about something important to both of us. I misinterpreted what you said, thinking it was dismissive."

"I was just joking around, Amy." Eric's voice was earnest, serious. "I'd never dismiss your ideas. Not ever. Even if I don't always agree with them."

She took a deep breath. Yikes, she was overreacting. Her past with Scott had triggered this anger and was bleeding into her exchange with Eric. She forced a smile. "Let's just say my feelings about the bridge are about what, in my opinion, is good for the town. She pointed toward the wooden mess. "I admit I have a certain emotional attachment to it. But I'm beginning to understand why some people in town don't feel the same way." "Well, that's good." His blue eyes softened. "I do have a fondness for some old things," he said, smiling now. "I care enough to invest my savings into rehabbing a worn-out eyesore of a house."

"And it's beautiful." She looked down at the river rushing past them, high from the rain and melting snow and sparkling under the afternoon sun. It swirled and bubbled as it passed over the clusters of stones in this section of the river. "I know it sounds corny to say this, but it touched my heart to see how you're bringing it back, old leaded glass and all. It's not an eyesore anymore. You've boosted the neighborhood."

It was awkward, her speaking those words, as if she'd made a confession of some kind. What was it? That she'd wanted a house like that herself, but couldn't make it happen?

The knot lodged in the middle of her chest expanded. So ridiculous, this reaction. "What I said stands," she managed to say. "We may not agree, but I do understand the other side of the argument."

Eric braced his foot on one of the barriers and stared at the river. "I think you're not only smart, but very brave."

Most days she didn't feel like either. But unsure what to say in response, she acknowledged his words with a single nod.

Eric opened his arms. "How about a hug to end the skirmish? Well, near skirmish."

Amy inched forward, ready to welcome being held in his arms and feeling the pressure of his cheek against hers. His mouth was so close to her lips. He was gently bringing her closer when her phone buzzed in her jacket pocket. "Uh-oh." She stepped back and pulled it out. The screen said Grandma Barb. "Oops. It's my grandma. I have to take this."

For a split second, Eric's face fell. "Of course, go ahead." He squeezed her shoulder before easing down the riverbank.

"Everything okay?" she asked.

"We're fine," Barb said, "but Scott dropped Cassie off half an hour ago. A little early. I guess they skipped dinner."

"Big surprise, huh? Silly me, I thought maybe he'd actually make the most of his day with her."

"Cassie's not that upset, though," Grandma said. "I'm watching her going up and down the sidewalk on her scooter. A handful of other kids are out doing the same thing." She paused. "Lots of noise in the phone. What's that I hear in the background?"

"Probably the river rushing by. Eric and I took a quick bike ride on the trails and stopped by the bridge." Her afternoon timeout, fun while it lasted. "I'll pick up dinner and come home."

"Take your time, honey," Grandma said. "I'm keeping an eye on Cassie. I just wanted you to know she was back."

"I know, but still…" Her grandparents watching Cassie after school every day was why Amy didn't leave them alone with Cassie on weekends, at least, not often.

When Amy ended the call, she went down to the edge of the river to tell Eric she had to ride home. She didn't hide her sarcasm when she said, "Something super-duper important came up for Scott, so no dinner with Cassie after the movie. He's already on his way back to Chicago." She shrugged. "My free afternoon was fun, though. *Really*."

"I'll come with you," Eric said, frowning. "I'm sorry Scott messed up your day."

"Oh, it's nothing new." She forced a cheerful tone. "And hey, I don't feel bad. I got the grand tour of your house and a bike ride on the trails. My first since coming back."

She stepped toward him and circled his neck with her arms. She planted a kiss on his cheek before releasing him and turning toward her bike.

They ended their ride in front of the diner. "Let me know if you ever need help with any of your house projects," Amy said.

His face lit up with pleasant surprise. "Will do. Thanks for the offer."

Half an hour later, with the carrier on her bike full of food, she looked up and down the street for Cassie. She wasn't among the kids, but her face appeared in the living room window. She waved and Amy waved back.

Grandma greeted her at the back door and took the bag of food out of her hands. "You could have invited Eric to join us. He's always welcome here."

She had to admit she would have liked to stay with him a little longer. But no matter what her heart said, the interruption of that moment between them was for the best. Otherwise, she could be sending the wrong message.

GEORGIA WASN'T ALL the way through the door yet, but was already shaking her head. Amy had a hunch she knew what was up with her boss. Amy had seen it, too, when she'd come in just before noon. A for-lease sign had appeared in the window of the exercise studio next door.

Georgia propped her elbow on the reception desk. "I had a feeling this was coming."

Amy agreed.

"The space is empty now. Someone removed all the treadmills and the other equipment when we weren't looking," Georgia observed. "I don't like having empty storefronts appear on River Street just when we've started to fill some prime spaces with new businesses."

Amy was aware Georgia had weathered a few storms to keep her business open, and where the exercise studio had failed, Georgia's salon was growing. Amy had her job because the business had expanded. Watching her boss was like taking classes on running a mini empire.

"It's a good retail space," Georgia said, remarking that the empty studio and her shop had been one store back in the day. It had sold men's clothing and had been family owned.

"Before my time," Amy said, "but Grandpa used to talk about how easy it used to be to walk down to River Street to pick up a new shirt. Driving to the mall in Clayton now is never his favorite way to spend an afternoon."

Georgia moved to the window and pointed to a storefront across the street. "All is not lost. A fudge and ice cream shop is on its way, or so I hear."

"And maybe a yarn and craft store," Amy added. "High-end, supposedly."

Georgia leaned against the window and studied Amy. "Do you mind if I ask you a personal question?"

How personal? Amy wondered, a little wary. But she said, "Sure. What's on your mind?"

"Do you like your job here? I don't mean only because it's straightforward and you know what's expected. I'm wondering how you feel about this kind of business."

Amy let out a light laugh of relief. "Ask me something hard, Georgia. This job is pure pleasure." She paused to scan the room and gather her thoughts. "It's not so different from retail, you know. I like to work in businesses where I see different people coming and going every day."

"You're good at what we do here." Georgia frowned. "Now, I don't mean just the basics. You can make appointments and take payments with your eyes closed. But you're great with our clients and making this place inviting. Since you changed up the displays of the makeup and skin care lines, we sell more of everything."

"That's a huge compliment, especially coming from you." Keeping her voice light, she added, "I'm glad I could use my experience to help out here. I like to think of salons like this one as part of the self-care trend. In this town, you're a big player."

Georgia stared at her with a faint, almost amused smile. "I like how you think."

Lately, Georgia had been quietly checking the number and frequency of appointments and comparing this year with last. She'd asked Amy's opinion on what spring specials the salon could offer. Georgia hired another nail tech to work Friday and Saturday and holiday weeks. Slowly but consistently, they were selling more and booking more services.

The door opened and her phone rang at the same time, bringing Georgia and one of the other stylists, Rita, to the front. Amy let her call go to voice mail. Another couple of women came in for lunch-hour haircuts. Those women were always rushed. As soon as they were in the chair with the cape fastened, they started scrolling through messages and gave Georgia or Rita quick answers to questions about what they wanted done.

If Amy could change one thing, she'd transform the salon into an oasis for women, and for the many men like Mike and Eric, who relied on Georgia.

During a lull, she checked her messages on her phone and played back one from Grandma Barb. Her voice was low and raspier than before. Grandma told her about the visit from Grandpa's home health nurse. Grandpa was fine, but the nurse was concerned about Grandma's sore throat so she set up an appointment with the doctor for the next morning. Meanwhile, Grandma was supposed to rest and said she was pretty worn-out. A rare admission. Earlier, she'd downplayed her hoarse voice and insisted she was fine.

Amy felt both concern and relief. She'd deliberately searched for a job that kept her mornings free for just this kind of thing.

Amy paused to greet another of Georgia's clients arriving. The salon was too busy for

Amy to go home at the end of Cassie's school day. Thinking out her options, she texted Kyra and explained the situation. Could Cassie go home with Lottie? It was several minutes before Kyra got back to her to say that was fine. Amy then texted the school, then her grandma, to tell her not to watch for Cassie on the bus.

When she finally put her phone down, she realized she'd been holding her breath. She let the air out of her lungs, painfully aware she was overreacting. This wasn't an emergency. Amy turned her attention back to the work in front of her, although thoughts about her grandma lingered. Even with Amy taking on a big chunk of the burden, Barb still ran the household and oversaw Grandpa's care. Amy stared at the open appointment program on the computer screen, but she didn't really see it. She'd taken a trip to the past, to a time Grandma waited at the window for the bus to drop her off and deliver a hello kiss on Amy's forehead. Only rarely did Amy hear stern words.

How hard it must have been to cope with a little girl asking about her mom, Grandma's own daughter, who proved too unreliable to be a parent herself. When word came that her mom and dad were presumed dead in a boating accident, Amy remembered her grandmother's soothing words, not just for Amy, a young adult by then, but for Grandpa Les, too. Only when Amy held Cassie in her arms did she fully understand that her grandparents were forced to mourn a daughter they'd held in their arms and who they'd loved and raised. At first, Amy had a curious absence of sadness over two people she'd barely known. Now she tried to comprehend the depth of her grandparents' grief and the courage it took to put on a brave face.

Deep in her thoughts, the sound of the phone startled her. "Good," she muttered to herself as she grabbed the phone, "enough with the past." Seeing Eric's name on the screen gave her a lift.

"Hey, I'm calling to check in. Kyra drove away with the two little buddies a couple of minutes ago," Eric said. "That's why I'm calling. Heidi mentioned your grandma. Anything I can do?"

The calm in his voice brought her stress level down another couple of notches. "Thanks, but I've got this. Once I covered Cassie after school, I could relax."

"Good. But you'll let me know if you need

something. You know, chicken soup or treats from Sweet Comforts."

"I promise I'll let you know," Amy said, amused.

"By the way, did you know Kyra put in a bid to do the design for the flyers, webpage and ads for the Fourth of July festival?"

"No, I didn't know. But that's great."

"I ran into Mike and he told me she was among the six that applied. The bids go through the city, but we make the decision."

"I'll try to remain neutral," Amy said dryly, wondering if that was possible.

"All the samples are anonymous, so we'll all be neutral."

"Good move."

"There's a knock at my door," Eric said. "I have to go. Don't forget the meeting tomorrow night. I had to remind myself it's on Friday this time."

"I won't forget," Amy said, amused. "I highlighted it in orange on my calendar."

"Promise you'll call me if you need anything."

"Promise."

The afternoon passed quickly, with clients in and out and a text from Kyra assuring her the girls were fine and busy playing a game on the computer.

Eric's mention of Sweet Comforts prompted Amy to swing over to the bakery-café near the highway to pick up soup and bread for their dinner, and enough cookies to share with Kyra and Lottie.

With her treats in hand, Amy drove over to Kyra's cozy house. She had seedlings in the sunporch windows. "You're putting in a garden this spring?" she asked as Kyra greeted her.

"Always," Kyra said. "I *need* to live where there's garden space."

"I'm going to help," Lottie said, proudly.

"Yes, you are," Kyra said, squeezing Lottie's shoulder.

"Good for you," Amy said, thinking back to the days when she helped Grandpa weed rows of lettuce and peas, and later in the summer, the peppers and tomatoes. "Here, these are for you." She handed the bag of cookies to Lottie, who let out a cheer.

"Thanks," Kyra said. "That's so thoughtful of you."

"My pleasure. I appreciate your help today."

Kyra nodded. "Hey, I put in a bid for the graphics for The Fourth on River Street."

Kyra seemed pleased with herself. "I've been looking for an opportunity to do more local work, a change from the large corporate projects that take up most of my time."

"Wonderful," Amy said. Cassie hopped up and down and announced she had a new joke to tell Grandpa and it couldn't wait a minute longer. On to the next thing, she thought.

Amy steered Cassie to the door and soon they were home. She started their dinner, stirring the beef barley soup and heating crusty peasant bread from Sweet Comforts. She thought ahead to the doctor's appointment in the morning and then all the rest of the next day rolling by without a free minute.

Once everyone was in bed, Amy made herself a cup of chamomile tea and went into her room and pulled out her journal. She didn't write in it every day, but she had the urge to tonight. Her chat with Georgia had triggered the visions she mulled over. Visions of the life she was building with Cassie.

Amy got satisfaction from writing down random thoughts about her dreams, too, even now when they seemed far out of reach. A business on River Street? Impossible. At least right now. But she wouldn't let it go. She smiled to herself. Georgia would understand her dream. Kyra, for sure. But what about Eric? She had a feeling he'd enjoy her vision of the future. Doing what she loved and building security for herself and Cassie.

Not that what Eric thought mattered one way or the other.

Amy let her head rest on the pillow, realizing that wasn't true. She cared very much about what he thought. She talked to him almost every day. She liked being close to him as she learned more about him. She saw him often and every time she looked at him, she saw a good man who'd matured out of the shy boy she'd known in high school.

She remembered how she felt down at the river when he held her close. Their almost kiss. She'd felt safe in his arms, even knowing her growing feelings for him weren't safe at all.

CHAPTER ELEVEN

ERIC LOOKED UP and waved when Amy came in. They'd started the committee meeting without her, but she'd let him know she'd be a little late.

"How's your grandma?" Emma asked after Amy mumbled a quick apology for not making it there on time.

"Bronchitis will cramp her style for a while." She glanced at Eric, but quickly shifted her gaze back to Emma. "Scott is with them. He came up to have a weekend with Cassie. Unexpectedly."

"*He's* keeping an eye on them now. While you're here?" Eric shifted in the chair, conscious his voice was louder than intended and echoed through the room.

Eric tried to ignore the bothersome jitters in his gut. Why be worried? Amy probably sighed in relief when he came for Cassie. He ought to be pleased for Amy—and for Cassie?

Amy looked around the table to include

everyone in her response. "I was lucky he wanted to change his weekend to visit. Otherwise, it would have been kind of a hassle to get here."

Lucky? Oh, yeah, real lucky. Why was she spinning the story to make Scott look good?

So what if she did? Not his problem.

"Are these the samples of the graphics?" Amy asked, eyeing the table as she shrugged out of her jacket. "Cool."

"We made them anonymous, as much as possible," Vivian said, "so we don't know whose is whose."

Eric cleared his throat, needing a second to regain control of his emotions. "We have to make a decision either today or sometime soon. We're in April now, the event's less than three months away."

They passed around the samples, including mock-ups of banners and flyers, and bantered about adapting different logos for the website and other PR pieces.

Eric settled on one bid that had bold block letters, bold like the holiday itself. But he said nothing, while the others narrowed down their choices to two, his favorite being one. Early on, they'd agreed to try to reach consensus rather than voting up and down on every issue.

Amy in particular seemed to gravitate to the other design, Eric's second choice. When Rick, Emma and Vivian spoke up, they'd also settled on Eric's favorite, although Emma liked Amy's choice almost as much. Eventually, the bold simplicity of the first design won out.

"Are you sure you're okay with this?" Emma asked, glancing at Amy.

"My favorite seems a little more modern and fresh, but the other one is good, too. Who's the artist?" Amy asked.

They all had to laugh when the winner turned out to be a senior at the high school, due to graduate in June. "That's as local as we could get."

"What a graduation gift," Emma said.

"Out of curiosity, which one was Kyra's?" Amy asked.

Eric checked and it turned out that Kyra's was everyone's second choice, and Amy's preference.

"I'm a little disappointed for her," Amy said with a shrug, "but she's so talented, I'm sure other local jobs will open up." Amy explained to the others that she'd only recently met Kyra at the salon. "Our girls are like two best pals now."

"You didn't know this was her work, did you?" Eric asked, immediately wishing he hadn't.

Amy's head jerked back in obvious indignation. "Of course, I didn't know."

Eric realized his rash comment and where it was coming from. He grimaced. This wasn't about her at all. It was about Scott. Showing up. Helping out? That's what threw him. Eric gave his head a little shake. *Get over it.* "Please forget I said anything."

"Hey, it's all good," Rick said, holding up a copy of their agenda. "Let's move on. We've got stuff to cover."

Eric coughed. "I mean it, Amy. I'm sorry."

Amy nodded and offered a smile, but the quizzical look in her eyes remained. "It's okay, Eric. Like Rick said, let's move on."

Emma took charge of the next item—the positive response Eric got from the principals of the town's schools.

"Most everybody was surprised to be asked," Eric said, explaining that between the teachers and support staff, fifty-five people signed up to be in the parade. "I told them we'd like to have a complete count by the time school's out in mid-June."

"This is such a unique feature," Amy said. "Not just honoring teachers in this way, but linking education and freedom."

"Maybe it will make it easier to fund schools," Rick said, dryly.

"I could argue the state of the *country* depends on it," Eric said with a grin. "Not that I'm being self-serving or anything."

When Amy smiled at him the stone sitting in his stomach got a little lighter.

Rick invited everyone to come to the diner for coffee and dessert on the house. That sounded fine to Eric and everyone else, but Amy begged off.

"I'll walk you to your car," Eric offered.

"No need for that, Eric," Amy said. With a quick wave to the group she was gone.

Later, the conversation in the diner revolved around The Fourth on River Street. Eric noted how excited the committee was about the planning, even though much of it was a matter of checking suppliers and comparing prices. Even the logistics of getting enough tents, finalizing the parade route and redirecting traffic was more involved than it had first seemed.

On the walk home, his spirits dropped along with the temperature. The wind picked up and April was beginning to feel a lot like March. More troubling was the realization that he'd upset Amy earlier with his offhand remark. He'd apologized. That's all he could do. In his determination not to scare her off, he'd failed to make it clear he was a guy falling in love with a woman who probably had no idea how he felt. And it was his fault. Seth would be the first to say so.

THE PREDICTED RAIN started on Saturday afternoon and by the time Amy finished up the dinner dishes, the spring storm's high winds and battering rain brought Bluestone River to a halt.

"I remember lots of storms like this," Amy said to Les when she sat with him in the living room. A gust of wind rattled the windows on the side of the house, followed by a couple of cracking, snapping noises that ended with a thud that shook the floor beneath them.

Amy looked at the window, where part of a fallen branch of the newly budding sugar maple brushed the glass. "Uh-oh, Grandpa, that whole limb broke off. No wonder we jumped." Amy went through the living room and stuck her head out the back door and leaned over the porch. The limb just missed the corner of the house and landed diagonally across the flower beds, crushing some of the daffodils shooting up from the ground. Half-broken branches rested against the house and the windows in her room. Smaller ones had broken in pieces and were strewn around the yard.

She went back to the living room and described what had happened. So far, so good. That limb wasn't damaging anything important and the rest could be cleaned up easily enough.

"Don't try to move that huge limb by yourself, Amy."

She glanced out the window again. "Not a chance of clearing the big one, but I'll be able to push it away from the window." Another gust rattled the windows. "When the wind dies down, that is. I'll call someone to come out and remove the limb and debris on Monday."

One more thing to add to her always expanding list. But at least Grandma was slowly improving and Grandpa was the same as always. The house seemed empty without Cassie. With Grandma Barb still resting a lot, she was okay when Scott showed up on

Friday night instead of Saturday morning. Cassie was thrilled to have the extra time with him, but Amy didn't trust anything about this early arrival, even his insistence on staying with her grandparents and waiting to leave with Cassie until after she came back from her meeting.

Why the sudden interest in her grandparents? He'd only begrudgingly visited them on occasional trips to Bluestone River. He mostly made excuses not to come along.

On the other hand, maybe Scott was changing for the better. Or, after hearing Cassie's stories about her school and her new friend, Lottie, Scott had finally gotten the message. With or without him, Cassie was adjusting to her new life. If Amy's ex wanted to turn over a new leaf and show more interest in his daughter, Amy would welcome the change.

Before he left with Cassie on Friday, he'd told Amy of his plan to meet one of Cassie's old friends and her parents for lunch on Sunday. They'd have time to squeeze in a trip to the zoo before he brought Cassie home. After she'd left Chicago with Cassie, Scott had left the studio he'd rented while they were separated and moved back into the apartment they'd once shared. Cassie's room remained almost exactly as it was on the day Amy packed Cassie's clothes and favorite things and drove away. That small apartment in Chicago was the only home Cassie had ever known before moving to Bluestone River.

Sometimes Amy worried that once Cassie was back in her familiar room, she'd want to stay. Maybe on this visit she'd wish for her old school where she knew other kids. On the other hand, she'd been settling in fairly well now that she had those meetings with Eric twice a week. He'd thought it best to keep them going. Cassie was still struggling with relating well to other kids, Lottie being the exception.

But for the steady rain and now the high winds, it had been a quiet, almost reflective day. She'd washed her grandmother's short hair. Barb had even fussed a little when she'd styled it. Amy smiled at the thought. She'd picked up a trick or two from watching Georgia and Rita cutting and curling hair so often. She gave both Barb and Les hand massages, and tried to accept the changes in them these last years. When she was a teenager, Grandpa wouldn't have thought twice about dragging that limb out of the way. She smiled to herself, recalling how many times Grandma had warned him to be careful and not break a bone or strain his back.

She finished storing the food she'd fixed for the coming week, before joining her grandparents in the living room. Grandpa wasn't big on movies, but he enjoyed sitting with her and Barb. He'd work on a crossword puzzle while they watched either romantic comedies or grisly detective dramas.

"What's it going to be, ladies?" Grandpa asked, grinning. "Is it a hugs and kisses night or are bodies going to float on the surface of a remote lake?"

"Oh, Les, stop." Grandma tried—and failed—to sound like he was being ridiculous. "What do you say, Amy? Hugs and kisses?"

"Let's have a few laughs, Grandma," she agreed, picking up her phone off the coffee table. She'd missed a call from Eric. "I'll check this and be right with you." She went into the kitchen and listened to Eric's message. "Just saying hello. Wanted to see how you and your grandparents were doing in the storm. Nothing urgent."

Maybe it wasn't urgent, but it gave her an excuse to call him later.

Amy stretched out on the couch and streamed a new comedy that took place mostly on a cruise ship. As she'd predicted, Barb enjoyed it from the first scene. Even Grandpa paid attention because the scenery and the ship brought back memories of a cruise he and Barb had taken a few years ago.

When the movie ended, Les and Barb went off to bed. Restless, Amy poured herself a glass of red wine before phoning Eric.

"Hey, thanks for calling," she said when he answered. "We're doing okay. No bike rides tomorrow, though. We have one limb down on that old sugar maple. It missed the house, so no harm done. I'll get someone to come out and take it away. And probably finally get rid of that tree."

"Where did it fall?" he asked.

She described the location, trying to keep her tone light. It really wasn't so serious, it was just one more thing to take care of.

"You don't need to call anyone. Seth and I can drag it out. He's got the equipment to cut it up and haul it away."

She might have known he'd offer to handle it. "No, no, Eric. I didn't tell you about it so you'd volunteer to take care of it."

"I know that," he said, in a casual tone. "But we can handle it. What if we stopped in tomorrow morning?"

It would take care of the problem. She'd get to see him again, too. "Are you sure you want to spend part of your Sunday dragging tree limbs around?"

Eric laughed. "Well, I suppose when you put it that way…but seriously, I'll bet it's not a big deal. We'll be in and out in no time."

"Okay, you twisted my arm."

"I prefer to think I sweet-talked you into it."

"Hmm…maybe you did." Amy chuckled. "In any case, I'll be happy to see you."

They settled on a time and when they ended the conversation, she went to her bedroom. Once there she realized she was too restless to sleep and too tired to read or write in her journal. She sipped her wine and tried to sort out the jumble of thoughts that refused to either go away or untangle. The last time she glanced at the clock on the nightstand it was after 1:00 a.m.

After a few hours of fitful sleep, Amy heard noises coming from the kitchen and inhaled the aroma of coffee. When she joined her grandparents and poured her first cup, she told them about the plan to deal with the fallen limb. "Eric and Seth should have it hauled away by noon."

"That Eric is a nice fella, isn't he?" Grandpa

said. It was a statement more than a question. "Not the first time he's come around at the right time."

Amy cut her gaze to Grandma Barb, who offered a smug and amused closemouthed smile.

"What's with you?" Amy asked.

"Nothing at all, honey," Grandma replied. "But Les is right. Eric is a very helpful guy. Can't help but like him."

"I do like him. He's a good friend." She blushed as if Grandma was psychic and knew how much he'd been on her mind.

"Wouldn't be such a bad thing if he wanted to be more than Cassie's principal and your friend."

Amy waved her off. "Please, Grandma, you know I don't have time for men and dating and all that." She carried her mug of coffee to the rattling window. "The rain may have stopped, but the wind has picked up again."

Barb opened her mouth to speak, but the sound of a strong gust stopped her. Then *crash!* Everything came to a stop.

ERIC AND SETH walked through the side yard, kicking away small branches. "This tree has had its day, I'm afraid. It needs to come down," Seth warned. "I can fix the shingles on the roof of the garden shed. No need to hire someone."

"I didn't know you work for free, Seth," Amy said. She was bundled up in a jacket with her hands hidden in her pockets. When her hair blew around her face, she gathered it up and twisted it into a knot.

Eric got a kick out of watching her.

"I mean it, Seth. We want you to repair the roof, but we expect to pay for your services." She pointed with her chin at what was left of the tree. "As for the maple, I know we waited too long. One limb crashing last night. Another one jolting the house this morning."

"This could have been a lot worse," Seth said, surveying the mess in front of them.

Eric agreed. It was a cold spring morning, with a bank of charcoal clouds threatening more rain. "You don't need to stay out here and freeze. Seth already has the chainsaw ready to go."

"I'd rather be outside." Amy did a little jog in place and stretched her arms to the side. "I was cooped up yesterday." She glanced at the smashed plants in the bed. "Maybe I can salvage some of the daffodils coming up."

"Have at it," he said, turning to the sound of the chainsaw. Seth had started without him.

Eric steadily stacked the cut wood into the truck bed, while Amy took garden gloves out of the shed and repaired what she could of the smashed and broken flower stems. Then she helped Eric load the smaller loose branches into Seth's truck.

When a car pulled into the driveway and parked behind the truck, Amy left the leaves and twigs she'd raked into a pile. Eric knew immediately it was Scott who had climbed out of the car and opened the rear passenger door. Scott noticed him, too. He was staring at Eric and Seth as he waited for Amy to reach him.

Cassie materialized from the back of the car and waved frantically, happy to see him in her nine-year-old way.

"Hi, Mr. Wells! Why are you here?"

"The wind knocked branches off your big old maple tree. Seth and I are just hauling it away for your mom and grandparents."

"My dad has work stuff, so he had to bring me home." Cassie shrugged. "That's why he's wearing a suit." She looked behind her. "He called Mom a little while ago, but Mom didn't answer her phone."

"She probably left it inside." In his dark blue suit and light blue tie, Scott looked like an expensive accountant on the way to meet a rich client, Sunday morning or not.

Keep it casual, Eric reminded himself. And civil. With Cassie following, he took the few steps to join Amy by Scott's car. It would be rude to pretend he didn't remember his old classmate. He held out his hand. "Hey, Scott, how you doing?"

The handshake was a little short of curt. "In a hurry, unfortunately. I was telling Amy that one of the firm's clients needs some last-minute help with an audit. My name was next on the list to take the weekend emergencies. I have to head back." He pulled back his cuff and checked his chunky sports watch. "It'll be midnight before I'm done." He looked over Eric's shoulder at the wood in the truck. "If I'd known about the tree, I'd have called someone to come right out."

Amy rolled her eyes, her expression of disbelief priceless.

Eric suppressed a laugh. "Hey, no problem. My cousin—maybe you remember Seth—has all the equipment we need."

"And the truck," Amy added.

Cassie grinned and her arm shot up as if

seeking permission to speak in class. "But you have a snowplow, Mr. Wells!"

Amy and Eric both laughed. "You're right, but it's small so we call it a snowblower." Eric turned to Scott. "We've had a few bad storms this winter. I'm sure Cassie told you all about them."

"And you came right over to lend a hand, huh?" Scott's challenge crept right up to the edge of sarcasm.

"That's right, Scott, I plead guilty." Eric tried to match Scott's smug expression with one of his own.

Amy distracted him when she put her hands on Cassie's shoulders. "I'm glad you're back, kiddo. Grandma Barb is much better today. She and Grandpa will be so glad to see you. Why don't you go in and say hello. Tell them I'll be right in."

Cassie gave Scott a quick hug. "Bye, Dad."

"Be good. I'll call you this week. Love you."

"Love you, too." Cassie grinned at her dad and then gave Eric a little wave as she hurried away. "See you tomorrow morning, Mr. Wells." Even Seth got a quick goodbye wave.

Feeling a little guilty about his grudging attitude toward Scott, Eric said, "Cassie seems happy. I guess she had a good time."

Scott nodded and started to speak, but stopped when Seth joined their group. The two shook hands and Seth made some small talk about being a couple of years behind them in school. "We're done here, Amy. You'll be okay until you can get the rest of the tree down," Seth said. "I'll text you the guy's number. I'll be back this week to fix the roof. I can pick up the shingles."

"That's great, Seth. Thanks so much."

The four stood awkwardly in place until Amy told Scott his car was blocking Seth's truck. "Oops, I guess we all need to go," he said, turning to Amy. "Say hi to your grandparents for me. Glad I got to see them the other day."

It wasn't until Scott's car rounded the corner that Eric released a breath. There was something galling about Amy's ex. Seth caught his eye and communicated a "what's with you?" look. Eric gave his head a little shake, and murmured, "Nothing. It's nothing."

"Thanks, guys," Amy said, coming to stand beside the truck. "Really, it saved me from having to make a bunch of calls to arrange for someone to come out."

"I'll see you at the next meeting," Eric said, climbing into the passenger seat. "Let me know if you need anything."

"I will."

When Seth had backed out and was heading up the street, he lifted one hand off the steering wheel and poked Eric's arm. "Guess you're not a fan of Scott's, huh?"

Eric snorted. "No kidding. Guess I don't hide it well."

"I hope what you were doing back there wasn't you trying to cover it."

"Tell you the truth, I don't really care," Eric said, rapping his knuckles lightly on the window. "I never liked him. So slick and smug in his suit. He was always like that."

"I don't know, I see it a little differently, Eric."

"Oh, yeah?" Eric closed his eyes, knowing exactly what was coming next. Seth was no fool.

"I bet you wouldn't like any ex of Amy's. They'd all be jerks who did her wrong," Seth teased. "Nothing wrong or even strange about that, of course. It's typical of the way we guys act when we really like a woman as much as you like her."

Eric snorted. "Think you're pretty smart, don't you?"

"Right. It takes a real genius to see through you."

Eric scoffed. He could hardly deny it.

CHAPTER TWELVE

DECISION TIME. SHOULD she steer Georgia to the two seats next to Eric and Seth in the town hall meeting room? Or would it be better to avoid Eric altogether? The community room was filling up fast, though. In the couple of seconds Amy debated with herself, Georgia took charge and led the way toward the two men. "Might as well make nice with a couple of clients," her boss said, "even if I don't agree with them on a thing or two."

"Got it," Amy said, secretly pleased.

Georgia flashed a lopsided smile. "Fair warning, though, sparks *might* fly."

Amy wished they could be exciting sparks. The kind that made her heart hum a little tune. She'd given up pretending she didn't welcome the sight of Eric. His smile did a number on her heart every time and her feelings didn't fit in the neat boxes she preferred. Black and white, in or out. Even so, she had goals and obligations. She couldn't afford to let her heart get soft. These feelings, simultaneously delicious and terrifying, had to stop.

Apparently, not tonight.

"Hey, you made it." Eric's face lit up with his smile.

"I didn't want to miss this. I left Cassie with Kyra so I could come." Amy glanced around the room. Mike and a couple of council members were setting up more chairs to extend the semicircle in front of the conference tables. Amy waved at Emma, Parker and Ruby who were sitting at the end of the front row.

Mike didn't use his voice to call the meeting to order, but the banging of his gavel on the lectern quickly quieted the room. The mayor's expression was uncharacteristically grim when he spoke. "Let me start by saying this meeting isn't going to be what I'd originally planned. I thought we were going to finalize what to do about the bridge and the direction of development in the immediate future."

AMY GLANCED AT Ruby, who gave Mike a thumbs-up. But Ruby wasn't looking especially happy, either.

"Oh, no," Eric muttered, when Wes Deerfield made his way to the microphone. On this they could agree. Amy cherished the covered bridge. Most people in the room did, but that's all Wes Deerfield cared about. He was working on a book about the founding of Bluestone River, and for him, the bridge was a symbol of the past that continued to serve the community.

"Uh, Wes. I know you have a lot on your mind," Mike said, "but the members of the council have agreed that we're not going to have yet another meeting where everyone airs their opinions and then we leave with nothing resolved. So, I'm going to ask you to sit down while I lay out the agenda for tonight."

A ripple of disapproving noises were balanced with sounds of approval.

"Whaddya know?" Eric said. "I'm not sure what he has in mind, but he's right. The other way wasn't working."

He tilted his head toward Amy and whispered, "Look at the serious faces on those council members. They're in on whatever this new strategy is."

"So, I made a mistake, and I'm apologizing for it." Mike's voice filled the otherwise quiet room. "The thing is, we asked for input, and we got some valuable information, but all the ideas came down on one side or the other. Bridge or no bridge, develop the acres or leave them alone. No compromise ideas came in."

"Something to think about," Georgia whispered. "I've been guilty of that."

Mike pointed to the council members sitting on either side of him. "We voted unanimously to do what I should have asked for in the first place, a commission to look at all the options for all the stakeholders."

A few people in the audience groaned so loud others laughed, including Eric and Amy.

Mike smiled broadly for the first time when he said, "No, no, folks, this commission will come up with a plan quickly. We're talking weeks, not years."

With the atmosphere in the room lighter now, no one raised too many objections. When hands went up to volunteer, Mike promised he and the town council would fill the commission with people without a direct financial interest in the outcome. "Our hope is to come up with a group of thirteen members, so we avoid a tie. And we're counting on getting proposals and plans based on compromise. Bluestone River is on the move. We all want progress to continue."

Only a few in the audience voiced objections, but they were the same voices that had clashed with each other before. Mike whacked the gavel again to settle things down.

"I hope this issue gets resolved before the Fourth of July parade," Amy said to Eric. "Everything we're planning is positive and fun. A real celebration."

"I agree," Eric said, "but I have a good feeling about what Mike is doing. In fact, if we weren't already planning The Fourth on River Street, I'd say we'd be good candidates for the commission."

A shiver of pleasure went through her at the notion. "Even if we don't think exactly alike, huh."

"When it comes to the school, for instance," Eric said, "if we waited for everyone to agree on policies, we'd never open the front doors or hire a single teacher. I learned the art of compromise the hard way."

Mike moved to adjourn and the meeting broke up. The four of them walked out together, but Georgia and Seth hurried off. Eric fell into step and they strolled down the street toward her car.

"It may seem odd," she said, "but I've decided I am cut out for doing my civic duty.

I've had a good time at all the meetings. This one was especially good."

"I was thinking the same thing," Eric said. He stopped and stared at the town hall with a thoughtful expression. "People who take the time to show up are committed to Bluestone River. I like being part of that."

When they reached her car, she didn't immediately open the door, but leaned against it instead. "No regrets, then?" she asked.

"About what?"

"Moving back here—investing in Bluestone River the way you have."

Eric reached out and caressed her cheek and then took both her hands in his and drew her into a hug. "No regrets at all. And you?"

Her breath caught in her chest. She had trouble getting her answer out, but she lifted her head and managed, "Nope. Not for a minute."

When Eric's kiss came, she leaned into it and him.

"That's good," he said, when he ended the kiss. "I'm glad we agree on that."

Amy opened her car door and slid into the driver's seat. "Matter of fact, it could be one of the best decisions I ever made."

Eric smiled as he closed her door and

waited nearby until she'd pulled out of her spot and drove to the exit. In the rearview mirror, she could see him turn and cross the street to head toward home. Had he always had that little swagger in his walk? She'd never noticed it before.

THE SUN BEAT down on Amy's bare arms. Her skin glistened from the mix of sweat and the sunscreen she'd slathered on. She watched Eric brush the sealer on the section of the deck, while she worked on the support planking below, first the sealer and then wiping off the excess. Even with a lot of interior work left to finish, adding this deck to the back expanded the space for the coming summer and was a final modern touch. His house was already a standout on one of the oldest streets in town.

At first he'd refused her offer to help. But she'd worn him down with reminders of all the times he'd helped her. *Between clearing my driveway and getting rid of falling trees, you've done plenty*, she'd said. *The least I can do is give you an extra hand on a project. And that doesn't even touch what you've done for Cassie.*

"How does it feel to scratch one more item

off your to-do list?" Amy called out. "You keep ticking off jobs at this rate, the work will be done this summer. It's already inviting and comfortable." *Too inviting*, Amy thought, *and way too comfortable*. The house was not only open and roomy, the abundance of light was like a welcoming committee.

Sadly, her grandparents' house spoke of days gone by. Amy suggested painting the living room and kitchen to brighten it up. She assured them she could do all the work. But she'd backed off when she sensed Grandma Barb got tired just thinking about upending their routine for even a few days. Amy had retreated and let the subject drop. For now.

"After living in an apartment for years," Eric said, "a sprawling comfortable house is exactly what I wanted." He glanced at the newly installed patio doors. "Now I've got it."

"Only a few feet left," she said, pointing her brush to the end of the base and its supports.

"After all this work, I think you deserve a burger and a beer."

"And with Cassie gone for the weekend, I am free to say yes."

"I'm glad," Eric said, "but maybe I should

start grilling now, huh? You never know when Scott could end the weekend."

Her jaw tightened. Maybe he was stating the obvious, but that didn't mean she appreciated hearing it from him. She didn't glance up, but kept her focus on sweeping the brush along a two-foot segment before dipping it into the oil can again. "Um, sorry. That was snarky."

It would be too easy to spew out resentments, for all the good it would do her. But nothing Scott did affected her in any important way any longer. His behavior was mostly an inconvenience. It was hard on Cassie, though. That's what mattered.

"Cassie hasn't given up on her dad," Amy said. "That's too much of a stretch. But she's not counting on him as much. She doesn't hang by the window waiting for his car to pull up in front of the house."

"That's good, isn't it?" Eric asked. "Sort of."

"Right. Sort of." Amy finished coating the last section and got to her feet and brushed grass and dirt off her knees. She picked up the sealer can and brushes and walked toward Eric. "Can I ask you something?"

Eric had worked himself off the deck and

down the stairs where he stepped away and held both arms up. "Done." He quickly added, "Ask away. I don't have secrets."

"Oh, it's not about secrets." She unloaded the supplies in her hands. "Did you ever stop hoping for more from your father? Or did you finally accept he wasn't ever going to be the dad you needed him to be?"

Silence. She looked on as he pressed hard on the lids of the containers until they snapped into place. She could see from the set of his slightly jutted jaw that the question had jarred him. "Did I overstep?"

Eric shook his head. "Not really. It's just that it brings back memories, not of my dad so much, but of me. All the acting out. I came so close to becoming a bully. I can still feel the sneer I walked around with. No lie. All that contempt changed the muscles in my face."

Amy closed her eyes and let her head fall back. "That's what I feared could happen with Cassie until…" She paused and realized she needed to say how much she owed Eric. "Until you intervened. The right way." There was nothing harsh about the steps Eric took with Cassie, or even the words he used.

"With me, being an angry kid was my revenge. In my distorted thinking, it was how I accepted that my dad was not only gone, but hadn't been there in the first place. I knew it was true, but I didn't have to like it. Or keep my feelings to myself."

Amy took in a breath, realizing how familiar his words sounded, even though her way of adjusting to her situation had been different.

"As kids, I suppose we have to find ways to adjust to things we have no control over," Amy said. "Sometimes people like you come along and lend a hand. You helped Cassie be open to liking her life." She ran that thought through her mind again, savoring the new lightness of Cassie's moods.

"It's your work with Cassie that's made most of the difference," Eric said. "Her disappointments with her dad aren't over, not by a long shot, but she's much happier now. We all see it at school."

What he said was true, so why was she agitated?

"What about you?" Eric said.

She pointed to herself. "Me?"

Eric scoffed. "Yeah, you. The girl in our high school who lived with her grandparents."

"Yep, lucky for me." She shifted her weight,

uncomfortable under Eric's gaze. That superficial answer wasn't going to work this time. "If it weren't for them, I'd likely have ended up shuffled around among strangers. Like Lottie." She loosened her hands and let her shoulders relax. "Or my parents might have taken me along and I'd have been moved from one place to another every month or two."

She'd thought about them so much since Lottie had come into their lives. She glanced at Eric, who watched her with an expectant look.

"The truth is, I wasted a lot of time secretly wishing they'd taken me with them," Amy admitted, looking down at her sneakers. "When you're a kid the life of a vagabond is adventurous. Exotic islands are the stuff of fairy tales."

"It had to have taken a toll. I had my mom. Cassie has you to make her feel secure and loved. I know Barbara and Les are wonderful people, and they obviously loved you, but they weren't your parents." Eric went to the cooler and got two bottles of water. "Let's sit a minute. My mom and Seth will be here soon and then we'll start up the grill."

She followed him to the picnic table positioned under a large swooping tree that offered plenty of shade.

"You never talk about it, Amy."

Amy let out a light laugh. "It's easier to change the subject."

He picked up her hand and held it in his palm. "You can't deny it, I've told you more about my dad walking away from me than you've ever said about your parents. If I hadn't asked you about Scott back when I was first meeting with Cassie, you'd never have mentioned anything."

His tone and soft look in his eyes touched her. But why was he bringing it up?

Eric twisted off the cap and handed her the open bottle. She swallowed a mouthful of water and touched the cold bottle against her forehead.

"I talk to Cassie and the other kids for reasons that go beyond keeping them in line at school, valuable as that is," Eric said. "Catch the anger issues early and they don't become a habit. My anger with my dad became that for me. I ended up believing I was born hostile."

"I get that, Eric. But it was so different for me. I had my grandparents."

"But still, you collected a diploma one day,

Amy, and a marriage license the next. You followed a guy who, uh, never mind." His face flushed and he let go of her hand. "When it comes to you and Scott, I don't know what I'm talking about. I'm sorry."

"Don't apologize. You were close enough," Amy said, reaching for his hand again. "I followed a guy who needed someone to make life look good on the outside, who would go along with him no matter what." She paused, debating if she should stop talking, but since they'd gone this far, she didn't want to bury it all again. "Let's just say I'm trying to undo the damage I did to myself and stand on my own."

Eric leaned forward. "So, maybe you were too eager to prove to yourself that you could have a family of your own and make it work. And maybe I've been so afraid to fail, I've never tried."

"Well, aren't we a pair?" Amy swallowed hard to stop herself from blurting what she really wanted to say about the great dad and partner she believed he'd be.

Eric didn't respond in words, but he put his hand over hers. They were silent for a few seconds before he stood and climbed over the bench and headed to the grill. "Let's get to work." He stopped abruptly and turned to her. "Hey, I've got an idea. I've got more food than the four of us could possibly eat. Why don't you see if your grandparents would like to come over and eat with us?"

Amy smiled, struck by how much she liked that idea. But almost immediately the reasons to say no started filling her head. She frowned as she studied the stairs from the yard into the side door. Would the wheelchair be okay on the grass? Could Les cover the distance with his walker? "It would be fun for them, but I'm wondering if I can make it work for my grandpa."

"The stairs? It's only three through the side door. He'd have you at his elbow." Eric gave her a reassuring smile. "I'm sure we can figure it out." He held up both hands. "But only if Les *wants* to join us, of course."

"My grandpa was always up for a backyard party." She pulled the phone out of the pocket of her shorts. "If I pick them up, I can change." She put both arms in front of her. I can see I'm wearing a lot of that sealer."

Eric left her alone while she made the call. Grandma raised no objections, at least not right away. But then she said, "I know Les would enjoy an afternoon away from home, but…"

Amy gave her all the reasons the plan would work, especially if Grandpa didn't mind being in the wheelchair. "The yard is only a little bumpy," she said lightly. "Let's try it. If Grandpa isn't comfortable or gets tired, I'll bring you home."

"We wouldn't want to interfere with your, you know, *evening*." She drew out the word.

"It's not a date, Grandma."

"Really? More's the pity."

"Grandma! Come on, I've been helping Eric finish his deck. I'm repaying a favor or two, that's all." Was she protesting a bit too much? Deliberately lowering her voice, she added, "I told you his mom and Seth are on their way over now."

"Oh, okay, I won't tease you. At least not now."

"I'll be right there. Tell Grandpa I'll take care of everything."

Eric came back out to the yard when she ended the call. "What's the verdict?"

"It's a go," she said, "so I'll head home and get them."

"Exactly the answer I hoped for," Eric said, as she wheeled her bike through the side gate and out to the street. She was feeling almost buoyant as she started pedaling the few blocks home. So, this backyard barbecue with his mom and her grandparents might not be a date, but it kind of felt like one.

And it wasn't the first time. A day at the Snowball Fair, a group dinner at the diner, a bike ride on a Saturday afternoon, even a hug and a kiss after a town meeting. She didn't want to admit it, but they'd all felt like dates.

LOOKING AT THE others sitting around his picnic table and in lawn chairs in the yard, Eric stayed out of the conversation for a few minutes and listened to his mom and Barb chat across the table. They sounded pretty excited about what was happening on River Street. Seth was in a lawn chair next to Les and the two were in a friendly debate over the newest development ideas. An initiative that had nothing to do with the bridge.

"I'm open to all the ideas," Eric said. "Mike texted me earlier and asked me to be on the commission."

"And?" his mom asked.

"I said yes. He wanted someone who was a teacher or a principal, and I'm it."

"Congratulations, Eric." Amy's pleasant

surprise was obvious in her expression. "I'm happy for you—and Bluestone River. Seriously."

"Since I have the ear of a commissioner," Les started, "I'd like to see something done with the old food processing plant," Les said. "It's rotting away. Nothing more than an eyesore on the edge of town. And if we're going to build more convenient shopping, we already have a road out to that site."

"You have a point," Seth agreed.

"Except that the conglomerate that owns that land, whoever it is, isn't selling," Barb said. "We've been down that route before."

"I remember you riding your bike out to work at the plant, Grandpa," Amy said.

Les responded with a sad tsk. "Guess I won't be doing that anytime soon."

Eric winced at his gloomy voice. But Amy and Barb just gave him a reassuring look.

"Check out that sky," his mom said, patting his hand to get his attention. She nodded to the sun setting behind the house and turning the sky deep fuchsia with lavender around the edges like lace trimming the bank of clouds.

"It's been a while since I've been outside watching a sunset," Les said.

"Maybe so, but summer is coming. We'll

go sit in the yard and watch the sunset, so you can enjoy it." Amy smiled at Les with love written all over her face.

There was so much to her, Eric thought. She didn't give herself nearly enough credit for handling all the demands that pushed her one minute and pulled her the next. Cassie had no idea the lengths her mom would go to in order to give her the security of a family.

"You're awfully quiet," his mom whispered. "Is everything okay?"

"Everything's fine. It's been a good day. I like having people here filling up the yard." If they'd been alone he might have opened up about being isolated for too long.

She leaned sideways and nudged his shoulder. "I'm not surprised you're enjoying yourself. You were born to be a grilling-in-the-backyard kind of guy."

He snorted. "So the real me is coming through."

His mom glanced at Amy, who had left the table with Barb. Now Amy was topping off glasses of lemonade while Barb settled into a lawn chair next to Les. "I think it is. Not showing my bias or anything, but you're a great catch."

"Oh, really? I have a job and a house, so

that makes me a good catch?" He knew his mom didn't mean it that way, but her words embarrassed him. Why couldn't he say it?

"Your friendship with Amy isn't all about her daughter, is it?" his mom asked, her voice serious now.

"No. We were friendly in high school. I had an enormous crush on her, but she didn't return my feelings," he admitted. "The first time I saw her in over twenty years was to intervene in a problem with Cassie. Not a good way to rekindle an old friendship."

"Maybe so," she said, nudging his arm again. "She's got a lot of spirit, that one."

Eric smirked. "I detect your matchmaker impulse is alive and well and on the job."

His mom shrugged. "So what if it is?"

Right. So what? His thoughts exactly, even though he wasn't ready to talk to anyone about his growing feelings for Amy. "Amy ran off with the other guy, Mom."

"Ancient history, my love." She tapped his arm. "That was high school. And it didn't turn out so well for her, did it?"

He didn't have a rational answer for that. Ever since he'd seen Amy in his office, ancient history seemed like yesterday.

Seth rapped on the table. "Hey, Eric, I need you to agree with me about something."

"Oh, and what would that be?"

"That Amy should enter the thirty-mile fundraising bike ride the sanctuary just announced."

Amy jabbed her thumb in the air toward Seth. "He's been trying to talk me into it."

"Why not, honey? You ride your bike most everywhere, anyway," Barb said.

"I do now that the weather is cooperating. You know I love my bike."

"You'd be raising money for a local cause, Amy," Les argued. "The sanctuary and nature center are expanding all their programs for kids. Takes money to do that."

Grinning, Amy thrust out her palms. "Stop, stop. It's a lot to think about."

"You know I'll be rooting for you," Les added, "and you always liked a little competition."

Eric wouldn't say it out loud, but the race could be good for her. He'd run a marathon while he was doing his student teaching and it did a lot to build his confidence. It got him out of his own head, for one thing, and expanded what he believed he could accomplish. Eric waited for Amy's argument that she didn't have time. But he'd bet that if Amy said yes, Les and Barb would be all in, maybe watching Cassie a little more while she trained.

Amy nodded toward him. "What do you think, Eric? The race is the end of June. I'd need to do some training to get ready by then."

"When's the first training ride?" he blurted. "I'll come along. Oops. If you don't mind company."

A smile spread across her face. "Hmm, let me think. Cassie's not due back until tomorrow, so how about later tonight?"

"All right!" Seth said, clapping. "She's in."

"I just hope I can finish the course. I'm not even going to think about competing to place."

"You'll do fine," Eric said with an encouraging laugh. "It's thirty miles."

"Didn't you ride road almost that far last Sunday morning before the rest of us opened our eyes?" Les pointed out.

"I bet your little girl will be proud of you," Monica added. "And it's for the nature center and sanctuary."

The smile she gave his mom proved his hunch. A part of her was doing this for Cassie.

CHAPTER THIRTEEN

"YOU'VE GOT THIS, Amy," Eric shouted as they made the turn on the unpaved road that led them away from the back of the sanctuary.

"I'm not struggling with this short distance, but I'm not that fast," she shouted back as she coasted to slow down. They'd made the trail circle twice, a little better than fourteen miles. The unpaved road led away from the center of town and took them out past Emma's log home. "I guess we'll need to double back to the road across the river to get back on the trails. I know a shortcut."

"Shortcut? What kind of training method is that?" he kidded.

"Hey, it's getting dark," Amy said, amused. "I don't want to be where we can't see the bumps and dips ahead."

"Good thinking. You set the pace and lead the way." Eric dropped slightly behind her as she led them down a short unpaved road she'd almost forgotten about.

Once they were back on the trail along the river, Amy gradually slowed down and came to a stop when they reached the park. "Well done," she said, getting off the bike. She took off her helmet and freed her hair from the elastic band and shook it out. Then she pulled it tight off her face and fixed it in a high ponytail. "If I can get my hair to stay put, I'll be in business."

"I imagine that'll be a challenge," Eric said, his breathing only slightly more labored than hers. He was fit and muscular, but hadn't spent much time on his bike in years. A couple of long bike rides would get him into great shape for the charity ride. She accepted the bottle of water from his hand and downed half of it. "I've got a terrific idea," she said, "but you might not like it."

He narrowed his eyes. "Try me."

"You should enter the race, too. We should do it together." Standing in the park at dusk with the reddish clouds slicing across the horizon as the sun set, her suggestion sounded more intimate than she'd realized. Maybe because the only other people around were couples walking hand in hand along the river. But she'd said the words and wouldn't take them back. She didn't mean it, as Grandma would say, like a date or anything.

Eric's face changed with the big smile spreading from ear to ear. "You think we'll push each other, right?"

"I suppose, although like I said, this ride is a lark. I'm doing it for the fun of it. And to raise money," Amy said. "Don't worry, I won't hold you back." She gave him a sidelong glance. "You don't fool me. I know you were holding back a little today."

Eric let out a self-conscious laugh. "Today, a thirty-mile charity ride, tomorrow the Tour de France."

"You know what I meant," she chided, although she couldn't help but laugh along with him.

His expression turned serious. "Not really. I have that treadmill sitting in my living room, but with all the work on the house I don't use it. My stamina has fallen off. I bet you have a chance of placing in the women's group. "*You're* the one who didn't ride full out just now."

He'd picked up on that, huh? She couldn't claim he was wrong. "I'm pacing myself." She'd had the idea to ask him to be part of this with her when they were pedaling along the empty unpaved road. It had seemed casual at first, but now she was taken aback by how invested she was in doing the charity ride with him.

"So, I'm jumping ahead, but let's work out the logistics." Eric's forehead wrinkled in thought. "We could bring your grandparents and put the wheelchair in your trunk. And I have a rack for our bikes. My mom and Seth could come together."

"You are such a good man, Eric," Amy said softly, touched by how easily he figured out a way to include her grandparents. "In no time at all we have ourselves a plan."

Eric stared at her with a faint smile. "I guess we do."

Amy looked at the sky framing the trees and water downriver. The cloud bank had darkened to a deep pink as the evening light faded. Something about this moment, this day, held a meaning she couldn't quite define. She only knew she wouldn't forget it.

Eric opened his arms and she stepped into them. "What a great day, huh?" He kissed her cheek and then her mouth and slowly let her go.

Amy got on her bike. How was she going to convince Grandma this wasn't a romance in the making? Fat chance. She couldn't even convince herself. She couldn't let this go on.

THE MUSIC BLARED from the jukebox, making it hard to carry on a conversation with Amy as they finished up their roast beef platters. "When I suggested we come back to the diner by ourselves, I hadn't thought about crowds and noise." Eric frowned. "Seth and I are usually here on weeknights when it's a little loud, but not deafening like this."

"Who knew?" Amy said with a laugh. "The diner has turned into a real weekend hot spot."

He leaned across the table and grinned. "Want get outta here?"

"You bet."

"I'll take care of the check and meet you outside." He slid his chair back.

"Deal."

A few minutes later he joined her outside on the warm night. "So, where to? Anywhere you'd particularly like to go," he asked.

"Since you asked, I haven't been on that new boardwalk at Hidden Lake Bird Sanctuary," she said. "We only ride bikes on the road behind the woods, but I wouldn't mind seeing this new showpiece."

Perfect, Eric thought. It would be special on a night like this. "Since we're raising money for it, we ought to have a look."

The sanctuary wasn't too far away and while they weren't completely alone when they left the parking lot and wandered toward the boardwalk, it sure beat the noisy diner.

Amy stopped to look at the lake, a pale shade of pink under the dusky evening light. "It's really something, isn't it?"

"I know. One of the town's most special places." He nodded to the pier where a couple with their kids stood watching the ducks paddling by.

They were alone in woods as they strolled along. Eric took Amy's hand in his as they followed the twists and turns of the boardwalk and ended up at a turnout positioned over the marsh at the far end of the lake.

"This is incredible, Eric," she said, squeezing his hand. "I'm so glad we came here."

"Me, too." He pointed to the bench. "Let's sit. I'm in no hurry to leave. Are you okay on time?"

"I'm good," she said. "Grandma almost shoved me out the door and said she expected to be asleep when I came in."

Once they settled on the bench, he slipped

his arm around her. She responded by resting her head on his shoulder. Then, as if he'd planned the moment, the strings of lights along the rails and slats of the boardwalk came on all at once and turned the woods into a fairyland.

Amy gasped. "Emma said lights in the woods on a dark night are enough to make you believe in fairies. I'm a believer."

Eric nodded. "It's like being in another world. And it's just us out here right now."

"So much of the time, we're dealing with all the real-life stuff." She released a long breath. "You know, fallen trees, crumbled bridges, work, people to take care of."

"This is real life, too." He stroked her cheek and kissed her softly on the lips. She deepened the kiss as she grasped his arm and held on tight. When they broke the kiss, he took her into his arms and she stayed silent, with her head nuzzled into the hollow of his shoulder.

When she finally spoke, she made no comment about what was happening between them. Instead, she said, "This has been a wonderful night, but we really should start back."

He stood and took her hand and they retraced their steps. When they got back to her car, he hugged her and kissed her lightly. And then she was on her way. As he watched her car disappear when she made her turn off River Street, he was conscious of his confusion, even a peculiar emptiness that took him by surprise.

WHILE ERIC GOT them each a beer, Amy stood at his beautiful window and unsuccessfully tried to make the fizzing in her stomach vanish. Anxiety, eagerness? How about fear of the unknown? Not really. She was aware what this was all about.

Even before they'd agreed to do the bike ride together, they'd been dancing around what they were to each other. The other night in the sanctuary showed her that the dance had to stop. All along he'd been interested in her, not like the teenager he'd been, but as the man he was now. A guy with depth and the ability to see beyond his own needs. It's what she'd always wanted. But call it bad timing, she couldn't take what she believed he was offering. The truth she finally faced was that she'd fallen in love with him.

He came back into the living room and handed her an open bottle of her favorite dark beer. They sat next to each other on the couch. Amy curled her legs under her so she could turn and face him.

"I suppose I can't entice you to tell me what's doing with the commission," she teased. "You've been mum."

"As I promised," he said with a grin. "Changing the subject here, I can see you're building strength and endurance every time we ride. If we do fifteen miles, you're pushing up the speed, always shaving off a few seconds."

"Same for you."

"I don't know. Maybe, but you're starting at a higher endurance level."

She took a sip of her beer, aware of her heightened senses and being almost light-headed. The feeling came over her often when they were alone and had fallen silent.

Eric reached for her hand. "We need to talk."

She put the bottle on the coffee table. She could pull her hand away from him, but she didn't. Keeping her voice light she said, "Do we?" Why had she said that? She couldn't keep putting off the inevitable.

He shifted in his seat. "Tell me, what are we doing here? We see each other, talk all the time, do things together. Exchange friendly hugs one day and passionate kisses the next."

"I don't… I can't." She groaned in frustration, knowing she was botching this conversation. Her heart pulled her one way, but the little voice in her head was flashing caution lights.

"Am I just an old high school friend, a guy who had a big crush on you? Is that all I am to you?"

No, no. That was the trouble, the dilemma she didn't know how to figure out. "It's not anything like that anymore."

"I'm going to take that as good news," he said softly. He lifted her hand and pressed her palm to his cheek.

Amy sighed with the touch. She closed her eyes and tilted closer to him as his lips brushed her lips, firm and sure. She gave in to the longing in her heart and pushed the doubt aside. She'd denied herself too long. He pulled her close and she clung to him, kissing him again, surprised by the rush of feelings threatening to overwhelm her.

Eric broke the kiss, but kept her in his arms. "I've wanted to hold you like this all my life."

She pulled away from him and held her

head in her hands, letting her hair fall forward. "You're free to have these feelings, Eric. I'm not."

He touched her hair, tucking it back over her shoulder. "I understood at first, but not anymore. Not with everything…"

He didn't need to finish the sentence. It had been so clear to her before. She'd come back to Bluestone River feeling diminished, even weak. Never again would she be caught scrambling to find a way to support herself and Cassie. She vowed she would stand on her own two feet.

"I'm not *done* yet. You've made something of yourself. But I'm just getting started. It's going to take time to stand on my own. I need to feel secure and know I make a good living for myself and Cassie…no matter what." She paused, realizing how much she wanted what he already had. "I want to feel proud of what I accomplish in my career like you do in yours. I haven't really made something of myself. Not yet." She heard the conviction in her voice. This was a promise she'd made to herself.

"All evidence to the contrary," Eric insisted, getting to his feet and walking away from the couch. "It's just so frustrating," he said, resting his elbow on the fireplace mantel.

"You mean I'm frustrating."

He planted his hand on his hip. "When are you going to stop being so hard on yourself?"

"I can't afford another failure. Cassie can't afford it."

Eric smiled warmly. "You know how I feel about your daughter."

Amy stood and went to the window to keep a distance between them. "But your fondness for her doesn't mean she'd be okay with…the two of us."

"Maybe not, but it's a good start." He sounded almost angry with her. At one time, she might have resented it, but she couldn't blame him anymore.

She moved to the door. Avoiding his eyes she said, "I should go."

"Okay." Eric nodded tersely.

"Thanks for understanding."

"Don't thank me for that, Amy, because, I don't understand. But we *are* friends. And we have a committee to serve on, and a race to finish." He opened the door, but turned away. "Good night."

She drove, desperate to get home, repeating her mantra, "I did the right thing, I did the right thing."

The sweet, warm kisses were lovely. Maybe one day she would let herself fall into that kind of mind-blowing love, but not now. By making a clean break with Eric now, he was free to move on. She couldn't expect him to understand her, even though the situation seemed so simple to her. He wanted what she wasn't free to give.

WITH MEMORIES OF Eric's kisses still on her mind every day, Amy didn't know if she was happy to get a text from him or not. But then she read it. And reread it, more slowly this time. It didn't help. The rising anxiety in her gut intensified. She was forced to put on a normal face when Rita's client appeared at the desk to pay for her haircut. Amy fumbled through the motions, pasting on a smile as she said goodbye to that customer and switched to a welcoming voice to greet the new one coming inside the salon.

Minutes passed in small talk and pleasantries as Amy helped Rita explain the products on display. On autopilot she talked about the different types of moisturizers as if that was the most important thing on her mind.

Amy didn't have many details to go on, but Eric was clear enough in his text message: Cassie was in trouble again. This time it involved Lottie and two other classmates. He would arrange a meeting, and he'd do what he could to make sure it was scheduled for a morning, so she'd be available.

As soon as the front of the store cleared and she'd worn out her mouth with social smiles, Amy replied to Eric to acknowledge his message. He immediately texted back, Let's talk tonight...call when you're free. Pls don't worry...really.

Don't worry? *Don't worry?* What did that even mean?

The afternoon crawled by and when she was finally home, the first thing she saw was Cassie's glum face resting in her palms and pushing the skin of her round cheeks up toward her eyes. Her legs were swinging in lazy circles as she watched Grandma Barb cutting a cucumber at the counter.

"I'm in trouble again," she blurted as a greeting.

"I heard that," Amy said, glancing at Grandma, who kept on slicing and didn't meet her eye.

"It wasn't my fault," Cassie insisted.

Right. It never is. "Really? Why don't you tell me what happened?"

Cassie's eyes filled with tears. "Robbie and Carson made fun of Lottie."

The series of somersaults in her stomach made it hard to speak, but she rolled her hand toward Cassie. "Tell me more."

"They told Lottie a lady was coming to her house to take her away, 'cuz Kyra isn't her real mom. They said lots of mean stuff."

Surely Eric must have known Lottie would be targeted. "I see. Then why are you in trouble?" Eric's words, *don't worry*, looped through her brain. She was trying to keep a lid on this.

"I yelled at them. I told them to stop." Cassie's legs were swinging fast and hard now.

"And?"

"They wouldn't shut up."

"And?"

"I pushed Carson into the fence."

"Did you hurt him?" Amy braced for the answer.

Cassie bunched the fabric of her peasant blouse. "His shirt ripped. By accident." She looked up, defiance etched into her face. "But he wasn't hurt. He cried like he was. He's mean. And then he acts like he's in kinder-garten."

Amy closed her eyes and sighed. "Oh, Cassie."

"They were being really mean. I told Mr. Wells that." Tears ran down her cheeks now. "Big bullies."

Amy grabbed a couple of tissues. "Here, blow your nose. Dry your eyes."

For the few minutes Cassie dabbed at her eyes Amy thought about how she wanted to respond. If the boys were being that mean, and she had a feeling the story was likely true, she had to choose her words even more carefully. She refused to make her daughter feel bad about reacting to anyone taunting Lottie, but she couldn't allow her to shove other kids.

"I believe you, honey, about the boys being mean, but you can't go around *pushing people*," Amy said, exasperated. "No matter what."

"I know."

Amy looked at Grandma Barb, who added the cucumber slices into the bowl of greens. She'd successfully avoided being pulled into this latest escapade. Something about this situation bothered Amy and nudged her to say more. "You're right to stand up to someone hurting Lottie's feelings, Cassie, but you have to tell the teacher. Or Mr. Wells."

Cassie wiped her eyes with the back of her hands. "Then I'd be a tattletale...a snitch. Carson already calls me teacher's pet because I'm better than he is at math—and at reading maps *and* spelling. Carson couldn't even find China on the big map on the wall."

Grandma Barb badly stifled her laughter with a phony burst of coughing. Amy tried hard not to join her.

Amy shook her head. "Does nothing ever change? Those are the same names kids called each other thirty years ago."

"Apparently they're stuck in the past," Grandma said, in control of her voice again.

Teacher's pet? Amy thought. Better than being the class troublemaker, but who could deny Cassie's point.

"Go wash your hands for dinner," Amy said, leaning back against the counter.

Cassie ran from the table and down the hall like she'd been let out of a jail cell.

"I'm torn, Grandma," Amy said when she heard the bathroom door close with a click.

Grandma nodded. "I'll bet you are. But

you're not alone. You have Eric. What do you suppose he'll do?"

She didn't exactly *have* Eric, but Amy wasn't up for quibbling over semantics. "Other than finding myself sitting across the desk from Eric yet again I don't have a clue." Her guttural sound of frustration communicated exactly how she felt. "But I know this," she said, jabbing her index finger toward the floor. "I'll be really unhappy if Carson's and Robbie's parents aren't brought into this. I have to control Cassie, but their boys need some work, too."

"What about Lottie in all this?" Grandma asked.

"And Kyra," Amy added. "She has to cope with Lottie's hurt feelings. It's probably not the first time that little girl has heard that kind of taunting."

Later, at bedtime when she was alone with Cassie, she asked what Lottie had done during the dustup. "Was she sad? Did she shove Carson? Or Robbie?"

Cassie hugged the dolls closer to her chest. "She didn't say anything. She pulled *my* shirt to try to get me to leave." Cassie lowered her voice to a whisper, and added, "She's afraid."

"Afraid Carson and Robbie will hurt her." It came out as a statement rather than a question.

"Nope. She's thinks if she gets in trouble, the people at that agency will take her away from Kyra. She wants to be with her." Cassie lowered her eyes. "Forever. Like you and me."

Amy squeezed Cassie's hand. Of course, Lottie wouldn't want trouble. "I don't know much about the way the foster care system works, Cassie. I can't say for sure, but I don't think a little trouble with mean boys would affect Lottie and Kyra. But I would imagine Eric... Mr. Wells...might have more answers. I'm sure he's talked with Kyra already." A lot of assumptions, Amy admitted to herself.

Cassie gave a slight smile. "I'll tell him about it myself. He'll believe me."

"Honey, Mr. Wells will get to the bottom of what went on. You need to let him handle it." Eric would insist Cassie shouldn't be Lottie's sole defender on the playground.

When she left Cassie's room, she took her phone to the back porch to make the call. Eric picked up on the first ring.

"I wish I was calling about our training schedule," Amy said.

"Yes, well, as I'm already meeting with

Cassie," Eric said, "I can deal with her about this fairly easily."

"She knows the pushing was wrong, Eric, but I can't very well tell her she was wrong to react."

He agreed. "Both things are true. Right to be angry, wrong to push."

"So, just to be clear, you're not letting the boys get off with only a warning."

"I'm getting to that, Amy," Eric said.

"You can't blame me for being upset. Besides, the little part of me no one can see is proudly patting Cassie on the back for confronting Carson." She scoffed. "Admittedly, in her nine-year-old sort of way."

"I have the same voice in my head. You know that," Eric shot back, "but I can't let the way I feel about her—or about you—get mixed in with what I have to do in my job."

She shivered at his words, surprising herself with how deeply they touched her.

"Neither of us wants another meeting about Cassie," Eric said, "but it's different this time. I'm calling all the parents in first and then I'm bringing in the four kids."

"Obviously, Cassie will see it as being punished," Amy said, "but what about Lottie? I mean, this all started because of her. She might be afraid to be put on the spot. What does Kyra think? Have you talked to her?"

"C'mon, Amy," Eric said, "You've got to trust me to do my job."

She filled her cheeks with air and blew it out. "I'm trying, Eric. But this is hard. Cassie's in the hot seat once again."

"That hot seat is crowded this time. There's Carson, and I'm not letting Robbie off the hook."

"Good."

Then she had nothing more to say. She didn't feel like talking about their next ride or the committee. Nothing. "I suppose I better go."

"Wait, I know you're concerned about Lottie. As I'm sure Kyra will tell you, Lottie spilled the whole story to her."

"That's good, isn't it?"

"It is, but right now she's trying to reassure Lottie no one will take her away."

Stinging tears pooled in Amy's eyes when she thought of Lottie leaving her house tomorrow morning possibly afraid and heartbroken. "That's terrible."

"Naturally, Kyra will be at the meeting. I'm going to ask her to speak right away," Eric said. "I can guarantee you at least a couple of parents will try to put all the attention on Cassie. I have a different take and plan to make sure we keep the focus on the real issue. Everyone needs to hear what Kyra has to say."

"I'm so glad you feel that way," Amy said, blinking back her tears. "That little girl has completely stolen Kyra's heart. When is the meeting?"

"I'm hoping for the day after tomorrow. In the morning. As it happens, it's the best time for everyone."

"I'm so glad we talked, Eric," Amy said. "This situation is so important. A lesson in empathy, I guess."

"That's the plan." He paused. "Uh, Amy, you can't imagine how much I'd like to high-five Cassie for standing up for Lottie. And you're aware how I feel about you. But I have to stay neutral. Especially because what I do in the meeting is all part of a plan that's bigger than just turning around Robbie's and Carson's thinking about Lottie."

"I hear you, Eric. I do. And believe me, I don't envy you." When they ended the call, Amy stayed on the porch alone with her thoughts. As much as she didn't want to admit it, Eric was right to warn her that he couldn't show any favoritism. It would be too easy to treat him like more than a friend and expect something special or extra for Cassie.

Without warning, Scott came to mind. *A wake-up call*, she thought. From the time she got Eric's text to this moment on the porch, she hadn't given Scott a thought. Lately, he'd become more predictable with his calls and visits. At the same time, he'd been more vocal about being shut out—his words. He claimed she didn't talk to him about anything that came up about Cassie. He was right when he accused her of making all the decisions on her own. She could list the reasons why that was true, but he still had a right to know. She'd call him after the meeting.

When it came to mulling over what was best for Cassie, though, she'd much rather talk with Eric.

CHAPTER FOURTEEN

KYRA AND AMY arrived at Eric's office together and claimed two of the three folding chairs he'd set up in his small space. Robbie's parents, Fran and Patrick Gibson, were already seated in chairs along the side of his desk. For Eric the worst part of meetings like this was actually getting them underway. The empty minutes of small talk were torture. He and the parents in front of him couldn't very well sit in silence, so they ended up chatting about The Fourth on River Street event.

Finally, Doreen Nolan knocked lightly before coming in. Doreen nodded to Eric and greeted the Gibsons like casual friends before formally introducing herself to Kyra as Carson's mom. She nodded to Amy. "My husband is out of town and couldn't be here."

In order to fill in some history, Eric explained that both Cassie and Lottie were newcomers to the school. On the other hand,

Carson and Robbie had been friends since kindergarten.

"I know Doreen from the salon," Amy explained.

Kyra remarked that she'd gone to school with Doreen's husband.

"It's a small world around here," Eric said, "which is mostly good. We're all neighbors and cross paths. We may be old—or new—friends. Let's keep that in mind as we talk over what happened the other day."

"Uh, I want to be clear about something," Doreen said, nodding to Kyra. "I don't have a problem with Lottie. She wasn't the one who pushed Carson. She didn't hurt him in any way."

"But *he* hurt Lottie," Eric responded, not missing a beat. "That's why Kyra is here and Lottie will be in my meeting with Robbie, Carson and Cassie later."

Lifting her chin a notch, Doreen said, "I thought we were here to deal with Cassie's aggressive behavior."

Eric glanced at Amy, who'd pressed her lips together and didn't respond. He knew exactly how hard that was for her.

"You're right, Doreen, it's why I asked to meet with you. *In part*. But I'm not going to let a good teaching moment pass us by here at Madison School. We find ourselves in the middle of one of these significant moments today. We could handle it as an isolated incident and walk away, or we can take advantage of it."

Robbie's dad cleared his throat and took out his phone and glanced at the screen. "Whatever you plan to *teach* us, could you get on with it?" He pointed to Robbie's mom and back to himself. "We have to get to work."

Eric made a choice to ignore the subtle attempt to trivialize what was going on. Checking their phones meant they thought he was frittering away their time. "It's pretty simple, really. According to Lottie and Cassie the two boys began teasing Lottie about being a foster kid. They escalated to taunting her, even telling her someone was coming to take her away."

Fran cut her gaze to Kyra. "Do you believe the girls?"

"Yes, I do. It's not the first time," Kyra said. "And it has to stop. It's made Lottie afraid to come to school."

"Then she better toughen up," Fran said. "I mean, she's going to have her feelings hurt now and then. Attacking Carson isn't doing Lottie any favors. Cassie needs to know that."

"I'd like to address that," Kyra said, her voice filling the room. "Lottie's already afraid of being taken away from my home. The teasing—the taunting—is cruel." In a few sentences, Kyra told the others how Lottie ended up with her, the child's fourth placement in twelve months. "It's taken a long time to build trust. She's afraid to take the bus and clings to me the way a younger child might. Lottie already knows she's different. She doesn't need Robbie and Carson to remind her."

"We don't know exactly why the boys are doing this," Eric said, "other than being kids who are making bad choices. But when I confronted them they didn't deny it." Eric paused to let that settle in. It was the heart of the issue. "So, what we've got here is Cassie being impulsive and Robbie and Carson showing a lack of empathy in line with their ages."

"They're nine. I doubt they understand Lottie's situation," Fran said.

A *good segue*, Eric thought. "Exactly. That's why we're here. We can't have taunting, and we can't have Cassie making it her job to set the boys straight."

"Good to know," Amy said, looking at him with a hint of a smile before turning to Doreen and the Gibsons. "Look, Cassie has had her own adjustment problems, so I'm not judging anyone. And I'm not making excuses."

"We'll speak to Robbie," Fran said. "I don't want him getting into trouble over a little teasing."

"This isn't about teasing," Eric said. "It's about kindness. Robbie and Carson were unkind to Lottie. And sure, Lottie might be a quiet child now. Who knows? She may always be on the shy side. Cassie was standing up for her."

"Even though Lottie tried to get her to walk away," Amy said, shaking her head.

"So, it comes back to kindness and that's what we'll work on with Carson and Robbie," Eric said. "And with all the kids in this school."

"I suppose they'll need to apologize," Patrick said.

"Not exactly," Eric replied. "I'm not bringing them into the office to force empty apologies. I'll talk about the rules, sure, but I'd rather have them thinking about how they made Lottie feel. If there's going to be an apology it will come from them. Maybe not today, but maybe one day. We'll see."

The room fell more than quiet. It was still. Eric waited a few seconds before he continued. "Cassie must come to understand that pushing and shoving another kid solves nothing. But both boys can join my Monday and Friday meetings. Cassie is already part of them."

"What about Lottie," Kyra said. "What should I tell her?"

"I was getting to that. She should join my small group, too. I don't focus on punishment in my sessions with the kids. It's more about how they're adjusting and making good choices." As he spoke, Eric finally gave voice to ideas that had been percolating for a long time. He was defining his approach in ways almost everyone could sign on to.

"All the kids are dealing with tough issues, so a little extra attention won't hurt." Finally, he added, "Lottie needs some extra reassurance that she's safe. I'll make sure she understands she can come to me."

"You're like the Pied Piper," Amy said, with a laugh. "You're going to need an extra room for all the kids you bring in."

"That's the plan," he said, getting to his feet. "We're done for now. But I'll let you know how the meetings go."

The Gibsons stood first, followed by Amy

and Kyra. Doreen was the last to stand and move toward the door. "This wasn't what I expected."

"Eric… Mr. Wells's meetings with Cassie have helped her a lot." Amy held up her hands as if warding off the protest she knew was coming. "I know, Cassie's at fault here, but overall, things have improved."

"Funny, I didn't think Carson had any so-called issues," Doreen said. "Now I'm being told otherwise."

Knowing he'd said enough, Eric let the remark stand and started the round of handshakes to end the meeting. He followed them out of the school office and left them by the exit with a quick wave. "I'm going to start my classroom rounds. I'll see the kids in my office later."

He was certain only Amy was likely not surprised by the way he bypassed the traditional "who should be punished more" approach to these problems. Walking down the hall to the kindergarten room, a shot of energy surged through him.

"FOR A MOM called to the principal's office you sure are in a good mood," Georgia said.

"I know," Amy said. "It feels weird even to me."

"Be honest, is it a little bit about the particular principal?"

Odd question, Amy thought. She'd said little about her and Eric. But she had no inclination to fib, either. "Maybe a little," she admitted, in a low and confidential tone. "Did I tell you Eric and I entered the charity bike ride for the sanctuary? We're training together to cover thirty miles by the end of June."

Georgia responded with a smirk. "Hmm… let me think. You might have mentioned it once or twice."

Amy's hands flew to her cheeks. "Really? I suppose I do talk about it. I'm excited to be part of something like that. And it's fun to do practice rides with Eric."

After giving her a long look, Georgia said, "You spend a lot of time with the blue-eyed principal."

Amy laughed. "That's how my grandpa refers to him." She lowered her voice and mimicked, "What's doing with the principal, Amy?'"

"Nice way to avoid the question," Georgia

said, flashing an amused look at Amy. "Now, why is it so hard to admit you're seeing him?"

No matter how gentle the ribbing, Amy still loathed these conversations. "Well, of course, I'm *seeing* him, Georgia, but we're friends."

"Ah, I see. You do things together, but you don't call them dates."

When Georgia put it that way, it brought up the foolish contradiction Amy wrestled with herself. "Let me explain, Georgia. I have to keep it casual." Her tone intensified with every word. "I can't afford to take my eye off my goals. I did that once, and I'll *never* do it again."

"Whoa, I surrender," Georgia said, pretending to push away from Amy, "but not without observing that your Mr. Wells doesn't strike me as the kind of guy who'd interfere with what you want in life."

Amy smiled. Mr. Wells. He sure was that serious adult man at the meeting this morning. Even Kyra walked away impressed by how he steered the meeting to what he wanted to accomplish. "I think you might be right, Georgia." Amy turned and touched the computer screen to pull up the calendar. "But he deserves someone who already has her life together."

"Sounds like you're describing yourself."

Amy didn't have a chance to even consider a response because Georgia promptly turned and walked to the back of the shop. Then a regular customer came in with her three pre-school kids, a set of twin girls and a younger boy. Georgia would have a full chair for the time it took to trim three heads of red curly hair, plus the mom.

Georgia came to the front again, but her attention was on the kids. "The carrottops have arrived," she said gesturing for them to follow her. The girls ran ahead and the boy toddled along as best he could to keep up.

"You're the happenin' place," a new client said when Amy told her Rita would be ready for her in about ten minutes.

Looking around at the busy salon, Amy admired Georgia's patience in building this business. It had all the qualities of the kind of business Amy wanted for herself. A business where people left feeling better than when they came in. Like she'd told Georgia, a self-care business.

She said as much later when she and Eric had finished their sixteen-mile ride and ended up at a picnic table in the park sharing a container of cashews and washing them down with a cold beer. This was the first chance she'd had to ask Eric how the meeting with the four kids had gone.

"Pretty well," he said, with a half-hearted shrug. "Carson was still complaining about his shirt and Lottie was awfully quiet, but otherwise it was okay."

"Only okay?" Amy mused.

"I didn't have high expectations." He unwrapped the towel from around his neck and ran it across his forehead. "It's never this hot in May."

"Oops, sorry. You seemed to be in such a great mood when we left."

"I was."

His tone was flat. Something had gone wrong. "I'm sorry. I've obviously annoyed you."

He grimaced, but reached out and touched her arm. "No, no, it isn't you. A lot came up for me while we were riding. I'm going to lose a teacher, and the school board added one more report I have to submit before the summer break. Trivial stuff. I'd rather meet with the kids."

"And now you have the commission work."

"I like the work better than I thought I would. Lots of facts and details to consider."

Eric pretended to turn a key over his lips. "I can't say another word. Sorry."

"Okay, then I won't ask. But earlier, I was mulling over all the little things Georgia does to keep her shop going." She stared out into the expanse of the park. "It would feel so good to run my own business one day." She immediately regretted her words. It was all a pipe dream, anyway. "I was just thinking out loud. Ignore me."

"So, where will your business be located?"

"On River Street. Big surprise." She smiled. "You know how I feel about our downtown. But forget I said anything. It's not imminent, so I shouldn't have mentioned it."

"Oh, I don't know. Dreams can come true. Like I told you before, my job was exactly what I wanted, and I got it." He paused, maybe waiting for her to say something. "Tell me more."

"Well, since it's not something I can put in motion now, I haven't thought it all through."

"But it's supposed to make people feel good. I've heard you say that about the salon."

"A new haircut or touched up color lifts our spirits. I see it every day." She stood and stretched her arms over her head and then bent in half and touched her palms to the ground.

"Looks like you could run one of those yoga studios."

She raised her head. "Uh, I'm pretty sure you have to study yoga first." On the other hand, she could bring someone in to teach yoga in her fantasy business.

Eric grinned. "You've got me there."

"I need to head home. I told Cassie I'd be back to say good-night."

"Our training is fun—it's only a few more weeks."

"I hope when the race is over we can still ride now and again—at least on the weekends, I mean." *Wow, that came out fast*, Amy thought.

"Sure, Amy, I'm always game to hang out with you." Eric led the way out of the park and down River Street until Amy made her left turn and they waved goodbye.

Grandma Barb was in her chair brushing Cassie's still-damp hair when Amy came inside the house. Cloud stretched and curled up in Grandpa's lap. "What a nice picture you three make." She rested her hip on the arm of Grandma's chair and lightly touched her back.

"Are you ticking off those miles?" Grandpa asked, peering over his reading glasses.

"We are. We're gaining speed. We'll do eighteen miles this weekend."

"You could win, you know," Grandpa said.

Amy gave him a pointed look. "I don't know about that. I should be okay in my age group."

"Don't underestimate yourself," Grandma said.

"You sound like Eric." It was as if the three of them were colluding to push her. "I didn't sign up for the ride to compete. It's fun to be part of something that's also for a good cause."

Grandpa shrugged. "I suppose. I can't wait to see you there. And the sanctuary and nature center is a good cause."

"Kyra's bringing Lottie," Cassie said.

"I'm glad we'll all be joining in," Amy said, hoping that would bring the talk of competition to an end. Still, it was something to think about.

Eric's attitude toward the race wasn't at all like what she'd expected. He took it more seriously, not for himself, but for her. She'd originally thought they would find a pace good for both of them and do the ride together. But Eric wanted her to exceed her expectations for herself.

Amy watched Grandma loosely braid Cassie's hair for the night. "Grandma used to brush and braid my hair, too," she said to Cassie.

"And put flowers in it on prom night," Grandma added, rubbing Cassie's shoulders. "I'll do the same for you when the time comes, sweetie."

Amy smiled at her grandma's words. Leaning sideways, she rested her cheek on her grandma's soft white hair. "Thanks, Grandma."

"For what, honey?"

Amy blinked back tears of nostalgia all mixed up with love for her grandma that threatened to overwhelm her. She managed to keep her voice light when she said, "For pretty much everything."

"THE NOISE IS overwhelming," Amy said with a laugh. "Worse than the diner on a Saturday night." She leaned toward Eric and put her hands over her ears.

"It's a really big night." And Eric's mood ran high, especially because Amy was with him in the high school auditorium and he had a feeling he'd like what was happening. They'd clashed over things related to the future of Bluestone River, but all through the winter and now in June they'd become closer and closer. She might have said no to something more serious once, but he wasn't giving up. When she and the rest of the crowd heard the plan, he could almost guarantee most people would leave happy about the future of their hometown. Even the bridge.

"You're quiet in the midst of all this noise," she said.

"I'm surprised that we might come close to filling the auditorium. When Mike said he was moving the meeting, I thought that was overkill. But looking at the steady stream of people coming, I was dead wrong." He grinned at her. "But I don't mind."

"I suppose you don't," she said, teasing, "since *you* already know what's going to happen."

"Hey, it's because I'm such a VIP." He laughed, unable to resist teasing her right back.

She playfully punched his arm. "Right."

"Don't worry. All will be revealed." He had trouble keeping the lid on his own excitement.

"Mike is trying to get your attention," Amy

said, nodding toward the mayor, who stood on the raised platform where the council and the committee sat.

When Eric turned, Mike waved for him to come up.

"I better go. Mike's in gavel-wielding mode." Eric squeezed Amy's hand and hurried to carry out a job he'd never imagined taking on. But since he'd come back to Bluestone River, so much had come together, not only for him, but the town. The storm was the lemon, but the plan was a pitcher of sweet lemonade.

When Eric joined him, Mike pointed to the chairs designated for the commission. "We'll start in a couple of minutes. I want to get us in place up on the stage." Eric grasped the back of the chair and looked up and down the row at the council and the commission. Maybe because this meeting was such a big deal, or because the venue seemed more formal, everyone on the stage had upped their appearance a bit.

In the audience, Amy, who'd come straight from work, took his breath away in her silky blouse and summery slacks. He had to laugh at himself. She took his breath away in her cycling shorts, T-shirt and helmet, too.

Like Mike, Eric had worn a suit, rather than black jeans and a jacket. Others had done the same. Watching Mike greeting the council members, it struck Eric that he and others in town were stepping up and taking on the future. Eric felt that responsibility in the way he ran the school. Sometimes the responsibility weighed heavy on him, even after asking for it. Knowing the compromise he and the others had come up with, he could go on with a sense of satisfaction at how they combined all the ideas to reach this conclusion.

As in the previous meetings, Mike was committed to hearing every voice who wanted to speak. To prove it, the meeting was scheduled for an hour earlier than usual and would last as long as needed.

Mike confidently brought the meeting to order and smiled at the council and commission members on either side of him. His tone revealed notes of gratitude and optimism when he introduced Eric and then Nancy Lundgren, a lawyer in town who would speak for the commission.

"We heard a lot of ideas," Nancy said, "and the comments from the previous meetings guided our direction. Even we were surprised when a compromise plan took form.

The more we worked on it, the more confident we were that we had something special that would please *almost* everyone." She paused. "Let's face it, nothing is one hundred percent."

The crowd responded with amused chuckles, and then Eric stepped forward and hit a key on the computer and an image appeared on the screen.

Eric cut his gaze to Amy. She held up two fingers and beamed as she mouthed the words, *Ha! Two bridges.*

"Now, this is what I call a compromise," Jim Kellerman said from the end of the table.

With a satisfied smile at Amy, Eric knew they'd done it. The buzz in the room, the exclamations of surprise, told him that the work of sifting through ideas, some bad, some better, had been worth it. The screen image showed the river in light blue, the park on one side, the empty acres on the other. The only change in this view was the second bridge. Everyone in the room saw that first thing and somehow the compromise hit home.

"So, step one is easy," Nancy said. "We can get the covered bridge repaired—more like rebuilt, given the extent of the damage. But we agreed we should keep as much of the old structure as we can, and we'll preserve some of the bigger pieces of the walls where for decades now, young people have carved or painted their initials." Nancy grinned at Mike. "Isn't that right, Mike?"

Mike raised his hand. "Ruby and I plead guilty."

Someone in the audience stood. Rather than going to the mic, he cupped his hands and called out, "What's saving that heap of lumber going to cost us?"

Eric snorted. He might not be all that attached to the bridge, but if that guy wanted to keep his friends, calling the bridge a heap of lumber was not a good start.

"I'm glad this came up early," Mike said, getting to his feet. "It won't cost the town anything. It's being covered by donations."

"Thanks, Emma," someone shouted.

"Wait, wait…that's only partly true." Mike pointed to Jim. "Why don't you explain? I'd like to clear up that concern."

Eric and Amy both recalled Jim Kellerman and his yearslong quest to build condos on Hidden Lake. Goodbye, sanctuary. But something changed.

Jim explained that he and his wife, Ruth, were teaming up with Emma to cover the cost of rebuilding the bridge. "We don't want to let our landmark rot away. But budgets are tight, and we knew Emma would fund the repair if we asked her to. But she shouldn't have to do it alone."

Jim snickered and pointed to his wife in the audience. "Ruth keeps telling me that we can't take our money with us, so we thought we could leave some of it behind in the bridge." Jim grinned. "Let's get going on it. I want to live to see it."

The audience broke into applause. Eric joined in, his chest tightening when he looked at Jim. He remembered the notorious Jim Kellerman of the past—and not in a good way. His mom used to joke that Jim would pave over the river if he thought he could make a profit.

Eric changed the slide to show details of the road and brand-new bridge. He explained the way they could extend River Street by using acres adjacent to the park. "We can build on the land across from the river, but without losing any park space. We can reconnect the trails on both sides of the river through the rebuilt bridge. And because that part of the project doesn't require taxpayer money or state grants, we can start taking bids and get this project underway. We'll fund the road through the highway fund."

As Jim walked away from the podium, the audience started clapping again.

Next, Eric brought up a drawing of a possible shopping area. Amy didn't know it yet, but this was Kyra's work. She'd been quietly brought into the project, but like everyone else on the commission couldn't talk about it. All the drawings were hers, but this vision of commercial development relied on the new bridge.

Eric glanced at Amy, who met his gaze and smiled. She gave him a thumbs-up sign—two thumbs. Must be extra good, he mused.

Nancy stepped to the podium and said, "This compromise really does give something to everyone. Preservation and development. Increased tourism. Convenient shopping for those of us who live here—potentially, anyway."

"You're destroying acres of prairie," an angry voice shouted.

Eric nodded. "Well, we're using the acres. You're right. But we came up with some fairly strict guidelines for development."

Georgia spoke up, surprising Eric with her

tone. "A lot is riding on what goes up on that land."

"We're getting to that," Eric blurted, a little exasperated. "By extending River Street and maybe providing a trolley from downtown, the other side of the river will come to be a vital part of town."

"We're just making sure River Street is protected, Eric. That's all," Georgia said in a softer tone. "This town is roaring back. You put The Fourth on River Street together with the Christmas festival, and it's going to end up a holiday town, as well. And our spring festival might have been, well, washed out, but we'll try again next year."

Eric could quiet Georgia's fears if she let him speak. But Georgia ran through the businesses, plus a few getting ready to open.

"The business owners will feel better when we go to the next stage, which involves more detail about the plans," Eric said. His earlier annoyance gave way to eagerness to talk about more ideas. But he'd lost the audience. They'd begun talking among themselves about what Georgia had brought up. They ran the risk of going back to the atmosphere of the earlier meetings where people with different positions talked past each other. He picked up Mike's gavel and gave the podium a decisive whack.

"Hear me out, folks," Eric said, changing the slide and putting up a more detailed sketch of a cluster of storefronts with landscaped walkways between them. "No one, *no one*, suggested a big mall of big-box stores on Bernie's acres. We never received so much as a one-page proposal for that. But the comment box we put online brought lots of innovative suggestions."

Eric went through some of them, including the demand for a small supermarket and a café, maybe connected under one roof. They had demand for a yoga studio and a sporting goods store. "As a matter of fact, we heard from a woman interested in opening up a shop selling athletic and camping gear. The guidelines we've posted on the webpage explain the architectural hoops store owners will have to jump through. If we learned nothing else from this process, we know that most people want to enhance the town's character—and beauty—as it grows."

Mike stood and explained the proposal and guidelines would be posted online and the council would vote on it next week. "We welcome more comments. We want ideas. Our plan was based on what all of you said you'd like. But this is only the beginning."

The meeting adjourned and Mike gaveled the meeting closed one more time.

The crowd broke into applause.

Eric stood with Nancy and Mike and glanced back at the others on the commission. "We did it," Nancy said.

"Looks like it," Eric agreed.

Mike waved to acknowledge the reaction and the crowd started filing out.

"Good for Mike," he said to Amy when he joined her.

"Good for you," she said, giving him a quick hug. "I don't know how you were able to keep secrets for so long. Especially the idea of the two bridges. So logical, really."

"The solution was right there in front of us, but Jim and Emma paying for it took away all the arguments against it. Keeping the bridge a secret was easy compared to knowing your friend Kyra was the graphic artist we used."

Amy's mouth fell open. "Those beautiful drawings were Kyra's?"

Eric nodded. "We needed a bid and wanted to go local, and this project is right up her alley. She'll be doing more work on this project."

Amy pressed her palms together. "I'm so glad. She's become such a good friend and she does great work."

As they wandered toward the door, Amy opened her handbag and checked her phone. "I can get back in time to tuck Cassie in." She glanced up at him. "I should do that since I'll be out tomorrow for our ride."

"One of our last," he said.

"Congratulations on the proposal." She reached up and gave him a quick hug and a kiss on the cheek. "I need to talk to Georgia for a minute on my way out, but I'll see you tomorrow."

Eric spotted Seth standing in the back watching him. His gaze followed Amy as she hurried to Georgia's side. When Eric approached, Seth was all smiles.

"You're in good with her now," Seth said.

"What are you? Like fifteen?" Eric could tease, but it was the truth.

"I'm thinking like a grown-up here," Seth said.

As they walked toward the door, Eric filled him in. "I've been quiet about it, but things are good between us. I don't need to spell it out. You know how I feel about her." Beyond that, Eric would hold his plans close to his chest.

CHAPTER FIFTEEN

THE NEXT DAY, Amy stepped inside the salon at noon on the dot, excited. To copy her daughter's words, she felt fizzy inside. In contrast, Rita and Georgia wore serious expressions as they stood behind the counter, looking at the computer screen.

Georgia glanced up and smiled. "We're in a lull, but not for long. We're doing a little revamping of the schedule. Rita is adding another half day."

"Good," Amy said. "Little by little you've brought in more business." With the proposal last night that both saved the bridge and extended River Street, that trend would continue for Georgia. Happy to be part of it on the one hand, on the other Amy envied Georgia's challenge.

"Quite a meeting last night, huh?" Georgia asked.

"I never thought I'd be so open-minded to new development," Amy admitted.

"You must have read my mind." Georgia curled her fingers beckoning Amy to come along with her. "There's something I want to show you in the back."

Another breakroom chat, Amy thought, *always interesting*. Flattering, too, that her boss liked to run ideas by her.

Georgia held up the coffeepot. "Fresh brewed. Want some?"

"Always," Amy said.

"Have a seat." Georgia gestured to the folding chair at the card table. "I've got something on my mind."

"Always," Amy repeated, accepting the coffee.

Georgia sat across from her. "Turns out the meeting last night was about so much more than listening to a proposal. For me, at least."

"For me, too. We got what we wanted. And the sketch of the two bridges and the road struck me as an amazing compromise. Possibilities everywhere."

"So, I'll get to the point. The way I see it, we really do have a nature town—outdoorsy. Parks and trails and all. Agree?"

"Sure. And the sanctuary adds to our reputation as a community that supports the natural world."

"And these things attract the kinds of people who likely try to take good care of themselves."

Amy mulled that over. "Or at least they think they *should* be health conscious."

"Right. Our visitors like their getaways. They believe in stress management." Georgia pointed to Amy. "You said it yourself. This little shop I run isn't just about beauty." Georgia snickered. "No ma'am, I run a self-care business."

"With a few more changes you can keep reinforcing that," Amy said, her sense of excitement rising. It was almost a game with her to imagine this business offering more services and becoming an up-to-date salon.

"I was thinking more along the lines that *we* could make some changes." Georgia's face lit up and she dramatically swiped her palms. "But not on a *small* scale. I took a risk before and I'm ready to do it again. I want us—" she leaned across the table "—the two of us, to take over the empty space next door and make this over as River Street Salon and *Day Spa*."

Amy's mind jumped to the vision she'd had all along. "We can offer facials and massage.

Oh, and infrared sauna. That's really popular now."

"Right, right," Georgia responded, "and I've been doing a little research. No one here in town offers it."

"Are you promoting me?" Amy's spirits shot up, but then dropped a notch. Georgia would need someone fulltime.

Georgia shook her head. "Absolutely not. No promotion. I want to do this right, and that means I need a *partner*. And that means you." Georgia leaned back in the chair. "If this is what you want."

Amy felt the pressure behind her eyes. But she willed herself not to let even happy tears fall. But Georgia couldn't know this offer was so much more than a new opportunity. It was her dream coming true in a way she'd never have expected.

"Oh, I want it. But…" Amy tried to find words that told the truth, but didn't douse the fire this idea created inside.

"Are you going to bring up money? The funds we need to make this investment."

"Of course. I want this. This very idea has been bouncing back and forth in my head since the day I greeted the first customer at the counter."

"I know. I see the look in your eyes. You're hungry for the challenge."

"But I have obligations beyond Cassie."

Georgia put her hand over Amy's. "I know the situation with your grandparents. We can figure it out as we go. I've thought this through, Amy, and I still want you with me in this venture."

Amy listened while Georgia filled in the details of the business arrangement she had in mind. It involved a bank loan and partnership papers, a plan to open the connecting store in the fall. The menu of services they'd offer was still up for discussion, but they'd sort that out.

Amy took out her tablet and jotted notes, including some promotional specials they could work out with other businesses. They could expand Georgia's services for wedding parties and offer spa days to small groups of women. It was so easy to picture Ruby and Emma coming in together for their facials and manicures. They already made most of their appointments together.

Georgia continued. "The list goes on. Holiday season spa weekends for sure, coupons at every River Street event, and promoting gift certificates as the perfect gift for the women you love—wives, sisters, moms...and we can't forget grandmas."

Amy looked up from her keyboard and laughed. "I can't believe I'm already making lists."

"It's only a start, Amy."

"I'm so happy I can barely contain it, Georgia. I may explode from joy."

"Exactly the reaction I'd hoped for."

Georgia wouldn't understand, not yet, what this meant to her, even beyond her business dream come true.

ERIC STOOD AT the window and watched Amy's car park in front of his house. She had him curious now. The days were long in late June, but it was late enough that it was getting dark. She got out of her car and ran across the lawn to the stairs. He hurried to the door to let her in.

"Wow, you're in a..." When her arms circled his neck he didn't bother finishing his sentence. She put her hand on the back of his neck and pulled his face closer and pressed her lips against his. He wrapped his arms around her back and held her tight. When she ended the kiss, he stroked her cheek, but kissed her again. Keeping his mouth on hers, he walked backward and took her with him, freeing one arm only long enough to close the door.

Finally, she drew back. "The most wonderful thing happened today."

"This is pretty wonderful right here." He was also curious.

"Aren't you going to ask? Oh, and can I have some wine? I've got so much to say."

He led her into the kitchen and took a bottle of white wine out of the fridge and poured them each a glass. "Want to go out to the deck? No furniture out there yet, but—"

"I don't care. Oh, yes, yes, let's sit on the edge." Giddy, she said, "It doesn't matter where we sit."

This must be some announcement, Eric thought, allowing himself to hope she'd changed her mind about the two of them. She was acting like it.

They settled in next to each other and let their legs hang over the edge. Amy raised her glass. "A toast."

"To?" he asked. To the two of them? Maybe?

"To lots of things."

He touched his glass to hers. "Okay, start the list."

She started her list with Georgia. He could feel her excitement when she described accepting the offer of a partnership. "It's exactly what I've dreamed of. And we can have the new space ready to open by fall."

He clinked her glass again. "This is wonderful news, Amy." He wondered how she'd balance it with Cassie and her grandparents, but she'd manage. She always did.

"I talked to Grandma about it, and right now, she can watch Cassie after school. Cassie will be in day camp for a lot of the summer, anyway. On Scott's weekends—the ones when he deigns to make an appearance—I can work on the spa side of our shop."

"You must have been doing an amazing job these last months, Amy." He pointed to her. "Georgia wanted a partner and she picked you."

She let out a giggle. "Speaking of partners, can I pick you?"

Eric's heart beat wildly in his chest. Had he heard what he thought he'd heard? He stared at her until he finally had the breath to say, "Yes, you can pick me. But why now...why..."

"I told you I had feelings for you."

"Well, yes, but you also gave me a bunch of reasons we couldn't be more than friends."

He leaned in and gave her a light kiss. "Don't get me wrong, but the turnaround happened pretty fast."

"I know," she said softly, "but some of my barriers are gone, or at least, are shrinking. Grandma and even Grandpa seem to see right through me when it comes to you. They don't want my helping to look after them hold me back."

Eric twisted his body so he could better face her and read her expressions. "Go on."

"I had to get over the idea that I let myself down in the past and couldn't let myself do it again."

Eric nodded. There had been no arguing her out of it. "And Georgia's offer changed that?"

"Yes and no," she said, taking his free hand and smoothing her fingers over his palm. "It's a development I couldn't have imagined when I walked in there on my first day. But I realized it wasn't just her choosing me for this venture. It was my confidence about saying yes." She tapped her chest with her index finger. "I've wanted to have my own business for a long time and now I'm sure I have what it takes to make it happen."

She took a sip of her wine and smiled before saying, "Do you remember when I told you I wanted to finally make something of myself?"

He groaned. "And I told you that's already happened, you've accomplished so much, and it's absurd to think otherwise."

"But I expected more from myself." She bobbed her head back and forth. "What I'm doing here tonight, Eric, is about taking a stand for myself." She leaned in to kiss him and ran her fingers lightly over his chest. "No more denying what's in my heart. You have the guts to take a chance on a woman with a daughter who has her own mind and doesn't always make, as you say, good choices."

"Not so risky, Amy. I love your spunky little girl." He looked out over the tops of the houses around him. Only a hint of a pinkish mackerel sky was left on this special summer evening. "I won't deny it. I wish Cassie was my child." He turned to look Amy in the eye. "But I also know she has a dad."

"Maybe, but in the last months, you've been more reliable than Scott has ever been."

He tried to protest, but she shushed him.

"I'm not happy about that. But it's true. When it comes to many of the decisions ahead, Scott will have to team up with me to make them." She smiled. "You know, Mr. Wells, you've got a big head start on winning that little girl's heart."

"Big heart, actually. Like her mom." He lightly captured a few stray strands of her hair and wove them through his fingers. "Have I ever told you what beautiful hair you have?"

"Nope."

"Well, I just did. If we ever have a child ourselves, I wonder what color hair he or she would end up with."

"A baby, Eric? Really?"

"I know things are happening all over the place in our lives, but let's think about it."

She took another sip of her wine and let out a happy sigh. "Okay." She sat up straight and said, "Wow, Eric, it just occurred to me I didn't ask if you were still open to me. For this." She batted her finger back and forth from him to her.

"Ha! Did you really think I'd have changed my mind? I was trying—and failing—to accept what you said about your struggle to be true to yourself."

"Now you don't have to try. You've got my heart. You did a while back, but I tried—and failed—to deny it." She reached out to touch his cheek. "But I'd like to keep this to our-selves for right now."

"You want to ease Cassie into the idea that her family will expand by one."

She nodded. "Something like that. I want to see how I'll balance things with my grand-parents and Cassie as the salon changes. This summer will be a good test, more or less."

"That's wise," he said, trying to envision the path ahead. "Cassie is your priority, and your grandparents, too."

"As long as you know I'm madly in love with you, we'll find a way to work it out."

As the time slipped by, he told her that Cassie and Lottie had been a big part of the tone of the work he'd done at the school in the weeks before the end of the year. "I've finally taken a lot of pieces of an idea and started on the theme for our school next year."

Eric explained his thoughts about kindness as the positive way to avoid bullying. "Maybe this wouldn't work so well in a larger school, but the families in our community so often know each other, at least casually. And I've wanted to stand *for* something, rather than only speaking out against bullying."

"Oh, Eric," Amy said, "you changed the mood in your office that day with the other parents simply by refusing to play the typical game. You offered up something new that wasn't all about punishments. I love your idea." Another soft kiss. "And I love you."

Amy eased herself out of Eric's arms. She patted the pocket of her linen pants. "My phone? I thought I put it in my pocket."

"You left your purse in the kitchen. I left my phone inside, too."

"I always leave it on vibrate," Amy said, hurrying inside. "Not that it should matter, but Lottie is sleeping over. It's a huge deal for the two of them. Grandma was making cookies with them when I left. Hours ago now."

She grabbed her phone and looked at her messages. "Oh no, I have three from Grandma." She scrolled through them, her eyes widening. "Oh, no."

Eric's phone rang, pulling Cassie's attention away from her screen.

"Kyra?" He listened. "I got it. No, Amy is still with me. We were out on my deck. We didn't hear the phone. She's got messages from Barb."

"Cassie and Lottie are *gone*," Amy said. "Grandma can't find them."

"We'll find the girls." He spoke to both

moms, Amy in front of him and Kyra on the phone. "I promise. We will."

ERIC INCHED THE SUV down another street behind Amy's house. "Nothing on Adams," Amy said to Kyra. She had her phone on speaker, so she and Eric could be in touch with Seth and Kyra as they all combed the neighborhood from Amy's house to River Street.

"I still can't believe this," Amy said. "I can't figure out why they would do this?" She couldn't blame Kyra or Grandma. Not even Scott. Amy alone had decided it was okay to leave the girls with Grandma Barb.

"We need to call the police," Seth said. "I know you wanted to see if you could find them right away, but we've searched the streets near your house, Amy. Or, we could follow River Street to the park. If we don't spot them, then we can call the police."

"Or we could head to the sanctuary," Eric said, pulling his SUV over to the curb.

"How could two nine-year-olds get *that* far in such a short time?" Seth said.

"We don't know how long they've been gone," Amy pointed out. "Grandma's first call came in at almost eleven. She'd checked on them around ten o'clock and they were asleep." For some reason, she'd opened the door again before she went to bed and that's when she discovered they were gone and the window was open. But without Amy seeing three messages before almost midnight, the girls got a head start.

"Seth is right," Eric said. "We need to call the police before we head to the park. We'll let the police know we're going there to look."

"Maybe they thought they could slip out of town on one of the farm roads." Hearing those words come out of her mouth stunned her. How ridiculous. Slip out of town? Cassie and Lottie? "Kyra, I know you're scared out of your mind, too. But, yes, let's call the police."

"This is all my fault."

"No, no, Kyra, this is not your fault. Please." Amy sighed. "Let's just concentrate on finding the girls."

Amy kept her phone on speaker when Eric made the call and quickly explained the situation. "And it appears the two girls left Cassie Morgan's house through her bedroom window."

"No, no," Eric said. "There is no obvious reason why the girls would have done it." Pause. "Uh-huh, yes, that's right. I'm the principal of Madison School. But that's not important. I'm a friend of Amy Morgan's. She was in my home on Oak Street when her grandmother called." Another pause. "We've been out searching. We assumed they couldn't get far on foot." A few seconds later, Eric said, "Here, I can put you on with Ms. Morgan."

She took the phone from Eric's hand. She gave the police her address. "My daughter and I live with my grandparents. She and the other little girl, Lottie—Charlotte—were having a sleepover." Amy kneaded her forehead in a vain attempt to relieve the tension.

Pulling onto the street, Eric said, "We'll head to the park by the bridge."

Amy nodded and answered the questions about Cassie and Lottie. She described them both, and heard Kyra's soft, heartbreaking gasp through her phone. Again, she said she could think of no possible reason for them to run away. Finally, in response to another officer's question, she said, "Her father is Scott Morgan. He lives in Chicago." Glancing at Eric, she said, "Yes, I was out for the evening with Mr. Wells."

Before ending the call, she said, "We're almost to the lot in the park right now. Please, meet us there. We can go to Kyra's house or my home later." Her heart pounding in her tight chest, she said, "Yes, we've got pictures."

Minutes later, Seth pulled his truck next to Eric's SUV.

Amy jumped out of his car and ran to Kyra. They pulled each other into a desperate hug. When they stepped apart, Kyra folded in half, resting her hands on her thighs. Seth put a hand on her back. "Kyra, it's really not your fault."

Kyra straightened up and shook her head. "It is. Lottie's afraid she's going to be sent away again. She has an uncle in Florida she's never met. He showed some willingness to take her, but now I'm told he's probably backing out."

Eric looked at Amy, who nodded. "Kyra and I talked about this the other day."

"I'm sure Lottie sensed my fear," Kyra said, her shoulders drooping. "She was asking questions, but I avoided them as much as possible. But that only fueled her anxiety."

Under other circumstances, Amy might have remarked it was exactly like Cassie to go along with Lottie so she wouldn't be alone.

"We should get down into the park," Eric said, pointing to Seth before turning to Amy and Kyra. "Why don't you two wait for the police?"

"I'm going to call Grandma Barb and let her know where we are." Eric and Seth took off as the cruiser came into view and Barb answered the call. "The police just pulled in to the park, Grandma." Her voice—and her hands—shook when she added, "Seth and Eric took off toward the river to search. On the trail."

"Oh, Amy, I'm *so sorry*."

"Grandma, no, no," she said, choking back a sob. "You have nothing to be sorry for. I never should have left the house on a sleepover night." Left unspoken was her selfish trip to Eric's house to share her news and admit, at last, that she was completely in love with him. And ready for him. They could be a family.

Right.

"Sweetie, the girls were fine. Whatever they'd schemed, they would have managed it one way or another," Grandma insisted. "I don't want you blaming yourself. I know you have to go, but how is Kyra?"

"She's doing okay, given everything that's

happening. We'll talk to the police now. Gotta go."

Kyra had already started toward the cruiser. Amy caught up with her and the two approached the officer.

"I'm Veronica Long," the officer said. "Right now, my job is to get as much information from you as possible. First, why you think the girls ran off?"

Before she answered, Amy quickly introduced herself and Kyra. "We don't know. Like we said when we called you, the girls were having a sleepover at my house. They were in bed."

Kyra jumped in to explain that Lottie had been her foster child for a few months. "Lottie is afraid she'll be moved again. And I'm concerned about that myself. I love her so much. If I could I'd adopt her today, but that can't happen. Not yet. I think she picked up on my fear and decided to run rather than being taken away again."

"And we believe Cassie, my daughter, decided to go with her." Amy wiped away sweat from her forehead on the still, humid night. "She and Lottie are really close now. She wouldn't want Lottie to be alone."

In answer to Officer Long's questions,

Amy explained that Eric and Seth were cousins. "We split up rather than the four of us looking together. We thought we'd find them wandering in the neighborhood right away."

The officer nodded and flashed a beam toward the river and the heap of wood and makeshift fencing that appeared to rise up from the water. The covered bridge.

"We came here because we thought they might think they could hide here," Amy said, gesturing toward the playground and benches. At some point it would have occurred to them they had nowhere to go."

"Did they take anything with them?"

"Lottie had her dolls and a change of clothes in her backpack," Kyra said. "But I don't know if she packed those things when they took off."

"My grandmother mentioned a box of crackers and some cookies were gone, but not enough to last very long."

"Lottie might have a few dollars that I gave her for an allowance. She saves it in a special box we decorated with..." Kyra brushed tears off her cheeks. "That doesn't matter. But no, they wouldn't have much money to buy food."

Amy brought up a photo of Cassie on her phone and Kyra did the same for Lottie. "Here they are. But really, how many nine-year-olds are going to be wandering around town in the middle of the night?"

Officer Long ignored the rhetorical question, but took Kyra and Amy's phones. "I'll send the girls' photos to the station right now. We've already alerted the state police and sent two cruisers out with a team. We'll do a public alert in the morning." She checked her watch. "Soon. Meanwhile, we want you two to stay put."

ERIC STILL REELED from the earlier conversation with Amy. It was the moment he'd been waiting for—hoping for—over the last weeks. And now this. Listening to Amy, a great mom, answer the officer's questions over the phone threw him, too. She was "with Mr. Wells" for the evening. As outrageous as it seemed, because of him, Amy was caught up in a situation where she thought she needed to defend herself. She'd only been gone a few hours. But those two little girls… He looked at the river on one side, the dark woods on the other. "I can't stop thinking about how scared they must be by now," he whispered.

"Would Cassie try to go to her dad in Chicago?" Seth asked as they jogged down the trail.

"I've thought of that. It seems impossible, but then, we thought we'd find them quickly and here we are." He and Seth had already taken the trail down to one of the major streets where the bridge crossed the river. Now they doubled back on the trail on the opposite side of the river. "On these biking trails with Amy, I saw hiding places down near the end of the woods and the start of the farm road and those empty acres. Amy said she showed Cassie our training route on the trail map. Apparently, Cassie likes drawing lines of our route and adding up all the miles we've covered."

"But would Cassie know the way back? Or Lottie?" Seth asked. "It's one thing to cook up some scheme and even take off. They might think they're running away, sure. But could they scratch together more than a few dollars?"

"And whatever they'd found when they raided the refrigerator."

Eric stopped and aimed the beam of his flashlight into a stand of oak trees that formed a wide border separating a neighborhood in town from the empty prairie acres due for development now. "Nothing." He looked ahead to the two unpaved roads. "One way would take them to Emma O'Connell's house. But the other way would lead out of town.

"They wouldn't know that, would they?"

"Cassie might. Just because she'd been studying the map with Amy. We can't say what Lottie would or wouldn't know." Eric rubbed the back of his head and then grasped his neck, now stiff from the stress. "Lottie's a mystery in some ways. She seems shy and quiet, but she's been moved around so much in the last couple of years. I can't say what she might think of or attempt."

The two stood staring at the road. "It's so deserted," Seth said. "And dark, especially on this cloudy night."

"The police are in cruisers, Seth. That's great for spotting kids walking on the street, but these woods have areas where a couple of kids could hide out."

Across the river, Eric spotted Amy and Kyra talking to an officer. "We could, maybe should, go back and find out what the plans are for a search. The thing is, something is pushing me to take a look down that unpaved road. Cassie might know it leads to a highway out of town."

"Then let's go," Seth agreed. "We can go back to the park if we don't spot them. It's iffy, but let's give it a try."

"Okay. We'll move slowly and flash our beams into the trees."

They peered down the dusty road, beams flashing to their left, covering the ground at a good pace, but not so fast they'd miss a couple of girls who could be asleep for all they knew. He was second-guessing Cassie with little to go on, but if it was all for nothing, they'd know soon enough.

They also scanned the prairie on one side, where the grasses were high in these summer months. Nothing appeared, though. Not a deer or a raccoon or anything else.

"How far are we taking this?" Seth asked. "We must have covered a half mile already."

"I'm not sure, but..."

Suddenly, it looked like a figure appeared in the dark up ahead. A deer maybe? Eric flashed the beam and picked up two figures in his line of sight. "It's them," he shouted over his shoulder, breaking into a run now and keeping the beam on the two girls.

As they got closer, two voices shouted, "Mr. Wells, Mr. Wells." The girls jumped up and down and waved their arms over their heads.

"It's me, Cassie. And Lottie."

The two girls ran toward them. Cassie threw herself against his leg and hung on tight. Lottie, not as bold, lowered her head and covered her eyes. "Kyra's going to be so mad at me."

"Don't let them take Lottie away," Cassie demanded. "Please, please."

Eric put his arm around her shoulders, but didn't respond to her pleas. "Make the call, Seth. Tell them we have them. They can drive to the bridge on the street. We'll meet them there."

"We're sorry," Cassie said. "We made a bad choice."

"You've got that right," Eric said, amused by her words in spite of the situation. He lowered himself to one knee. "We'll get into that later. But first we're going to meet your mom and Kyra." He put his hand on Lottie's shoulder, but kept a respectful distance between them.

He looked from one to the other. "You have no idea how worried we were about you. We had to call the police. Your grandma Barb is blaming herself. Kyra and your mom blame themselves, too." Being honest with them wouldn't be all bad.

"Oh, no," Lottie said, nervously.

"Do you know how much Kyra loves you?" Eric asked, holding the beam to the side to get some light, but not blind them with it.

Lottie hesitated, but then nodded.

"That's why she was afraid something could happen to you. You and Cassie were out here in the woods in the dark all alone." He decided not to talk about the bad choice. Cassie had already brought it up. It was a conversation for another day.

"Lottie is afraid the social worker is going to come and take her away."

Not an easy fear to quiet, Eric thought. And he was in no position to make promises. "Well, I can only say one thing for sure. Kyra wants Lottie with her, and right now, that's the arrangement."

"Okay, you two, let's get you back," Seth said, coming closer. "Two happy moms are waiting."

"My mom might be happy now, Mr. Wells," Cassie said, "but she'll be really mad later."

Eric and Seth exchanged a glance, but they didn't say anything. They both knew Cassie was right. *My stepdaughter*, Eric thought, knowing he had a long road ahead with her. He couldn't wait to tell her that one day, maybe soon. Then he'd no longer be Mr. Wells.

CHAPTER SIXTEEN

"YOU'RE ENDING THIS on the phone, Amy. Seriously?"

"Better than drawing it out," Amy said, keeping her voice low. "If I was with you, I'm not sure I could do what I know I have to. I love you. I meant it when I said it. I mean it now."

"Terrific, I love you, you love me. I love your daughter and I'm already attached to your grandparents." His anger and confusion seemed to rise with every fact he stated. "We have one glitch. One mistake—that ended without anyone being hurt, by the way. And you call it off...call us off."

"There will always be something, Eric. Things have tended to send me running off." He had no way to comprehend last night's fear. "I was there when Grandma was sick, and I was with them when the tree branches fell on the house."

"And we got all that fixed, too, didn't we?"

From the moment she first explained why they had to go their separate ways, Eric had been incredulous. He wasn't buying any of her arguments. He simply didn't understand.

"Do you think I wouldn't drop everything and rush over there with you if something like that happened again? Or, I should say, *when* things go wrong."

"I told you once before that I can't afford a mistake. Cassie can't afford it."

"And you and I both know we are *not* a mistake."

"You say that now. I certainly thought that, too. But then, I left Grandma Barb with Cassie and Lottie and rushed off to you. I couldn't wait one more day to tell you what Georgia offered and how it made me feel."

"A mistake, Amy," he said impatiently. "Yes, we got caught up in ourselves and didn't hear our phones. You didn't commit a crime."

Her shoulders slumped, along with whatever good spirits she'd ever had. "It felt like a crime when the police grilled me about my whereabouts, my evening with *Mr. Wells.*"

"I caught that. It was totally unfair."

"It wouldn't have sounded unfair to a judge if Scott decided he wanted custody of Cassie." She replayed that scenario over and over in her head. The more she did it, the more fright-ening it was.

"Isn't that a bit extreme?" he challenged. "You could list a string of dates when he never showed up and all the times he prom-ised to call and didn't."

"You bet it sounds extreme, but it hap-pened." She sighed. "I can't take that chance."

"I'm… I'm… I can't find words for this. I know we can make this work. Amy, I'm not my dad. You don't need to worry, ever, that I'll walk away."

She knew that, she did. But, like she'd said earlier, something would always come up.

"It isn't about you walking away, this is about what I have to do right now." She winced, and pressed her fingers against her eyes to force back tears.

"I'm not going to pretend that I'm not upset, Amy. My heart is aching right now. I adore you." The silence that followed was loud and long. "But I'm not going to argue with you. I do need you to do one thing for me, though."

This is it, Amy thought. He's accepted it's over. "What is it?"

"I want to do the race. We trained together. This was *our* thing. So, I want to do it the way we planned it. Your grandparents, Cassie, my mom and Seth are all set to go. And Kyra and Lottie, too."

It was little enough. And exactly what she wanted. "Of course. And, Eric, I'll never stop caring about you. We started out as friends."

Eric spoke slowly when he responded. "So we did."

More silence.

"I'll pick you up next Saturday morning."

"Okay." The call ended, and Amy slipped under the covers. She'd known this would hurt, but she'd had no idea how much.

"WE HAVE FANS," Eric said, lifting the wheelchair out of the back. "Seth and my mom are on the way to the starting point, but I told them we'd catch up with them."

"I want to get my grandparents settled in before we go off to register."

"Are you nervous?" he asked, only because a few butterflies were having their say in his stomach. He'd have given anything to be able to change his mind and back out of this. But even though Amy had walked away, he'd made a promise and he'd keep it, no matter how bad he felt.

"A little," she admitted. "I don't want to come in last."

She hadn't looked into his eyes yet. "Absolutely no chance of that."

She smiled sadly. "So you say."

He couldn't talk himself out it. She didn't give herself any credit and it annoyed him to hear her talk like she couldn't compete. No serious racers were participating in this charity event. The riders were all local, regular people. Then why was she hesitant to put it all on the line? He knew, if she wouldn't admit it, that she could pick up her pace and outlast him.

He wheeled the chair around to the passenger door and helped Les settle into it with Barb and Cassie standing on either side. "Here I go," Les said, testing the motor and maneuvering the chair to make a tight circle.

"Yay, Grandpa," Amy called out. She stood a few feet away with their bikes.

"Did you know Lottie and Kyra are coming today?" Cassie bounced on the balls of her feet.

"I heard that, Cassie. You and your best pal can cheer for your mom."

"And for you, Mr. Wells."

With a little bow, Eric thanked Cassie and grinned at Barb.

"Let's go see if we can grab a good spot

where Lottie and Kyra can find us," Barb said, leading Cassie toward the start of the route.

He enjoyed this a little too much, a little voice in Eric's head warned. Amy's grandparents were so easy to like. Cassie had her moments, but she was skipping ahead now and looking back to see if her grandparents were following. Amy was by his side, wasn't she? At least for a couple of hours.

"I think we'll have quite the cheering section," he said, wheeling his bike next to Amy on their way to the registration tent. A few minutes later, they attached their race bibs to their T-shirts. They were both in the under-forty age group. The bright yellow block on Amy's bib designated the women's group, and the men wore light green. It was a ten-mile route that went through woods and residential areas and took many twists and turns. They'd cross the starting point twice during the race.

Amy was quiet while they waited with the others, almost seventy-five teenagers and adults gathered near the starting point. She stared down the stretch of the paved trail. What was she thinking? She'd disappeared somewhere deep inside her own head. She didn't seem to notice Kyra approaching with Cassie and Lottie.

"Amy, calling Amy back from wherever she is," Eric teased.

She looked at him, startled, but then she saw her friend and the girls. She waved both hands. "You found us. We want to hear you yelling really loud."

"Oh, you'll hear us," Kyra said in an exaggerated tone that made Lottie giggle.

Eric looked on as Amy hugged Lottie and Cassie, who'd joined them before Kyra directed them back to the grandparents. This ride was so uncomplicated for Cassie and Lottie. He wished their lives would always be like that. He wished that for him and Amy, too. Riding a bike to help others do more for the local environment...what could be simpler?

"Let's stretch," Amy said, bending forward and back. When it came to stretching, Eric followed Amy's lead. Every move showed off her agile, graceful body. He was strong, but had none of her flexibility. If she wanted to take up yoga, she'd be great at it. She rolled her shoulders one at a time, then both together and then extended her arms over her head and twisted at the waist. "Don't forget the ankle circles," she said. "Just a friendly reminder."

On their first ride, she'd chided him, in a teasing sort of way, about not paying enough attention to warming up.

"Are you loose?" she asked. "Feeling good?"

"I am. What about you?"

Lacing her fingers behind her head she thrust her elbows back. "I'm fine."

That came out flat and showed little enthusiasm. Should he say something? In another few minutes the starter pistol would fire and it would be too late. Keeping his thoughts to himself would be a lot easier, but then he'd regret not being honest with her. What he wanted to say had nothing to do with how much he loved her. His thoughts were only about her.

He touched her arm to get her attention. "You know, Amy, you're too good—too strong—not to push yourself and give it everything." She looked like she was about to protest, but he held up his hand. "Let me finish. When we've trained, you've held back on my account. I'm not as strong a rider as you are. But I don't want you to do that now that we're here for real. Win or lose, give it your all."

Amy looked away. "Now you're sounding like Les. We started out doing this for fun, Eric. A lark. Why all the pressure now?"

"That's easy," he said, as if stating the obvious. "When we started, I had no idea how persistent, how focused you already were. Covering thirty miles is nothing for you." He nodded to the banner serving as both the starting point and the finish line. "Doing it at your top speed doesn't mean you can't have fun with it."

"Eric, come on…"

"No, it's true. When we've done our longer practice rides, you'd slow down to match your pace with mine. You barely break a sweat." He saw her getting ready to protest, a knee-jerk reaction. But that wouldn't stop him. "Granted, my stamina and speed got better in the last month. The same is true for you." He looked into her puzzled eyes. "Do this for yourself, Amy."

She looked away and fixed her gaze on the long straight trail. "That doesn't mean I'll win, Eric."

"I never said anything about winning, Amy. Do you think Cassie and Lottie care if you win, or if I win? Two little kids seem to get it. Winning this isn't what matters."

"I'm glad we agree on that."

"We do, but it matters that *you* see what you can do." He gave her a lopsided grin. "Admit it. This is what you'd tell Cassie. That's why it's important."

She cocked her head to the side. "I'd also tell her to try a lot of things just for fun."

"Right," he shot back, "and you've already done that. Turns out you're pretty good at it." He paused, but then added one last point. "Just think, this is one thing in your life that doesn't involve Cassie or your grandparents or your new business venture. This is your chance to do one thing for yourself."

She nodded. "You're a good principal, Mr. Wells, but you must have been amazing in the classroom."

"I held my own." He feigned smugness and it lightened what was for him a heartbreaking moment. He felt as if he was letting her go for good. When she didn't question any point he'd made, he kept quiet. He'd said his piece.

AMY ROUNDED THE curve with a couple of other women in her group flanking her. One woman had taken off immediately and opened up a huge lead. She shared that front-runner status with a couple of men. They were soon out of sight, but that left the bulk of the crowd fighting for position. One other woman was ahead of Amy, but not too far. Amy didn't try to close the distance. Not yet.

Eric followed. Even before she passed the starting point after the first ten miles, his words echoed through her mind, triggering questions she couldn't brush off. Why hadn't she trained for this ride with the idea she could place—or even win?

For years, she cycled on the many miles of unbroken lakefront trails in Chicago. She'd never entered a race, but she rode for speed sometimes, as if competing with herself to improve her time. She hadn't entered races because Scott flat out refused to cooperate and commit to making himself available to take care of Cassie so Amy could train. To Scott, Amy's cycling was all a waste of time and inconvenienced him. Besides, it was unlikely she'd ever be good enough to win, so why bother?

Buoyed by Eric's encouraging words, Amy passed mile fifteen. The halfway mark. Her legs were a little tired, but they didn't ache. She breathed easily. She had plenty of reserve energy left to burn. If she decided to give this ride everything she had, now was the time to pick up her pace. She kept her eyes on the pavement in front of her and the one woman she could see ahead. The really fast woman wasn't even visible anymore. Amy pedaled slightly harder. The woman ahead maintained her speed, but didn't step it up. Matching her pace, Eric was only slightly behind her on the right. She knew he'd stay with her. His presence would help her focus. She couldn't think about how empty she was when she'd told him she loved him, but had to leave him. Today she chose to follow through on their shared goal.

Amy focused on the trail and talked herself back into the headspace she needed. She'd feel sad over missing their evening rides another time. Later, she'd mull over how she'd finally dropped her barriers and let herself fall in love with Eric. Then she'd convince herself—again—that she'd done the right thing, the fair thing, to cut things off with him.

Rounding another corner, Amy picked up the pace again and pulled farther ahead of the two women on either side. A man broke out of this second group of leaders, but another rider fell behind. She set the pace now. She widened her distance a little more than three bike lengths at first, but about three miles later she was a good half a city block ahead. For a short stretch she had empty spaces in front and behind. Eric yelled, "Keep it up," from behind and then fell off her pace when she'd pushed her now straining leg muscles to pick it up again.

The banner across the trail at the starting line came into view along with the music of cheers and loud applause. Off in the distance she saw Cassie jumping up and down and as she got closer she heard her holler, "Way to go, Mom!" Lottie was next to Cassie shouting, "Way to go, Mr. Wells!"

One more round to go and she'd found the sweet spot that separated her from the crowd behind. A couple of men moved ahead, a few more lost their pace and fell behind. Only two women had created distance. One was still unreachable but Amy was closing in on her.

Do it for yourself. Give it your all. Eric's words were like messages to her body to send adrenaline, find the energy to keep going. Eric had been right. Grandpa had been right. Time and time again, she'd held back. Swallowed her dreams and went along to get along. *Not this time, not this time, not this time.* She pumped harder now. The muscles in her legs burned and seemed to scream, *How much longer?*

Not long. She was so close.

Nothing mattered now except the work, pumping her legs, gauging her breathing, ignoring her sore arms and the sweat rolling down her back.

Then the banner appeared in view for this final time. *This is it, hold out.* People lining the homestretch were cheering wildly now. A handful of the fastest riders had already crossed the line. Amy knew the first woman who had shot so far ahead and disappeared must have crossed the finish line by now. A couple of men rode in a cluster. They gave life to that one more sprint she needed to maintain her position. Ignore the muscle pain, ignore it all. She was living in her head now, where the thrill of what she was doing took over. She anticipated the last woman she passed would come up on her right side. But she didn't appear and Amy held the lead.

The line in clear sight, Amy could read the numbers on the race bib of the man in front of her. But he was slowing, unable to maintain his pace. She grabbed the moment and veered the bike to her left to give herself space next to him and using the last of the fuel left in her body, she made it across the finish line half a bike length ahead of him.

Stunned, she struggled to reorient herself as her speed dropped fast. She finally took a couple of deep breaths and let her mind absorb the noise around her, especially the happy screams of two little girls. As soon as she could she straightened up and waved at them as the bike slowed almost to a stop.

Maybe she hadn't broken a sweat on some of those training rides, but she was drenched now. She got off the bike and wheeled it to the walkway, looking up in time to see Eric cross the line and slow down. The woman behind her waved her congratulations. Only then, did Amy realize she'd placed in the race. *Second* in her group.

"You did it," Eric shouted as he came alongside her and took her in his arms. "Look at everybody. They're all cheering for you. My mom and Seth are overjoyed. You made us all proud."

"You didn't do so bad yourself," she said, stepping back to take off her helmet and loop it over the handlebars. She stood on her tip-toes and kissed him on the cheek. "Don't mind my wet jersey, but I have to thank you for this. It was you. I pushed because you finally got through to me. I needed this. Not even to place, but to do it for me."

"I'm so glad. And your training buddy didn't completely humiliate himself. But the last five miles made me question my intelligence." He laughed and leaned over to hug her again. "Come on, let's ditch the bikes by the tent and join the others."

They went to the registration table and grabbed a towel, and they received their official time and Amy's official placement. They learned the program would start soon, but they still had time to join their group. As they crossed the grass, Kyra and the girls met them halfway. She warned the girls she was damp, as she put it, but they hugged her anyway.

Amy spotted the woman who won and waved. When she caught her eye, Amy cupped her hands over her mouth and yelled, "Congratulations."

"Hey, same to you," the woman shouted back.

As they all walked along, she wiped the towel across her damp forehead again, but at that moment, her aching legs caught up with her and she bent over and grabbed her thighs above her knees.

"Hey, you okay?" Kyra asked.

"Yep, but I need to stretch." She glanced at

Eric. "So do you, but not until we get to your mom and my grandparents."

"Hey, what did I tell you, Amy?" Les said. "I'm taking credit for that ribbon you're going to get."

"You all share it." For the next few minutes the girls watched them stretch and imitated some of their moves. She couldn't stop smiling. "What about you? How do you feel?"

"I'm more wiped out than you are." He grinned. "You may be second in your group, but you did well overall, too." Before she knew what hit her, a couple of sweaty arms had pulled her close. "I'm taking all the credit," he teased.

"I'll give you half," she conceded, "but Les gets a share."

"Oh, okay," he said. "I suppose you should get a little credit, too."

He started walking toward the race booth.

"Wait, Eric, wait."

He turned around. "What?"

"Thanks, again."

"You made Cassie proud. We're all proud of you."

Amy nodded. With her arm around Cassie's shoulder, she watched him walk away.

CHAPTER SEVENTEEN

SHE RODE THE roller coaster of emotion for almost a week. Not pleased with her decision, at least she wasn't second-guessing herself. Alone in her room, Amy closed her journal and pushed it across her desk. Writing about her feelings wasn't helping, especially with Grandma's words echoing through her head. Before the race she'd told Barb and Les that she'd broken off her relationship with Eric. She'd expected them to be a little surprised, but she wasn't prepared for Grandma's fierce reaction. *You better not be turning away from love because of some notion of your obligation to us.*

Since then Grandma had noticed how listless and moody she'd been. *You can't fool me, Amy. Twenty years ago, I hoped you wouldn't marry Scott. Now I'm hoping you're not refusing to accept Eric's love. A good man, Amy.*

She couldn't deny it. Only yesterday, Barb had approached Amy again, reminding her that if she and Les needed major help, they'd all work something out. Besides, they weren't penniless. They could hire someone to take on some of the chores Amy was covering.

She ran through the scenario in her mind once again, knowing it was all about marrying the wrong man, wanting to do right by her child and her grandparents, and standing on her own two feet. Love hadn't been on her to-do list. Grandpa Les had laughed when she told him that. *Love found you, honey, ready or not.*

Amy continued her internal battle until she sifted through all that she'd done these last few months, including planning the upcoming Fourth on River Street and doing the bike race. Right now, her grandparents and Cassie were okay. But she finally had a man who loved her. And she loved him back.

She picked up the phone.

ERIC WALKED THROUGH the kitchen and waved at Les and Barb in the living room.

"Is Cassie in bed?" he asked Amy.

"She should be asleep. She needs her energy for the big parade tomorrow." Amy smiled. "I guess we all do. Come with me. We can sit out on the back porch."

"Okay." She'd sounded excited on the phone, but he stopped himself from speculating. "You seem to have a thing about these late-evening calls."

"I had to see you. It can't wait until tomorrow. We'll have too much stuff to take care of then."

They sat in lawn chairs on the small porch on the cloudless, still evening. The earlier thunderstorm left an earthy scent in the air. With all that had happened between him and Amy, Eric couldn't trust his feelings or the thoughts bouncing around his head.

He gestured toward her. "So what's this all about?"

"Here's the bottom line," Amy said, putting her hand on his arm. "You know I love you, Eric. I've said the words out loud. In the last week I've had realizations. Lots of them."

He waited, still not trusting his hunch.

"I changed my mind, Eric, I want another chance…with you, I mean." She cocked her head and looked at him with an intensity that made his nerve endings tingle. "I want to go back to what we talked about the night the girls ran away."

Reeling from the reality of what was happening, he swallowed hard, but didn't quite know how to answer.

"It's my fault we're even having this conversation," she said. "I know that, and I'm so sorry."

It would be easy to tell her she didn't have to apologize, but he didn't feel that way. Instead, he got out of the chair and perched his hip on the railing. "It's not about an apology, Amy. It's about trust. Falling for you and being open was the first time I've trusted myself to love that deeply. When Cassie ran off you trusted me to help you find her, but not enough to know we're on the same team always."

"I can see why you'd feel that way, Eric, but I didn't trust myself. I ran scared. I was too worried about Scott to trust that one mistake wouldn't mean I'd lose Cassie. It sounds so extreme." She rubbed her cheeks. "But I learned a lot in the last few days. Even our bike ride showed me that I don't want to give up on myself. Or love."

"You're an incredible woman. I'm glad you know that."

"It's been a hard journey, but I've realized I can be a good mom and care for my grandparents and still be myself. I don't have to give parts of myself away in order to love other people. That's why I'm asking you if you'll still let me love you."

It took all of a second for Eric to get off the railing and take hold of Amy's hands. He pulled her to her feet and held her close. "Oh, Amy, let's love each other for good." He kissed her soft lips and held her cheeks and gently tilted her head. "I want to look into those beautiful brown eyes every day of my life—even in the dark. Hmm...especially in the dark."

"Oh, really? Count me in for gazing into your blue eyes that shine so bright."

"Then let's launch this you-and-me life as soon as possible." He took a deep breath and spoke the words he'd wanted to say for so long. "Marry me?"

"Yes," she murmured, letting her head rest against his chest. "Oh, yes."

He closed his eyes and ran his fingers through her hair until the urge to kiss her overwhelmed him. Her mouth eagerly sought his and she wound her arms around his neck.

When they stepped back from their embrace, he held on to her hands and brought them to his lips.

"What now?" Amy's voice was full of joy.

"I want to tell Cassie, but when we're with her alone. Maybe after the parade?"

Eric didn't mind that the conversation turned to real life and all the arrangements. This is what their lives would be like. It was what he wanted. It was why he bought his house.

After a few more kisses, it was time to go. She walked him to his car. As he pulled out of the driveway, he waved and in the rear-view mirror, he saw the love of his life waving back.

CHAPTER EIGHTEEN

ALMOST SHOWTIME, AMY thought as Cassie held up the poster she'd made, this one with book covers pasted on a bright yellow background.

"This really stands out," Amy said, holding the poster at arm's length.

"I'm done with mine, too," Lottie exclaimed.

"And it's beautiful." Amy patted Lottie's shoulder. She'd drawn a good likeness of Madison School and added children's smiling faces looking out the windows.

"Do you think Mr. Wells will like our posters?" Cassie asked.

"You bet he will. I'm one hundred percent sure of that." Amy grinned at the girls. "Let's go outside. You'll be lining up for the parade any minute now."

The girls gave their posters to a volunteer and followed Amy out to the park grounds where teachers and kids were gathering. The earlier drizzle had stopped and the sun was out. Now the raindrops on the trees glistened in the sunshine.

"There's Mr. Wells." Cassie pointed to Eric towering over the crowd of children who formed a rapidly expanding circle around him.

"You two go ahead and join the kids," she said, giving them each a send-off kiss on the cheek. "Kyra's going to be in the parade with you. You'll see me in front of the salon." The girls ran off, but instead of leaving, Amy couldn't keep her eyes off Eric. He was tending to the children, but when he saw Cassie and Lottie, he scanned the area and she waved wildly to get his attention. When she caught his eye, everything and everyone fell away and for a few seconds it was just the two of them smiling at each other.

The spell broke when a parent came to his side—but not before he touched his chest over his heart. Everything happened quickly after that. Some of the high school student volunteers carried piles of posters to the teachers who would lead the parade. Other teenagers were dispersed among the younger kids to literally keep them in line.

The posters the kids and teachers carried

were handed out randomly, so Cassie and Lottie ended up with the ones the little kids made with big heads on stick figures. Some of the younger children carried posters with more high-minded messages, like the elaborate script spelling out things like Teachers Make Our Country Great. One group of kids had their posters revolve around a literacy theme—teachers reading to kids, a couple of kids staring at a laptop screen with text.

"Laptops and phones," Kyra said, coming alongside her. "Modern literacy symbols."

Amy pointed to a boy, a little younger than Cassie, holding a poster that simply said, Yay, Teachers, in huge bright red and blue letters against the white background. "That could be my favorite."

"Mine, too," Kyra said.

Up ahead, behind the teachers, the high school band lined up two abreast. Two police cruisers and a fire truck were getting in place in the parking lot to lead the parade.

"I love the float the students came up with." Amy nodded to the floral display of all fifty stars from the flag.

The newly energized Bluestone River Historical Society had collected enough volunteers to wear period clothing, starting with the nineteenth-century prairie dresses and bonnets and moving on to flapper-style dresses from the 1920s. A woman wore a 1940s jacket with padded shoulders and captured her hair in a hairnet. Her male counterpart wore a fedora and a suit with lapels that came almost to his shoulders. A couple of young people had dragged out some vintage hippy-era tie-dyed T-shirts and bell-bottoms.

"Hey," Kyra said, "they stole my jeans."

When Kyra left to help the children line up, Amy was alone for a few minutes. With her secret. Yet it wouldn't be secret for long. Amy could hardly wait to tell Cassie about her new stepdad.

Amy went to get her car and headed downtown to the lot behind River Street. Hurrying to the seniors' seating section near the stage, she looked for Barb and Les.

"Go, go," Grandpa shouted as she approached, flapping his hand to shoo her away. "We're fine and you've got work to do."

Okay, then, she thought, amused to be so readily dismissed. When she arrived at the salon, Georgia was setting up a table with their soap samples and coupons, along with an announcement about the River Street Salon's expansion plans.

Georgia gave her a quick one-arm hug. "Time to share our exciting news with the world."

"I know, which is why I dressed up a little," Amy said, looking down at her loose white cotton dress and sandals. "No shorts today."

"Good thinking," Georgia said, looking crisp in a pale yellow linen pantsuit despite the sticky day.

A couple of seconds later, sirens and horns in the distance quieted the crowd that lined the half mile from the park to the grassy area at the end of the commercial downtown where the town hall's lawn and sidewalk were crowded with residents and visitors.

With a cruiser leading the way, the principals were next, followed by teachers and school staff in a line of about five across. They waved their posters at the crowd, who greeted them with loud cheers that went on and on. Amy got as close as she could to take pictures of the teachers as they passed by. Georgia was filming the event with her camera. Eric and the other principals waved right at her and she caught them on camera—forever.

The marching band stopped along the route a couple of times to perform, and the histori-

cal society folks paused to greet the specta-
tors and shake some hands. Finally, the kids,
over three hundred of them, walked past the
cheering crowd. Her camera caught Cassie
and Lottie waving like little superstars. Mike
and Ruby's boy, Jason, walked with them.

Ruby, with Emma following, came alongside Amy to capture pictures. Ruby's baby
girl sat in a stroller decorated with balloons.
Amy's two oldest friends would eventually
hear her exciting personal news. She knew
they'd be pleased for her.

Amy lost count of how many pictures she
took, but she had all the proof of that special day she needed. From that moment on,
it would become known as the launch of the
annual Fourth on River Street Festival. She
was certain of it.

The rest of the festival passed in a blur
from the talented teenagers in the drama club
dressed like eighteenth-century colonists
reading the Declaration of Independence to
Eric and the principals reading the statement
honoring the teachers. Mike and town council
members were stationed at the model of the
new development set up outside the town hall.
Cassie and Lottie joined the high school chorus to sing "You're a Grand Old Flag." Then

they led the crowd in "America the Beautiful" with the high school students providing perfect harmony.

Later, after Cassie and Lottie had eaten their fill of hot dogs and cotton candy, Amy could see Barb and Les were worn-out. Time to drop them off.

Amy helped them into the house, where they sat in their reading chairs and put their feet up.

"Time for my nap," Grandpa Les said.

Grandma agreed.

"Well, then, if it's okay with you, Cassie and I have been invited to Eric's house for a little while."

"Oh, really?" Grandpa Les said, smiling.

"And there's going to be a surprise," Amy said to Cassie.

"What kind of surprise?" Cassie asked, eyeing her with a hint of suspicion.

"A great big one, so let's go. You haven't been to Eric's house yet. You're going to like it. Trust me." Amy could hardly contain herself. She sent Eric a quick text to let him know they were on their way. She turned to her grandparents. "We'll see you later." And she and Cassie were out the door.

A five-minute drive later, Cassie spotted Eric waiting for them on the front porch.

"Would you like to see my house, Cassie?" Eric asked, holding the front door open for her.

"It's pretty," Cassie said. She moved farther inside and pointed to the kitchen. "Can I go in there?"

"Uh, sure," Eric said, glancing at Amy. "Any particular reason?"

Cassie didn't answer, but ran to the refrigerator. "You do have my picture on your fridge. Like you said, it's the same one we have of me and Miss Sparkle." Her face was lit with a delighted smile.

"Of course, Cassie," Eric said. "I put it up right after the Snowball Fair."

"I just wanted to see," Cassie said.

"Why don't we go upstairs? I'll show you some cool rooms." He winked at Amy and led the way.

At the top of the stairs, Eric told Cassie to go ahead and poke around all the rooms and look out the windows.

"Really?" Cassie said, cutting her gaze to Amy. "Is this my surprise?"

"Part of it, sweetie," Amy said, following

Eric into a room with a wall of windows that looked out to the trees on the street.

"What would you think of this being your room, Cassie?" Amy asked.

Cassie frowned. "But why?"

Eric squatted in front of her and said, "Because I asked your mom to marry me and she said yes."

Cassie's eyes turned into huge brown saucers. "You mean you'll have a wedding?"

Amy clapped her hands together. "That's right, Cassie. And after the wedding you and I will move into this house. It's empty now because Eric is fixing it up."

"What about Grandpa Les and Grandma Barb?"

"We'll see them all the time," Amy said, cupping Cassie's chin. She leaned over and kissed her forehead. "I know how much you love them. Like I do. We'll still have lots of fun with them, and we'll help them with their house and the garden all the time."

"We're making our families bigger, so we have more people to love," Eric said. "Your grandparents are important to me, too. And my mom will think you're pretty special."

"We came over today, Cassie, because I

want you to see where we're going to live soon. I want you to be happy here."

Cassie frowned. "Can I come to the wedding? And Lottie?"

"We can't have a wedding without you," Eric said. "And Kyra and Lottie will be our special guests."

Amy saw the love in Eric's eyes when he looked at Cassie. Even with all her foibles, he got a big kick out of her. Amy took a few steps to the window and looked out to the street, feeling bubbly and tingly inside and out. "This is a wonderful room in a special house. I think we'll be so happy here, Cassie. I love Eric very much."

Cassie crossed her arms and narrowed her eyes. "So, if there's going to be a wedding, where's the ring?"

"Oh, sweetie, we haven't thought about…" She stopped when Eric reached into his pocket and produced a square velvet box.

"Not so fast, Amy." He made a funny face at Cassie. "Your mom doesn't think I've got it covered."

"But how?" Amy asked.

"You know…we talked a few weeks ago…" She nodded. She got it.

"Can I see it?" Cassie asked, getting up on tiptoes to get a look at the box.

"Show it to *somebody*," Amy said, laughing. "I'm jumping out of my skin here."

Eric approached and brought Cassie with him. "Okay, here goes." Eric kept the box low so Cassie could see it when he opened it and an oval diamond in a gold setting appeared.

Amy's hands flew to her cheeks. "Oh, Eric, it's gorgeous."

"Put it on, put it on," Cassie squealed.

Amy held out her hand and with Cassie looking on, Eric slipped the ring on her finger. Perfect. She leaned forward and kissed him on the cheek. She gestured around the room. "Thank you for this…for everything."

"So, we're almost a family," Eric said, squeezing her shoulder. "Why don't you go check out the backyard, Cassie? Your mom and I will be right down."

"Okay," Cassie said, twirling on her tiptoes toward the door.

When Cassie was gone, Amy couldn't hold back a chuckle as Eric gathered her in his arms, lifted her up and spun her in a circle, imitating Cassie's move.

"This is the best day of my life, Amy. I love that kid of yours. And her mom."

Amy tilted her face to accept Eric's sweet kisses. "And I love you. Always."

* * * * *

For more Back to Bluestone River
romances from Harlequin Heartwarming
and Virginia McCullough,
visit www.Harlequin today!

Get 4 FREE REWARDS!

We'll send you 2 FREE Books plus 2 FREE Mystery Gifts.

Love Inspired books feature uplifting stories where faith helps guide you through life's challenges and discover the promise of a new beginning.

FREE
Value Over
$20

YES! Please send me 2 FREE Love Inspired Romance novels and my 2 FREE mystery gifts (gifts are worth about $10 retail). After receiving them, if I don't wish to receive any more books, I can return the shipping statement marked "cancel." If I don't cancel, I will receive 6 brand-new novels every month and be billed just $5.24 each for the regular-print edition or $5.99 each for the larger-print edition in the U.S., or $5.74 each for the regular-print edition or $6.24 each for the larger-print edition in Canada. That's a savings of at least 13% off the cover price. It's quite a bargain! Shipping and handling is just 50¢ per book in the U.S. and $1.25 per book in Canada.* I understand that accepting the 2 free books and gifts places me under no obligation to buy anything. I can always return a shipment and cancel at any time. The free books and gifts are mine to keep no matter what I decide.

Choose one: ☐ **Love Inspired Romance**
               Regular-Print
               (105/305 IDN GNWC)

☐ **Love Inspired Romance**
  Larger-Print
  (122/322 IDN GNWC)

Name (please print)

Address   Apt. #

City   State/Province   Zip/Postal Code

Email: Please check this box ☐ if you would like to receive newsletters and promotional emails from Harlequin Enterprises ULC and its affiliates. You can unsubscribe anytime.

Mail to the **Reader Service:**
IN U.S.A.: P.O. Box 1341, Buffalo, NY 14240-8531
IN CANADA: P.O. Box 603, Fort Erie, Ontario L2A 5X3

Want to try 2 free books from another series! Call 1-800-873-8635 or visit www.ReaderService.com.

*Terms and prices subject to change without notice. Prices do not include sales taxes, which will be charged (if applicable) based on your state or country of residence. Canadian residents will be charged applicable taxes. Offer not valid in Quebec. This offer is limited to one order per household. Books received may not be as shown. Not valid for current subscribers to Love Inspired Romance books. All orders subject to approval. Credit or debit balances in a customer's account(s) may be offset by any other outstanding balance owed by or to the customer. Please allow 4 to 6 weeks for delivery. Offer available while quantities last.

Your Privacy—Your information is being collected by Harlequin Enterprises ULC, operating as Reader Service. For a complete summary of the information we collect, how we use this information and to whom it is disclosed, please visit our privacy notice located at corporate.harlequin.com/privacy-notice. From time to time we may also exchange your personal information with reputable third parties. If you wish to opt out of this sharing of your personal information, please visit readerservice.com/consumerschoice or call 1-800-873-8635. **Notice to California Residents**—Under California law, you have specific rights to control and access your data. For more information on these rights and how to exercise them, visit corporate.harlequin.com/california-privacy.   LI20R2

Get 4 FREE REWARDS!

We'll send you 2 FREE Books plus 2 FREE Mystery Gifts.

Love Inspired Suspense books showcase how courage and optimism unite in stories of faith and love in the face of danger.

FREE Value Over $20

YES! Please send me 2 FREE Love Inspired Suspense novels and my 2 FREE mystery gifts (gifts are worth about $10 retail). After receiving them, if I don't wish to receive any more books, I can return the shipping statement marked "cancel." If I don't cancel, I will receive 6 brand-new novels every month and be billed just $5.24 each for the regular-print edition or $5.99 each for the larger-print edition in the U.S., or $5.74 each for the regular-print edition or $6.24 each for the larger-print edition in Canada. That's a savings of at least 13% off the cover price. It's quite a bargain! Shipping and handling is just 50¢ per book in the U.S. and $1.25 per book in Canada.* I understand that accepting the 2 free books and gifts places me under no obligation to buy anything. I can always return a shipment and cancel at any time. The free books and gifts are mine to keep no matter what I decide.

Choose one: ☐ **Love Inspired Suspense Regular-Print** (153/353 IDN GNWN)   ☐ **Love Inspired Suspense Larger-Print** (107/307 IDN GNWN)

Name (please print)

Address _____ Apt. #

City _____ State/Province _____ Zip/Postal Code

Email: Please check this box ☐ if you would like to receive newsletters and promotional emails from Harlequin Enterprises ULC and its affiliates. You can unsubscribe anytime.

Mail to the **Reader Service:**
IN U.S.A.: P.O. Box 1341, Buffalo, NY 14240-8531
IN CANADA: P.O. Box 603, Fort Erie, Ontario L2A 5X3

Want to try 2 free books from another series? Call 1-800-873-8635 or visit www.ReaderService.com.

*Terms and prices subject to change without notice. Prices do not include sales taxes, which will be charged (if applicable) based on your state or country of residence. Canadian residents will be charged applicable taxes. Offer not valid in Quebec. This offer is limited to one order per household. Books received may not be as shown. Not valid for current subscribers to Love Inspired Suspense books. All orders subject to approval. Credit or debit balances in a customer's account(s) may be offset by any other outstanding balance owed by or to the customer. Please allow 4 to 6 weeks for delivery. Offer available while quantities last.

Your Privacy—Your information is being collected by Harlequin Enterprises ULC, operating as Reader Service. For a complete summary of the information we collect, how we use this information and to whom it is disclosed, please visit our privacy notice located at corporate.harlequin.com/privacy-notice. From time to time we may also exchange your personal information with reputable third parties. If you wish to opt out of this sharing of your personal information, please visit readerservice.com/consumerschoice or call 1-800-873-8635. Notice to California Residents—Under California law, you have specific rights to control and access your data. For more information on these rights and how to exercise them, visit corporate.harlequin.com/california-privacy.

LIS20R2

THE WESTERN HEARTS COLLECTION!

19 FREE BOOKS in all!

COWBOYS. RANCHERS. RODEO REBELS.
Here are their charming love stories in one prized Collection:
51 emotional and heart-filled romances that capture the majesty and rugged beauty of the American West!

YES! Please send me **The Western Hearts Collection** in Larger Print. This collection begins with 3 FREE books and 2 FREE gifts in the first shipment. Along with my 3 free books, I'll also get the next 4 books from The Western Hearts Collection, in LARGER PRINT, which I may either return and owe nothing, or keep for the low price of $5.45 U.S./$6.23 CDN each plus $2.99 U.S./$7.49 CDN for shipping and handling per shipment*. If I decide to continue, about once a month for 8 months I will get 6 or 7 more books but will only need to pay for 4. That means 2 or 3 books in every shipment will be FREE! If I decide to keep the entire collection, I'll have paid for only 32 books because 19 books are FREE! I understand that accepting the 3 free books and gifts places me under no obligation to buy anything. I can always return a shipment and cancel at any time. My free books and gifts are mine to keep no matter what I decide.

☐ 270 HCN 5354   ☐ 470 HCN 5354

_____

Name (please print)

_____

Address   Apt. #

_____

City   State/Province   Zip/Postal Code

Mail to the Reader Service:
IN U.S.A.: P.O. Box 1341, Buffalo, N.Y. 14240-8531
IN CANADA: P.O. Box 603, Fort Erie, Ontario L2A 5X3

Get 4 FREE REWARDS!

We'll send you 2 FREE Books <u>plus</u> 2 FREE Mystery Gifts.

FREE Value Over **$20**

Both the **Romance** and **Suspense** collections feature compelling novels written by many of today's bestselling authors.

YES! Please send me 2 FREE novels from the Essential Romance or Essential Suspense Collection and my 2 FREE gifts (gifts are worth about $10 retail). After receiving them, if I don't wish to receive any more books, I can return the shipping statement marked "cancel." If I don't cancel, I will receive 4 brand-new novels every month and be billed just $7.24 each in the U.S. or $7.49 each in Canada. That's a savings of up to 28% off the cover price. It's quite a bargain! Shipping and handling is just 50¢ per book in the U.S. and $1.25 per book in Canada.* I understand that accepting the 2 free books and gifts places me under no obligation to buy anything. I can always return a shipment and cancel at any time. The free books and gifts are mine to keep no matter what I decide.

Choose one: ☐ **Essential Romance**
(194/394 MDN GQ6M)

☐ **Essential Suspense**
(191/391 MDN GQ6M)

Name (please print)

Address   Apt. #

City   State/Province   Zip/Postal Code

Email: Please check this box ☐ if you would like to receive newsletters and promotional emails from Harlequin Enterprises ULC and its affiliates. You can unsubscribe anytime.

> Mail to the **Reader Service:**
> **IN U.S.A.:** P.O. Box 1341, Buffalo, NY 14240-8531
> **IN CANADA:** P.O. Box 603, Fort Erie, Ontario L2A 5X3

Want to try 2 free books from another series! Call 1-800-873-8635 or visit www.ReaderService.com.

Visit *ReaderService.com* Today!

As a valued member of the Harlequin Reader Service, you'll find these benefits and more at ReaderService.com:

- Try 2 free books from any series
- Access risk-free special offers
- View your account history & manage payments
- Browse the latest Bonus Bucks catalog

Don't miss out!

If you want to stay up-to-date on the latest at the Harlequin Reader Service and enjoy more content, make sure you've signed up for our monthly News & Notes email newsletter. Sign up online at ReaderService.com or by calling Customer Service at 1-800-873-8635.